LOOK AT THE SUN

DON CARSWELL

Print ISBN: 978-1-48359-209-1

eBook ISBN: 978-1-48359-210-7

TO THE READER

This may well be the world's first coming-of-middle-age novel.

The passage through midlife is unmapped. Like anyplace off the grid, it can be rocky and treacherous, with unexpected hazards. No wonder so many of us develop "quadragenarian angst." As challenging as this period of life may be, it is comforting to know that these challenges are universal; we all must navigate them, regardless of financial or social status, background, level of education or family situation. During these years, many of us will come face-to-face with the dark specter of depression.

I have done my best to treat these heavy topics in a light manner. The goal of this book is to make you think... to examine your life, your purpose, your possibilities... and to help you to see the beauty and color in everyday life. And maybe, to find your path through this uncharted territory.

Though the story is fictional, many of the events in this book are based on real experiences I have had during many years of travel around the world.

Enjoy the journey, and be careful if you *Look at the Sun*!

—Don Carswell

ACKNOWLEDGEMENTS

I would like to thank Elsa Todd for her patient encouragement and support. Also thanks to Lisa Priebe of Virginia for her editing suggestions. Finally, I would like to thank my daughters, Amanda Devine and Lindsay Carswell, for making my passage through mid-life wonderful!

Happiness is to be found along the way, not at the end of the road, for then the journey is over and it is too late.

Robert R. Updegraff

Probably a crab would be filled with a sense of personal outrage if it could hear us class it without ado or apology as a crustacean, and thus dispose of it. "I am no such thing," it would say; "I am myself, myself alone."

William James

LOOK AT THE SUN

By Don Carswell

CHAPTER 1
The End

I've just made a fatal mistake.

Not just fatal in the abstract sense of a major error, but an actual and unfortunate miscalculation that will now literally cost me my life.

A barreling tractor-trailer is but a few yards in front of me with no chance of veering away, and I've got no time to move out of its path and no place to run. Within three seconds, my body will burst like a punctured water balloon, and my living essence, whatever that is, will either disappear or somehow find its way to the next world.

The feeling is oddly familiar, a thousandfold analogue of that unnerving moment in a game of chess when you make what you consider to be a routine move, suddenly realizing only as you release the piece from your grasp that you have positioned yourself just one move away from being checkmated. Except that this is no game of chess.

Two seconds until impact. If the movies have it right, maybe this moment will expand into all eternity and I will have the opportunity to review my entire life in tedious detail, with its scattered achievements and disappointments dispersed like swirling bits of flotsam in a vast, gray sea of dreary mediocrity. Maybe I'll at last find some purpose or sense to this existence that I've struggled so hard to understand. Maybe I'll experience a deathbed epiphany, a realization of what it was all about for all these years. But the thought that hits me first is, what a *waste*. What a waste of these good solid legs that still have many miles left in them, these strong hands and arms that can still touch my daughters' shoulders, stroke my wife's hair, or shake an old friend's hand. A waste of these eyes that can still see (though I now have trouble reading without extending my arms), and these ears that can still hear (though not so well anymore in crowded rooms).

I think of my family and friends, at this moment most likely safely draped in classic American repose across their easy chairs and recliners, eyes and brains unflinchingly fixed on their televisions, looking forward to long, easy lives as they glide through the sedentary, routine pointlessness of middle age. I wonder what they will think of me now, leaving my comfortable home and loving family behind, taking this crazy trip that seemed such a fantastic idea to me and so strange to them, and now having it all end like this in a tragic, disastrous mess. Will this reinforce their generational drift toward becoming spectators in life rather than participants? Might they feel just a twinge of I-told-you-so satisfaction along with their grief? "I told Doug that it was a crazy idea. It's dangerous down there! But he wouldn't listen. No, you know Doug. An armchair and a TV weren't good enough for him, and now look what happened…"

But this is not the story of my death, or the day of my death, or the events leading up to my death, except in the sense that all of the events of one's life eventually lead to one's death. But enough of the macabre. This story is about life…

CHAPTER 2

Topical Depression

Two months earlier...

A writhing, vaguely reptilian mass rose from the putrid, lightless depths, its stench rivaling that of the open sewer in which it lived. When it moved, it moved not as a living creature; instead, it seemed to ooze like the very sewer itself. Upon reaching the surface, it twisted its hideous serpentine neck, then wretched, hacked, choked and spat out a thick black glob that slid down the wall and became... the day.

My doctor just looks at me, tapping a pencil against his lip, his eyes narrowed in concentration, his mouth slightly ajar. He draws in a deep breath across his teeth, making a sharp hissing sound, then puffs his cheeks and blows it all out in a sigh.

"Doug, I think we're gonna up your dose," he finally says, "That was the most uniquely foul description of someone's day I've ever heard in my life."

"Oh, come on, Doc, I was just joking. You doctors do joke, don't you? My day was fine. In fact, it's good, in a way, that I can tell jokes now, right?"

"Huh," he snorts. "Well, I wouldn't quit your day job to do stand-up comedy just yet— not till you get some better material than that."

"Doc, if I could quit my day job, I probably wouldn't even need to see you!" I stand up.

"Really, I'm doing fine. The pills might be helping, after all."

"You're sure?" The doctor looks doubtful. "Well, let's give it a few more weeks. I want you to come in again next month anyway, just to see how you're doing."

The doctor opens the door and walks out of the examination room, flipping through my charts as he goes, and for a moment I have to wonder— was he shaking his head? It was just a joke, for God's sake. Depressed people can tell jokes, too.

I walk to the reception desk, schedule my next appointment for one month later, and continue out to my car. It's a routine I'm getting to know pretty well these days.

How did I get to be depressed? I wonder this all the time. Really, I wouldn't even call myself depressed. That's the doctor's term. It's not the word I would choose. Stoic. Cynical, maybe. Realistic. These are words that better describe me. OK, maybe I don't laugh as much as I used to. Or have as much fun. But I have good reasons for that.

A 'chemical imbalance.' That's how my doctor explained it to me. Who would have thought? Apparently, if I understand his theory correctly, I have been wasting my time all these years pursuing happiness through such traditional means as raising a family, setting and trying to achieve life goals, and putting money aside for a brighter future. In the biomedical world, happiness is all about brain chemistry. You can achieve every goal you ever set, you can be rich and famous and surrounded by the most beautiful women, you can have a great, close-knit family and everything else you might conceivably want, but if your brain chemicals are out of balance, you won't be happy. Conversely (and this is by my own conjecture now), you could live the most pathetic, failure-plagued, most sorry-assed life that anyone has ever lived, but a few squirts of serotonin in the right place and you'll be happier than a swine in excrement and will die with an implacable grin of serene contentment plastered across your face.

Do I believe this? The thought of taking pills to make me happy came out of left field for me. I still bristle when I think about it. Initially it seemed to go against everything I was ever taught, and that puts me far outside of my comfort zone. That's because when I was a young kid, I was a teacher's dream. It sounds ridiculous now, but I was a very gullible child. I had the proverbial damp sponge of a brain, ready to soak up enlightenment from my elders on the mysterious ways of this world, an empty canvas waiting for the paintbrush of their wisdom... "Do not, boys and girls, DO NOT take drugs to make you happy." This commandment was locked inextricably into my mind along with many, many more directives through the years. I was never one to question authority. If my parents, teachers, minister, scoutmaster, big brother, or anyone else with an impressive title or a few years of seniority on me told me something, I accepted it as gospel. But now my doctor, a licensed physician with dozens, even baker's dozens, of years of education, qualifications and experience, backed up by the reams of diplomas and certificates hanging on his wall in fine, matted frames, is telling me otherwise, and he appears to be acting in my best interest. You can't argue with science. And this is big business! The U.S. pharmaceutical industry has spent even more time developing, studying, and of course marketing, these products, for my benefit. The whole U.S. economy depends on it! This is a matter of civic duty!

I wrestle with this conundrum on a daily basis. I don't want to come to depend on pills for my happiness, regardless of the theoretical, *in vitro* sense it might make. Do the pills really make you happy, or do you just *think* you're happy? Is there a difference? Like a twentieth-century throwback, I still believe deep down inside that happiness comes from the way you live your life, and I prefer mine marbled with the gray hues of occasional melancholy rather than hidden behind the artificial, robotic smile of a doll.

Medications aside, the real problem for me is that I live my life on automatic pilot, going through the motions, but not really feeling it. My routine has become so invariable of late that I barely need to think to get through my day, and the only deviations from the norm are the frustrations and annoyances of things not going right. I can't help but yearn in my stressed-out heart for something more than my nine-to-five job that somehow defies simple mathematics and gobbles about sixty hours of each week, leaving me to collapse every evening, exhausted, in front of a droning television that tirelessly pumps out recycled nonsense, canned laughter, and depictions of lifestyles incomprehensible to me. What I really need is a change, some way to breathe new life into my aging soul.

Let's get one thing straight. There's nothing special about me. I am just one of tens of millions of very ordinary middle-aged American worker bees in business-casual khakis. A director-level executive, if that's of interest, with a wife and kids and a house in the suburbs. In retrospect, nothing seems to have precipitated my condition; it was more like a long, slow fade-in, like a sunrise on a dreary winter morning. Before I hit my mid-forties, my life was exquisite. My thirties were a long, pleasant drift down a sleepy river- the blissful early days of marriage, the warm, soft caresses of my two daughters, who were then as much affixed to my side as cookie crumbs were to their sticky hands and apple juice stains to their frilly dresses. My life flowed as easily as wine from a bottle in those days. The passing years led my daughters from diapers to dinosaurs to dating, and me from quiet contentment to quadragenarian angst. Upon reaching my early forties, I suddenly awakened with a frightful start to find my kids almost grown and myself wearing a wrinkling mask with gray at the fringes. I then saw that the wine bottle was already half empty. The book of my life was half written, and it seemed to me that the story was not so interesting. Each tick of my watch was a wasted moment, lost forever. Eventually, I suppose, I exhibited subtle symptoms that a good physician could recognize and diagnose as clinical depression, such as, for example, my firm conclusion that everything I had ever done in my life up to that point had been nothing short of a complete and absolute failure.

Where did the expression 'Time is on my side' come from? Time is never on our side. From earliest adulthood, time is playing against us. Slowly, relentlessly, time is beating on us, tearing away the very fabric of our lives, fiber by fiber, even while we are sleeping. And it will always, always win.

For some reason, my subconscious has decided that the middle of the night is the perfect time to review the negative aspects of my life. The tenuousness of my finances, my mistakes and lost opportunities of the past, my missteps with my career- all my demons parade before me in the very early hours of the morning. When I should be sleeping, my mind is running through all my past failures in tedious detail, meting out a kind of extemporaneous self-punishment for foibles long buried in the sands of time, and checking the foundation of my being for weak spots, with a sledgehammer. How did I get to this point? What mistakes did I make in the past that led me to the inescapable realities of middle age?

After considering questions like these during many sleep-deprived nights, I have determined that living life is like swimming in the ocean on a stormy day: from the first moment you enter it, strong currents are carrying you toward your destiny. You can swim and kick like crazy to move in one direction or another and you will make some progress, but you cannot avoid the pull of the current, and no matter how much you struggle, where you end up will have a lot more to do with in which direction the currents are carrying you than your own efforts. And unfortunately, where the currents are carrying you has a lot to do with where and when, and under what circumstances, you entered, and with life these are things that are entirely outside our control. It is also obvious that the earlier in life you start swimming in one direction, toward a goal, the greater by far your results will be in the end. If, on the other hand, you paddle about aimlessly until middle age, just trying to keep your head above water, there will be a lot less of an opportunity to change your course significantly. I discovered this a little too late in life, and now I find myself floundering mid-ocean, battered by relentless, belligerent whitecaps. Perhaps it is because of these frightful nighttime thoughts of the sea that I cling to my wife in the night like a drowning man to a float. (Perhaps it is also why I need to get up to use the bathroom so many times?) I'm tired of floating in the currents. I want to set my own direction. I want to shed these manacles that were wrought on the forge of other people's expectations, of other people's ideas, infused into my head since childhood by those older and more powerful, those well-meaning and otherwise.

There are plenty of good reasons to want to think for oneself. A lot of the things you are told when you are young are just not true.

I must have been a young kid when I first heard the expression, 'he got out on the wrong side of bed this morning' as an explanation for someone's day not going well. I remember being terribly worried if, for some reason, I got out of bed on the opposite side than the one I usually did, for example, if I was spending the night at someone else's house. Through the entire day I would fret that all manner of things would go wrong. At home, I would always ensure that I got out of bed on the same side every morning. As long as I did that, everything would be fine. It was not until I was older that the thought one day struck me that, what if the side of bed that I've been getting up on all this time has been the wrong one, and my life would have been so much better if only I had been rising from the *other* side every morning? I became petrified each morning as I debated from which side to exit my bed. Always the logical one, I tried to do comparison studies for a short time, but I soon realized that this was impossible since each different day provided a different set of circumstances that could have been either better or worse than they were. Fortunately, I outgrew this ridiculous worry once I got older, say about age thirty-five. Well, maybe not quite that old.

Then there's the mortality thing. I don't mean to be morbid about it, but as a practical, logical thinker, I have to consider it: one day I will meet my end. I will cease to be. I may receive a certain amount of advance warning about this, or I may not. If I do receive advance knowledge of the how and the when of it, which I am not sure would be good fortune or bad, it may be any time between six months and a few seconds. It could happen at any moment. It could be sickness, accident or foul play. Even if there is a warning, it would be impossible to be absolutely sure of it until it actually happens. My doctor could tell me I've got six months to live, and then I could get hit by a bus the next day. I can't imagine how anybody could write an autobiography while being completely unaware of how this key moment of his or her life will pan out.

Recently I have come up with the unorthodox line of thought that I might not die. I was reading an article some time ago that explained that the population of the earth has grown so rapidly in recent decades that half of the people who have ever lived are alive right now. This is because, the article claimed, throughout prehistory, there were relatively few people alive at any one time. So if half of the people who have ever lived are alive now, we are basing our conclusion about the inevitability of death on the experiences of only 50% of humanity, the half that has already died. What if, say, five percent of people had a condition that prevented them from dying of natural causes (or probably more accurately, *didn't* have a condition that allowed them to die)? Throughout all of prehistory and most of history, the chances of dying in animal attacks, war or natural disasters were so high that this five percent was very likely to be killed anyway, before their ability to resist natural death was revealed. But in modern times, now that many of those hazards have been minimized, wouldn't it then be possible that five percent of us who are alive now, could remain alive forever more?

There are times when I have to admit that my logical argument favoring the possibility of everlasting earthly life may be flawed, and might contain a slight touch of disingenuous wishful thinking. This concession usually occurs in the morning, at about the time I am ready to start shaving, as I wipe the condensation from the shower off the bathroom mirror with my towel and look at myself, wondering for a brief second who that gray-haired guy with the crows' feet is, that's staring back at me. Still, there's that *slight* chance, isn't there?

We all unintentionally set in motion the course of our lives the moment we choose our uniform. Just as a person who chooses to decorate himself with leather, chains and unkempt facial hair has left himself little option other than to ride motorcycles, so it was with me when I saw the suit. I remember seeing my graduation present lying there draped over a dining room chair, the hook of its hanger curled toward me like a beckoning finger. I heeded its call and it led me here to middle-class suburbia.

I turn into my development and observe that the unacknowledged competition for 'finest lawn' continues. I have long ago excused myself from this competition, believing that my grass-farming abilities should bear no relevance to my social status in the neighborhood. My abstention has been quietly noted.

A familiar figure is bouncing along the road ahead in feigned haste; as I get a little closer I see that it is my good friend Rod, out for a jog. His green sweatshirt with the rolled-up sleeves bears the characteristic 'Rod pattern' of sweat- the lower armpits and a triangular patch on the upper chest. This, along with his 1970's 'porno-style' moustache, allows for his easy identification from a distance. I wave to him and he flags me down.

"Hey, Rod, what's new?" I ask.

"Well, let me think for a bit," he says with deliberate sarcasm, "Uuh, let's see… oh yeah, Lisa served me with divorce papers last night."

"What? Rod, what happened?"

"Mold," he says.

"What?"

"My marriage was ruined by mold."

"Your marriage got moldy?"

"Well, not exactly, although maybe that is a good way of describing it. Our summer house at the shore got moldy. We forgot to turn the water off when we closed it up for the winter last year. We didn't realize that there was a leak in one of the pipes upstairs, and it dripped down into the ceiling. When Lisa went down to open up the house in May, there was mold, so we had to get some remediation guys in. In the meantime, Lisa was invited to stay at her friend's house down there, and through this friend she seems to have met Mr. Wonderful, or some guy she likes better than me, anyway. So, yeah, my marriage is shot because of mold."

"Rod, I'm really sorry. Can I help in any way?"

"Well, not at the moment anyhow. Unless you know something about mold remediation." He gives me a forced half-smile. "Listen, I've got to run. I've got to squeeze two more miles in and then get to the gym. I just wanted to give you the news so you didn't find out through the grapevine."

"Are you sure you're OK?"

"I'm fine for now."

"All right. I'll call you tonight, OK?"

"Great. I'll see you later, Doug." He trots off into the sunset, no doubt chasing after his marriage.

Another one down. Lately it seems as if my friends' marriages are being swept along the wayside like cut grass from their sidewalks. The simmering, understated drama of suburban life goes on. The denizens lovingly tend and cultivate their lawns into lush, fertile showpieces, while their marriages wither and die from neglect and malnourishment.

I slowly pull into my driveway, taking stock of my designated piece of living space on the earth. An acre of land, an oversized house

and a couple of trees. What more could anyone want? I've been fortunate in terms of physical possessions—our family has everything
we need and most of the things we want. I'm not sure whether the
effect of this abundance on my daughters has been all positive. When
they were very young, their birthdays and Christmas holidays were
an endless parade of presents from us, from their grandparents, their
extended family and even our neighbors. All of the latest, trendy,
must-have toys arrived for them in pretty pastel packages, done up
with bright little-girl ribbons and bows. Many people would imagine
that such holidays would be a dream come true for the young recip-
ients. This unfortunately wasn't true, as such days invariably ended
in tears. The trouble was, I believe, that the focus of the day fell not
on the gifts that were received, but of the *receiving* of the gifts as an
activity. The number of gifts was too large for the children to comprehend; when they opened one gift that they liked, well-meaning
but impatient adults directed their attention away from their new toy
to the next unopened gift. The fun was thus derived from the process
of opening gifts, and when at last there were no more gifts to open,
the fun ended and the result was tears. We had passed the peak of
the affluence bell curve, beyond which each new possession made us
less and less happy.

I enter the house, and there is nobody in sight, as usual. Our
family has become somewhat like a club. Although we all use the
same clubhouse, our lives tend not to intersect in too many other
ways. Still, it is comforting to have that membership, that feeling of
belonging.

Everybody in the family has their own important functions that
keep the household ticking along like a finely-tuned Swiss watch. My
functions, for example, are to bring the almighty paychecks home, to
hold my wallet open and to act as second-string chauffeur when my

wife is otherwise occupied. I am thankful to hold such a key position in the household and to know that, without me, the whole system would grind to a screeching halt. Unless, of course, another source of income could be found.

My wife, Dawn, is an encyclopedia of knowledge about school events, meetings, doctor and dentist appointments, sports practices... she is the go-to person for anything requiring scheduling or a due-date. She also handles things of incomprehensible complexity, like laundry, shopping and meal-planning. How she keeps all of these juggled balls in the air at one time each and every day is a complete mystery to me, and I hope I never have to pinch-hit for her. Dawn and I have been together for many years, almost since before I can remember, it seems. We know each other to the level at which we can finish the other's sentences and we can tell by the look on the other's face what their reaction is to any event or idea, almost before we know our own. Our relationship has gone from boil to simmer to warm, and in spite of our best efforts to keep it otherwise, it is tending toward lukewarm these days. It is a comfortable relationship, though unfortunately at this time we seem more like friendly roommates than anything else.

Celeste, my oldest daughter, is, at age seventeen, a selfless giver of unsolicited fashion advice, particularly to me. Her favorite expression is 'Hi Dad; Bye, Dad,' generally said in passing as she makes a pit-stop in the house between social engagements, in order to refuel on junk food, change clothes or borrow money.

I'm pretty sure that somewhere in this house there lives another daughter. I remember raising one named Estelle into early adolescence some years ago, until such point that she mysteriously disappeared. I do notice some occasional signs of her now and then, such as blaring music from her bedroom, telltale crumbs on the counter, soda pop cans and snack packaging lying around the house, and even the occasional fleeting glimpse of her as she travels between the front door, her bedroom and the bathroom.

The most important member of the family, as everybody agrees, is Bonita. Bonita is the lynchpin of the family, the keystone that keeps the whole family from splitting at the seams, bursting into broken fragments flying in all directions. She is the one who consoles after disappointments, shares the joy after achievements, absorbs the troubles and frustrations of this widely disparate crowd, patiently listens and silently understands every emotional nuance spoken and unspoken, all the while wisely withholding judgment. She eats a bowl of kibble twice a day and, when the kids remember, gets taken for the occasional walk.

There are times when I have to admire Bonita for her steady, predictable personality (or dogality), but then again, if she senses that I am about to take the trash cans outside, she is over the moon with excitement. So much for canine stoicism.

I could really use a quick snack, which means it's time for what I call a "Survival-of-the-Fittest Cookie Hunt." This odd family quirk developed over time due to the different views on cookie consumption among the various members of our household. Celeste and Estelle tend to favor the 'no time like the present' school of thought, and will completely consume entire packages of cookies within a maximum of two days of when they are brought home from the store. I tend to be a bit more conservative in my cookie-eating habits and prefer to have just a few each day over the course of a week or so. The problem is, if the cookies are there, my daughters will find them and eat them, and the house will be devoid of cookies after day two. Therefore, to prevent this sad situation from occurring, Dawn has taken to hiding the cookies as soon as she brings in the groceries. In the early days, putting the cookies in a high cabinet was sufficient to give me a fighting chance. But soon the girls discovered the secret hiding place. This forced Dawn to become more creative in sequestering the sugary snacks. Of course, the girls improved their sleuthing skills as well, and the whole thing became a cat-and-mouse game of Dawn hiding packages of cookies in ever more obscure places. Unfortunately, Dawn's memory is not what it used to be, and as she generally avoids sweet snacks, the location of the cookies is of negligible importance to her. The result is that there are now unopened bags of cookies stowed in ridiculous places throughout this house, and if I am hungry, I must then prepare myself to undertake a quest of biblical proportions to locate these crunchy, chocolate-chip-filled holy grails. I'm in the midst of my search when Dawn walks in.

"Hi honey, what are you doing with the heating vent?"

"Nothing, I was just hungry. Hey, do you have any idea where the cookies might be?"

"Here, I just picked up a new pack. Chocolate chunk OK?"

"I'd rather just have chocolate chip," I tell her. "The chunks are too big. If I wanted that much chocolate, I'd just get a chocolate bar."

"Well, then you're going to have to keep searching."

"Forget it. I'll try the chocolate chunk. Hey, I just saw Rod, and he said that Lisa just served him with divorce papers."

"I know," she says. "I talked to Lisa last night. I don't know what she's thinking. It's like she wants to start all over again with her life—just erase the whole last eighteen years with Rod. She's acting like she's back in middle school again. What the… Oh, my God!"

"What?"

"I told the girls not to paint their fingernails at the dining room table. Look at this! Look at these drip marks! GIRLS!" Dawn runs upstairs to commence the evening's usual series of confrontations. I prepare my ears for the approaching onslaught.

Although it may not be obvious to the outside observer, our family rides the waves of an estrogen ocean. Judging from the amplitude of the emotional sine waves in our house, even the wallpaper must be saturated with it. As the lone male living in a house of females, I have become accustomed to this, although I know that according to the laws of nature I will never understand it. I have my ups and downs; I'll certainly admit that, particularly lately, but generally my disposition is fairly steady. There would be a relatively modest increase or decrease in my excitement level if, say for example, I won a thousand dollars in the lottery, or if the water heater broke down. But the others pass through as many moods in a day as I do doorways.

One thing I've learned from living in this estrogen sea is that there is no possible weather circumstance that does not warrant the use of either the heat, a fan or the air conditioner. It would seem that to the other members of my household, nature itself is incapable of producing a temperature that is comfortable for a living being. I've also found that there is no room in the estrogen sea for my eminently logical way of thinking. Logic is not the decision-making tool of choice here; emotions rule this roost, or better put, this nest. The verbal battles that take place here on almost a daily basis therefore find me at a marked disadvantage, armed with the wrong kind of weapon for this type of environment. The end result is that I find myself on the losing side more often than not, regardless of how much sense my point makes.

I often wonder what the girls will be like when they are grown, what occupations they will choose, how successful they will be, and whether they will have families. Sometimes I get so concerned for them that I wish I had a way to peek into the future, just to be sure that everything turns out OK. The day that Celeste came home with a tattoo on her shoulder was one of those times. It was a Saturday afternoon and one of those rare occasions when things seemed to be going quite well. I had just finished up a major project at work, installing a new software system for inventory control and over-seeing the staff training sessions that went with it. The family also seemed relatively harmonious, with no slammed bedroom doors or raised voices for several weeks. Although I had long ago learned to beware this kind of calm as a precursor to an impending storm, I absent-mindedly busied myself with minor projects around the house, disingenuously satisfied with myself as captain of the fam-ily ship for such smooth sailing. Celeste stumbled in the back door with her friend Katie. At first I didn't notice that their usual boister-ous and energetic entrance had been replaced with an embarrassed slinking, muffled giggles, and sideways glances at each other. Their brief pit stop in the kitchen was even briefer than usual, and I barely had time to get out a 'Hi, girls' before they scooted off upstairs. A couple hours later, Dawn called me over to the computer.

"Doug, take a look at this picture one of the girls uploaded. That looks like Celeste's shoulder... but it's got a *seahorse* on it!"

"What? What are you talking about?"

"Look- that's a tattoo of a seahorse on a shoulder that looks like Celeste's." I squint at the screen and see what looks like a small pink seahorse, complete with curled tail, outlined in telltale tattoo-blue ink.

"How can you tell whose shoulder that is? It could be anyone's shoulder."

"Trust me. I've seen Celeste's shoulders enough to know. That's her shoulder. Her right shoulder, in fact." Our eyes locked. Three seconds later, as if our voices were driven by the same impulse zipping through our neurons, we both yelled, "CELESTE!"

The spaghetti noodles lie steaming in the colander, the last drips of boiling water dripping through into the sink. Dawn says, "Estelle, please feed Bonita and give her fresh water." Dutifully, wordlessly, Estelle fills the bowl with dog food. None of us foresee the culinary catastrophe that looms like a crouched leopard waiting to pounce. Estelle's cell phone rings. Distracted, she turns while carrying the day-old dog water, frothy with backwash and peppered with biscuit crumbs, and dumps it into the sink, but unfortunately directly onto the noodles, through which the dirty dog water washes, leaving its kibbly residue to decorate our dinner. A jumble of emotions flashes through each family member's head; incredulity, anger, hilarity. But which one will percolate to the surface first? What will be the final display on the emotional slot machine? Estelle's lips curl upward at the corners ever so slightly.

"Uh, sorry?" she says, as if it were a question. A resounding laugh ripples through the kitchen, pulling the whole family into convulsions. This light-hearted reaction assures me that we are indeed a healthy family unit after all, despite all of our challenges. If I am depressed, perhaps it's only on the surface- a 'topical depression' as it were. Deep down inside, I'm fine. Right?

CHAPTER 3

Spectrum of a Shattered Prism

6 :00 AM. The alarm rings.

Didn't I just do this yesterday? And every other day stretching back to the moment I took my first breath? Already, at this early hour, I can basically predict every major move I will make throughout the day. The showering, shaving and dressing routine. The commute. The traffic. At the office, people doing the same inane things, and me fixing the same stupid problems. A rushed lunch at my desk, followed by more of the same. The commute back home, more traffic, the dinner routine, exhaustion and television. On bad days, there will be some fight with one or both of the girls about something they've done, something they haven't done, or something they want to do that we don't want them to do. Doors will slam, music will blast to drive away reality, and the family will sulk, not as one but as four lone individuals, each of us feeling misunderstood until the next morning, when the cycle will start all over. The alarm rings again. Morning has arrived. Like a swordsman in Tennyson's light brigade,

I must get up; I must see this day through. *Mine but to do and die*, I remind myself.

As it turns out, it isn't a good day at all. Work doesn't go well, and it has nothing to do with clinical depression; it has everything to do with corporate idiocy. Dawn listens patiently to my rants about work, but she really can't offer much advice, as her position as a school music teacher insulates her somewhat from the ups and downs of the corporate world. Lately I have been relying on my best friend Ted for this sort of thing.

I've known Ted since we were kids. We grew up together from the days of pickup baseball games and ice cream to the nights of picking up girls and liquor. In our teens, we counseled each other with misguided but well-intended girlfriend advice and even survived the occasional brief fistfight when our tempers flared. Toward the end of our high school years, we came up with the brilliant idea to throw a swinging beer party for all of our friends one weekend while Ted's parents were away. We made all the plans with such thorough precision that, at least of this one isolated aspect, our parents would have been proud. No school project ever received so much careful attention to detail as this gathering did- obtaining and sequestering the sacred beverage, removing costly or easily damaged furnishings and décor, slip-covering and protecting those pieces that did remain, selectively inviting those friends who were capable of keeping a secret and were reasonably responsible in other people's houses (but still fun when drunk) and even unearthing his parents' favorite collection of beer mugs, normally reserved for the rarest of occasions, and stashing them in the freezer to frost them ahead of the big event. The party was a tremendous success, the frosted mugs a huge hit, and a massive number of canned beers were carefully poured, passed around and guzzled. The next day, with the utmost care, Ted and I cleaned the post-party house from top to bottom, removed what must have been hundreds of empty beer cans, scrubbed the mugs and returned them to their rightful resting place, and carted out the trash. It was the perfect crime. We high-fived each other for a job well done. One week later, a special occasion arrived. It was an occasion so special for Ted's parents that the prized beer mugs would be broken out, for the first time (to their knowledge) in two years. Upon removing the mugs from their cabinet, Ted's parents noticed the most amazing thing— after roughly two years in storage, there was not so much as one microgram of dust on the entire collection! Unfortunately, their amazement quickly turned to suspicion, as it often does with parents, and a contrite confession was leveraged out of Ted. Not long afterward, a chain-reaction of groundings befell the neighborhood like an avalanche careening through the Himalayas.

More than a quarter-century later, Ted is still here, acting as a sounding board to my crazy ideas (and as generator of a few of his own), a marital and family advisor when I need it, and lately, a therapist for a certain troubled pal of his.

In the evening, I give Ted a call.

"Hey Ted, Doug," I say flatly.

"Hey, old pal! What's shakin' bro?" Ted hasn't changed his reflexive telephone greeting since high school.

"I've had better decades."

"Oh, Doug, come on, pal, your life can't be that bad. Did you ever stop to think that it might be you? Why don't you see a doctor? I know lots of people on depression medication now, and they're all doing better."

"I *have* seen a doctor, Ted. But just listen. This time my mood is justified, I swear."

"OK, OK. What happened?"

"My company is really pissing me off. You know, they made me their IT Director. You'd think they'd at least give some credence to my recommendations, as far as IT goes. You'd *think*. But they don't. They wanted to get some new software to do the customer account maintenance. I'd been looking at the different options available for months. This one package, *4mul8er*, is so much better than all the others. It's exactly what we need. I spoke with everyone in Customer Service that would work with the system. Not just the managers, but the people that would actually work with it every day. I know exactly what they want, and I know exactly what the company needs, and 4mul8er would be perfect. I did a great presentation to the management committee, answered all the ridiculous questions they had, walked them through the whole deal, and a week later, today, I find out they decided to go with this other program because it's cheaper. This program isn't anything like as good as 4mul8er. It's *stupid*. And guess who has to implement it? Me! It's *ridiculous*! I've been working with these things for twenty years, since they were basically electronic slide rules. They hire me to direct IT, and when I try to direct it, they don't listen to me."

"Doug…"

"I'm so pissed off. I've put my whole life into that place. I *live* there!" By now, I'm pacing the kitchen floor like a caged zoo animal.

"Doug… Come on, man, calm down. When you work at a place that long, you're bound to have times like this. You know they respect you. I'll bet you're a highly regarded person there," he says.

"Obviously not anymore."

"Doug, what's going on, really? This is the third time in the last two weeks you've called me to gripe about something. You never used to worry about this stuff. You used to just let it wash over you like a rogue wave. You're just taking one incident and blowing it up into a representation of how the last twenty years have gone. Think about it. There's been good times for you during those years. Remember how happy you were when you got the Director position?"

"That was a long time ago," I say. In fact, it was only about two years ago, but since then, my future career prospects seem to have evaporated.

"Look Doug, you know what you've got?" he asks. "Midlife crisis. That's what it is— midlife crisis. Everyone gets it. Here's what you need to do— go online and have a look at the flashiest new cars… Did you see the one Cal got?"

"Not the sports car thing!" Our mutual friend Cal had recently purchased a very expensive imported vehicle that he treats better than any of his family members, and since then his prospects of remaining happily married seem to have dropped off astronomically.

"It seems to work for other guys. Cal's real happy with his."

"What's next, the 21-year-old sex kitten?" Ted seems to think I'm going through the stereotypical midlife crisis and therefore require the stereotypical treatments. Can't he see that my situation is different?

"Well, since you mention it, that is another possibility… 'Course I don't know if Dawn would go for it…"

"What kind of best friend are you? You're supposed to be helping me, not putting my marriage on the rocks!"

"All right, well what do *you* think would help?"

"Certainly not these little pills. All they do is make my head feel funny. I don't think they're doing anything for this depression I supposedly have. Besides, I think the doctor's wrong. I have *reasons* to be upset. *Good* reasons."

"It takes time for the pills to work. You can't just take them for a week and say they don't work. And as for your *reasons*, well, they're not that good. Plenty of people have things a lot worse than you, and they're still a lot happier, and do you know why?"

"Their best friends are more helpful?"

"No, they look at things in a different way. They look at what they have, not what they don't have. They look at what has gone right in their lives, not at what has gone wrong."

"Well if I did that, I wouldn't have very much to look at."

"Doug, listen to me. You need to take a break. When's the last time you had a vacation?"

"Just last year. We spent a week at the shore. Dawn and the kids loved it."

"Did *you* love it?"

"I dunno… it was fine, I guess. If the family's happy, I'm happy."

"That sounds great, but that doesn't explain why you're *not* happy then, does it?"

"My problems have nothing to do with whether I spent a week at the shore or not."

"Fine, but do me a favor; just think about it, will you? Just think about taking a little time to yourself to chill out. Go someplace nice. Someplace you've always wanted to go."

It takes me a couple of days to figure out that maybe Ted is right. Maybe I *do* need a vacation. I need *something*. But I think it should be something different than what I've done before. Something I can do by myself, just *me*. Something that I choose, not something that I am doing for somebody else. It's been so long since I've done something I've really wanted to do, that the whole idea is almost alien to me. Don't get me wrong; I have done a lot of things I've enjoyed; it's just that there was always some other reason to do them. Going out to dinner to make my wife happy, vacationing at a certain place to make my family happy, playing golf with a client to make my boss happy—it's almost to the point at which I draw a blank when asked what I really want to do. My thoughts are so intertwined with work and family, with what others expect of me, that I wonder if I even know who I am anymore. What would I do with a beautiful spring day if I had one, and could really do *whatever* I wanted? Would I do things that are new to me? Would I be creative, or would I do nothing at all? Somewhere between age nine and now, I have lost the ability to fill a nice spring day with fun.

One evening I decide to go through my various frequent-flyer accounts, in which I've accumulated all sorts of mileage points from my past business and vacation travel. Most of the travel I have done has been within the United States, but I've also had a few business trips to Canada and Europe, plus trips with the family to a couple of resorts in Mexico and the Caribbean over the years.

As I review the statements, I find that most of the frequent-flyer accounts I have are either expired or contain too few miles to obtain any reward tickets. Unfortunately I have a knack for joining the club of whatever airline I fly on at the time, rather than concentrating on just one. However, much of my travel has been on one particular airline, as the nearest airport, Newark, is that airline's hub. I check their website and it tells me that I have enough miles for a free roundtrip fare 'within the United States, or between the United States and Canada, Mexico, the Caribbean or Central America, or selected destinations in Europe.' I should be able to find something interesting in that list.

Half a world of options, yet so difficult to decide what I want. I feel like a vegetarian at a barbecue buffet- I see more things I don't want than things I do. A cruise? The last thing I need is to be marooned at sea on a giant, floating shopping mall loaded with the same bland things I'm trying to escape. A Caribbean beach resort? Also out- an oasis of American culture and over-the-top affluence surrounded by barbed wire and safely cocooned from the looming harsh reality of third-world life would be unlikely to offer me any new insights. Nor would the kitschy tourist centers of Europe that have all but transitioned into theme park versions of what they might— or might not— once have been. For me, no phosphorescent umbrella drinks served by tuxedo-clad waiters or warmed, round pebbles strategically placed up and down my spine like a Monument Valley for frogs, or pair of limp, damp cucumber slices wilting over my eyes, are going to do the trick.

I review the list of potential destinations again. United States… Let's try something different…Canada… nah, too cold— I definitely want some sunshine… Mexico, just went there last year… the Caribbean— by myself?… Central America… well, what? No first impression comes to mind. The idea of Central America begins to buzz around my head like a pesky fly, until I stop and think about it. My eyes had skipped over that region as if it were the fine print on the bottom of a contract. But why? In fact, it seems, the Central American countries are a lot like me. Their best days are probably gone; nobody pays much attention to them; they've been pushed around a bit by bigger powers; they're not particularly pretty. Above all, they're stuck in the middle, both physically and temporally, like me in the middle of life, a skinny, awkward isthmus between old and new. I amuse myself with these forced, ridiculous analogies in my mind as though it were the ultimate inside joke, but the truth is, I find the idea intriguing. Nobody I know has ever gone to Central America except for a pair of adventurous pals of mine who traveled to Costa Rica on a rafting trip. The rest of the region draws a total blank. Probably very few tourists, I would think, at least as few as you'll likely find anywhere these days. Someplace *different*. That it is. And to top it off, an element of danger. The most dangerous activity I've undertaken in recent years is eating fatty foods. It wouldn't hurt, I imagine, to get some adrenaline flowing in this aging body before it dries up.

Central America actually makes sense for me for another reason. Although my major in college was computer science, I minored in Spanish and never really had a chance to use it after that. But I occasionally listen to the Spanish-language radio stations in the car on the way to work just to exercise my brain. I never reached a level of fluency by any means, but I could get by. The more I think about it the more I like the idea of having a look at Central America, for every reason and for no reason. Why not? Within minutes I have decided.

Now that I've settled on the region, where, precisely, should I go and what should I do there? A quick look at my atlas shows that Central America is composed of seven small countries squeezed in between Mexico and South America. Which one shall I pick? Should I book a five-star hotel that might as well be in New Jersey? Over the week that follows, I kick the idea around in my brain a thousand different times. The thin, winding shape of the land and the small size of the countries get me thinking about making an overland journey along its backbone to see all of them. A little research reveals that although there are no rail services to speak of, the countries are crisscrossed by several long-distance bus companies that seem at least relatively safe, convenient and inexpensive. After considering it, I decide to start my wanderings in Panama, and then proceed onward by bus to Costa Rica, Nicaragua, Honduras, El Salvador and finally Guatemala, from where I'll return home. Belize is a bit off of that path, so I'll save Belize for a future trip. As far as what to do, I think I'll just explore and let the chips fall where they may. To do too much reading and planning in advance, setting itineraries and booking tours, would take the spontaneous, serendipitous edge off the trip. I want to experience life, not have it spoon-fed to me.

I keep the idea to myself for a few days, just to be sure it isn't a passing whim, and to rehearse the points of my justification speech, knowing I am likely to meet some resistance from my wife and kids, and possibly from my friends at work. It turns out I am right about my friends. Unbeknownst to me before, they are all very well informed about Central America. Not that any of them have ever been there. And not that any of them could give me the slightest bit of useful information about traveling there. No, the thing they all know about it is that it is dangerous— so dangerous, in fact, that it is ridiculous even to consider going there for any reason. From their descriptions, it is amazing that anyone is capable of living there at all. Where did they get all of this information? From the news. There certainly is some bad news from Central America from time to time, and at times it is interesting enough that the US news media will devote a few inches of newsprint to it, or take a few seconds away from the pop culture gossip coverage to mention it. OK, it's dangerous. I won't argue that point. But there also must be some good things that happen there- things that go unnoticed by the American media. What kind of good news from Central America would merit coverage from our media?

The time arrives to discuss my plan with Dawn. I choose a Saturday evening when both of the kids are out. Estelle is away at a sleepover at a friend's house, and Celeste is missing in action, as usual. Dawn has an interesting habit of collecting the evening newspapers each weekday, when she is too busy to read them, and placing them on the end table in the living room. Then on Saturday evenings, when she does have time, she skims through all the newspapers of the previous week. The only trouble is that the newspapers are stacked in reverse chronological order, so she ends up reading the most recent newspaper first, and the previous ones afterward, traveling back in time, as it were, through the headlines. She reads out loud the ones she finds interesting.

"Oh, look— 'Herd of Sheep Gets Loose on Route 80'!"

I decide to present my idea at face value, as a way of dealing with my current situation, hoping she'll understand. "Dawn, you know I've been going through this depression thing. I've been thinking about it, and I think I really just need to take some time out to work my way through it."

"Time out of what?" she asks, her eyes widening. "Oh, no, Doug, is this about our marriage? You were talking to Rod- What are you saying?" Dawn has a tendency to overreact and fear the worst.

"I'm not saying anything- not like *that*. Our marriage is fine; at least I think it is. I just need some time to myself. I don't mean to get away from *you*; I mean a break from the day-to-day routine, you know. I'm getting so sick of it. It's hard to explain. I feel like everything I'm doing is for other people, and I'm just running on the same boring treadmill, getting older. It's like I'm watching life go on through the window, but I can't go outside. I work; I come home; we watch TV. And I don't even *like* TV. On the weekends I'm doing yard work. It's been like this for over fifteen years. Not that it's been bad, but… I just need a break. I don't know how else to describe it. I need something different."

"OK, spill it. You've obviously got something on your mind. What are you thinking of?"

"Well, I've got a lot of air miles in my frequent-flyer club. Enough to go to Central America. And I really want to do it."

"Doug, please tell me you're talking about Kansas…"

"No, really Central America. I really do want to go. A guy needs to have some adventure in his life. That's what we were made for. It won't be dangerous. I'm not the type of guy that gets into trouble."

"No, but you're the type of guy that decides he wants to go to Central America out of the blue. And you're the type of guy that's been on depression medication for the last month. For me, that's something to worry about." She places her hand on my shoulder affectionately.

"Look, honey, I know you've been going through a lot lately, but you'll get through it. We'll get through it. It happens to a lot of people our age. These are tough years. But we all get through them, and most guys don't need to risk their lives to do it."

"I'm not risking my life, Dawn. I'm taking a trip. If I don't go, I'm risking my sanity."

"Honey, I know you. You get exhausted from a couple of days of camping with Ted and Rod every year. And from what I can tell, you guys spend most of the time sitting around drinking beer. What are you going to do in a rain forest by yourself?"

"It's not a rain forest. Not most of it, anyway. I'll be traveling by bus from one country to another, staying in low-cost hotels."

"*By bus.*" She spices these words heavily with a tone of sarcasm that I rarely hear from Dawn. I consider the possibility that she really thinks I'm losing my grip.

"I know what you're thinking. It's really very safe. Lots of people do it. I've been reading about it."

"Nobody *I* know has done it."

"Lots of people down there do it. *I* can do it. I studied Spanish in college. I never got to really use it. That resort we stayed at in Cancun was nothing. Everybody there spoke English."

"Doug, if you really feel you need to go, I'm not going to stop you. You know I've never stood in the way of your dreams. But I want you to think carefully about this one. Is this really something you want? Or are you just trying to feel younger?"

"Maybe a bit of both, but what's wrong with that? Look at it this way— what's the worst that could happen?"

It wasn't the best choice of words. Dawn gives me a look that I instantly understand. I muster up my cutest little-boy smile to lighten the moment. She gets up and walks toward the bedroom door and then turns around again to say, "By the way, Celeste just got another tattoo."

I go outside to check on the lawn with Bonita. As soon as we step outside I see them— my enemies. I just dispelled them yesterday, but their comrades are again lined up on my lawn, their golden crowns glinting in the sun as if in mocking admiration. Dandelions! Dandelions are the cheap whores of the DNA world. They are interested only in reproducing themselves as prolifically as possible, without contributing any beauty to the world, save for the one fleeting moment in which they flower a brilliant yellow. They then quickly mutate into gnarled, thick-stalked monstrosities, and then giant, white-haired puffballs, like skinny little Einsteins who stuck their fingers in the electric outlet. I sigh and pick up my weeding trowel, Bonita trotting at my heels.

Bonita has learned the boundaries of our yard very well. To aid in her quick education, and especially to keep her out of the road, we installed an electric fence several years ago. The 'fence' is actually invisible, as it is only a system of electric wires buried underground. Should Bonita overstep her bounds, the system will trigger a harmless but noticeable electric shock through the collar she wears. After a few months with the system in place, Bonita had learned the boundaries so well that I took off the electrical collar device. Now, if a squirrel or rabbit runs by, Bonita will chase it, but she will run only up to the line and then will skid to a complete stop.

Bonita and I often walk around the yard together as I pull weeds, mow the lawn, or just survey the property. I have never worn an electric collar, nor have I ever received an electrical shock for crossing the line, but I know where those boundaries are too. As we approach the edge of our property, both Bonita and I will stop at the same place, often without realizing it. We'll look out over the neighboring yards for a minute or two, then turn around and walk in the other direction, neither of us with even the slightest thought of venturing beyond. It is funny, the things we learn in life and how deeply ingrained in our psyches they become.

I'm not so sure that Dawn is enamored with the idea of me traipsing off to Central America on what must seem like a moment's notice. I know she doesn't really understand what I've been going through lately, and it must have hit her out of the blue when I brought this up. After dinner the following evening, we are relaxing in the living room, and I try again.

"Dawn, I know this Central America thing seemed to come out of nowhere for you, but I really have been thinking about it for a while. I just want to do something that I came up with on my own, and decided to do for myself. This is something I never got to do while I was in college, when some of the other guys did, backpacking around different parts of the world. Remember my folks didn't have a lot of money and I could only put two years in at college before I had to take a break and work a couple of years to save up money so I could finish."

"I know. I've heard that story a thousand times. I know you were never happy about how that all worked out, but at least you got your degree. You should be proud of that."

"I am proud of that, but I never got to travel, is the point. I did everything because I *had* to do it; I never did anything because I *wanted* to do it. And still, even now, everything I do, every move I make, is for somebody else."

"It's like that for everybody at this age. Don't you think that I wish *I* could take some time out for myself? We just have obligations to our jobs, to our spouses, to our kids… these are just normal. Think of it as an investment for the future. When the kids are grown, when the house is paid off, we'll have more time to do what we want, and hopefully more money to spend on it."

"We'll be old by then!"

"Well, thank you for that enlightening thought."

"No, you know what I mean… It's more than that, though. I'm not just talking about obligations; I'm talking about everything… the whole way I live my life… the smallest things I do, the way that I think, my reactions to things… I'm starting to realize that even these things are all reflexive. They were taught to me, or infused into my brain by someone else. I try very hard to think for myself, to not be a sheep. You know, like… Politically I'm an Independent, so I evaluate the political issues for myself. I try to be open-minded on the issues, but the issues themselves are chosen by someone else. I'm just a flesh-and-blood robot that was programmed by society to give preconditioned responses."

"Don't you think you're exaggerating a bit? You don't look like a robot! Although your nose *does* look a little like a light bulb!"

"Dawn, I'm serious. It's hard to explain. I don't know if I ever even wanted the things that I have now… a big house in the suburbs, a job where I basically fix other people's screw-ups day after day…"

"…Me?"

"No, I don't mean you. Would you calm down about that? You and the girls I am sure about. But, I mean, I don't think I ever even thought about what I wanted. I just went for these things because everybody else did. I've been a good little sheep that followed the crowd, and I'm tired of it. Things have to change, and I have to change them now!"

"I don't know; you make a pretty cute sheep. Maybe I should call you 'Lamb Chop'…"

"You know what I'm saying, though, right? What would I be like if, instead of being raised here, I had grown up on a desert island, or out in the woods in Alaska or something?"

"You'd probably be the same as you are now, but your legs would be even skinnier!" She gives me a crooked smile.

"You're definitely the weirdest person I ever married!" I reply with mock exasperation.

I stare out the window for a moment, then shut my eyes and my mind wanders. I'm sitting at my desk in elementary school. The desk has a flat wooden top that is attached by a hinge to the back of the metal desk frame; my books, papers, pencils and crayons are inside the desk. I must be in first or second grade. The teacher has the class's attention; she is explaining why the number five must be written with two strokes, the first stroke being the lower or 'body' portion of the figure, the second being the straight line or 'hat' on top. "Now," she asks the class, "Does your father put his hat on before he gets dressed in the morning?" The class is in stitches. "Does your father get out of bed and put his hat on right away, then get dressed afterward?" Guffaws from the young students as they picture this ludicrous scenario in their heads. "So why would you draw the top of a five before you draw the bottom?" she concludes, and the entire class sees the point. Thirty-five or forty years later, I am still drawing my fives this way. Why? Because my father didn't put his hat on before he got dressed. At some point in time I must have realized that there was a disconnect in the logic (confounded by the fact that my father never even wore a hat!), but I still continue in this rote function like a robot, because some teacher had nothing important to say one day, and decided to enrich my eager, malleable brain with this nugget of wisdom. I briefly consider that with a concentrated effort, I could change the way I draw my fives, but it strikes me that to start drawing my fives 'backwards' after thirty-five years would be one of the most pathetic attempts at rebelliousness that I have ever heard. So it becomes just another of my idiosyncrasies, lumped on the shelf in my brain with many more.

Was it school that closed my mind to thinking for myself? I remember the old adage about history being written by the victors. Even in victory, however, the final version of facts is not decided.

There is constantly a struggle between those with political agendas about what to include or not to include, and what to emphasize or de-emphasize, in school textbooks. Then there are the stories we were taught that are flat-out untrue. If George Washington were really a heroic and gifted leader, as I believe he must have been, why was it necessary to supplement his real historical feats with myths like the one about him chopping down his father's cherry tree and the story about him throwing a silver dollar across the Potomac? All that's missing from his background is a virgin birth and he gains a shot at becoming a religious figure. I believe it's in our best interest to keep him mortal, because then children who learn about his life can aspire to his achievements.

I feel a hand on my shoulder and it's Dawn. "Doug, life is just perception. It's all in the way you look at things. You have so many good things in your life to be thankful for… a good family, a good job, a comfortable life, good health… I just wish you would get over this restlessness, or dissatisfaction, or whatever it is that you're going through. Try to look at things in a positive way. Think of yourself as a prism, with the sunlight of your life shining through you. It's up to you to make it into a rainbow. Those colors are all there, hidden in the sunbeam; you've just got to see them. Make that rainbow, Doug. It's here." She's right; the spectrum is there; unfortunately, my prism has shattered.

Well, Dawn seems to have given me the green light for my trip, or at least the yellow light. As for the kids, they probably won't be too bothered that I'm gone, if they notice at all. I'm not so sure I'll be nominated for the father-of-the-year award anytime soon. If my memory is not too distorted by time, I believe I was a fairly popular member of the family back in the early days. Then the girls hit their teens. I can't quite put my finger on what happened next, but my approval rating as a parent seemed to take a nose-dive soon after that. Maybe it was because I wasn't able to spend as much time at home anymore due to demands on my time at the office. Maybe I became a bit withdrawn when the chemical imbalance struck. Then again, maybe it had something to do with my idea of creating a fifteen-page date application form to evaluate their male suitors. Or maybe, it was the associated idea of a non-refundable application fee. It will likely always be a mystery to me, but for whatever reason, the family situation, which I still wouldn't describe as 'hostile' is a bit less cozy now than it once was. I could probably get away with taking a several-week-long trip without too many tears being shed.

As my departure day approaches, I begin to have second thoughts. What if I get lost? What if I get robbed or kidnapped, as seems so common in the headlines? Maybe I've made the wrong choice— maybe it's a bad idea. That's why nobody else is doing it. If it were a good idea, there would be lots of others doing it, instead of saying, "Wow, Doug, are you sure you know what you're doing? Why would you want to do that?"

A few days before I am to leave, I watch a video with my family. Another hormone-laced high school movie, exactly the same as all the others, with only different characters, actors and names. Whoever came up with the line 'high school never ends' must have been talking about Hollywood. I went to high school for four years and spent the next 30 years watching it on television. There are comparatively fewer movies about college life or young singles enjoying the dating life. By the time you reach my age, you have absolutely no on-screen peers except quarreling divorcées and bitter, clueless or dysfunctional parents. Life at my age is too boring even for a television show. Maybe that's because I spend most of my non-working hours watching television shows. This isn't a life. I've got to go. There is a lesson I learned while playing tag as a child. If you want to, you can stay on 'base' through the entire duration of the game, and you will have no worries of ever getting tagged. However, such a strategy makes the game dull, pointless and devoid of fun. That's not the way life should be. Get off base, and live a little. Do some running; have some fun. That's the way to play. I've been on base too long. It's time to play the game.

CHAPTER 4
Tequila Moonrise

I t takes two flights to get from New Jersey to Panama City, and I'm
not much of a flyer. At the airport, I am somewhat relieved to see
that the first plane is medium-sized- not so small that I think, 'How
the hell is this thing ever going to make it all the way to Florida,' yet
not so large that I wonder, 'How the hell is this thing ever going to
get off the ground?' The first flight takes me to Miami, where I have a
layover of a couple of hours and spend most of the time at the news-
stand, distractedly browsing through books and magazines.

Fortunately, I haven't had to act as airline policeman today.
Usually I am forced into this uncomfortable position. Before take-
off, the lead flight attendant will always announce over the public
address system that all cellular phones must be turned on to airplane
mode as they can interfere with the plane's navigation equipment.
There is always some idiot sitting near me (and probably several
more that aren't near me) who thinks that he or she is exempt from
this rule. As the flight attendants make only a cursory check, and this
person either hides the phone or pretends to be turning it off as they

pass, enforcing the rule is usually left to me. The choice I am faced with is either to assume the responsibilities of an unpaid flight security person and inform this individual that they must turn off their phone, or to take my chances with an unspecified safety incident, possibly leading to the aircraft going down in a flaming wreck. After some consideration of the pluses and minuses, I usually end up with the unpaid policeman role. Luckily, today it seems I have the day off. I am thankful to avoid this added stress.

I regard the sunny Miami weather as a preview of things to come, and I look forward to days of brilliant sunlight and nights of soft, silky breezes. A second three-hour flight (on another medium-sized plane), and I'm in Panama.

After arriving in Panama City, I take a taxi to the coastal town of Balboa and book a middle-class hotel right next to the Panama Canal. Twenty-plus years of business travel have left me soft and I don't want to overdo the roughing-it on the first day. For me, the hotel will serve during the daytime mainly as a repository for my luggage. For the few other Americans staying there, it appears to be a sanctuary, a refuge or "secure zone" isolated from the imagined terrors of the Panamanian outdoors. I note a number of fellow Americans, both businesspeople and some that appear to be vacationing, sitting by the hotel pool, seemingly with little desire to leave the hotel grounds. Panama is unlike the United States; therefore, Americans need to insulate themselves from it. That seems to be the line of thought. I can't understand it. If the idea of travel is to broaden yourself and see the world, why on earth confine yourself to an island of American culture and sit by a pool that may as well be five blocks from your home?

I, on the other hand, can't get outside soon enough. I take a long walk along the paved footpath that follows the canal's entrance. The first thing I notice is the humidity— I feel as if someone has sprayed me with the mist from a warm hose. My shirt is soaked after the first ten minutes of walking. The sun plays hide-and-seek in the clouds above me, and when it comes out, the heat is intense.

The second thing I notice is the green- the vivid, stunning greens that surround me in every direction. Who could have imagined that there could be such incredible variety within one single color? I see every green that I can name: the deep, cool greens of the forest, the burning golden-tinged greens of leaves in the sun, creamy char-treuse, shades of lime, flecks of Kelly, thick fronds of mint… until I run out of words to describe the colors and yet the spectrum con-tinues, unabated. Then, as if nature were trying to outdo itself with color, there are flowers on the trees: here pink and orange and amber like tulips, there yellow and white like daisies. I look down and think I see half a nutshell walking a wobbling path in front of me; a closer inspection reveals a leafcutter ant hoisting the precarious load.

Puffy white cumulus clouds of towering magnitude drift above, their bloated gray bellies pregnant with moisture. Banana trees and coconut palms hiss as a gentle breeze ruffles their fronds. Dozens of slack-jawed, yawning brown pelicans fill a skeletal tree. I spy ant-hills as big as upturned serving bowls with tunnels the diameter of a half-dollar; birds twitter; butterflies flit; I note the faint whiff of rotting fish and engine oil, and there is… life! Life everywhere, struggling and succeeding in every niche! It is hard to be melan-choly when you have a front-row seat to life's inevitable success. Any doubts I had about taking this trip melt away as I walk.

In the canal, the occasional container ship meanders by. A basin of anchored yachts rocks and sways in unison to the rippling wakes. To the east, the Pacific Ocean gently massages the shoreline. The ser-pentine twist of the Panamanian isthmus makes this the only place in the world where the Pacific Ocean is to the east and the Atlantic is to the west. This means that it is possible to watch the sun rise over the Pacific, enjoy a leisurely day, then take a short drive, and watch it set over the Atlantic that evening. That, however, is a joy I will leave to someone else.

I step closer to the water to admire its beauty. I gaze at the sparkling sunlight tripping across the waves for a few minutes, and then suddenly a searing pain sends a jolt through me; both of my feet feel as if they are being jabbed with flaming hot needles. I reflexively bend over and grab at my ankles, then jump up and stamp my feet on the ground like a tap dancer gone raving mad. I look down and see nothing but tiny red dots— ants— *red* ants— *Fire Ants!* Somehow I have stumbled near a fire ant nest and, through nothing other than incredibly bad luck, have managed to plant my feet on a piece of property that they had claimed as theirs. The pain has now climbed up my shins, and I leap as quickly as possible away from the source of my agony, slapping and brushing at my feet and legs until I can't see a single ant anymore, and even then I continue, as I feel phantom ants crawling on my body for some time afterward. Once I am back in the hotel I peel my socks down and count only eight raised red welts- five on my left foot and three on my right. They burn like hot cinders and look like tiny red gumdrops. Luckily my thick cotton athletic socks and quick reactions have protected me from a much worse experience. I alert the desk clerk and he sends someone out for hydrocortisone cream, and this helps a lot.

Later, I go out for another walk. The air is still warm, but the heat has lost its blistering edge from midday, and it is now much more comfortable to be outside. I find the perfect little restaurant in which to pass the evening. It is an open place, constructed inexpensively of wood and a thatched roof, but it looks very welcoming, with colorful lights strung along the trim and candles flickering on the tables. Classic rock music and lively conversation in staccato Spanish fill the air. Inside, a bar is stocked with all the standard international liqueurs. Most of the crowd is inside, but I am drawn to the front patio that overlooks a green strip of forest and the canal beyond.

This section of the canal is a natural inlet, and it is much wider than the excavated trench that links the inlet with Gatun Lake further inland. A long, narrow wooden pier juts over the water, and scattered groups of yachters walk its length, having moored their boats along the various docks perpendicular to the pier. Their laughter echoes off the water. I order a locally-brewed beer and relish the moment and my newfound paradise.

As the sun sets, half of the canal turns orange, then bronze, and the buoys began to blink with red and green lights. The rolling green hills on the horizon fade to gray silhouettes. I am amazed by how much difference the angle of the sun makes on the scenery- the colors, the shadows, the sparkle and sheen of the water.

The sun is the central feature of the Panamanian day. Its intensity is so powerful that its position in the sky controls just about every sensation that the body perceives: the brilliance of the surrounding colors, the prickle of heat on the skin, the heavy grip of the humidity in the air, the earthy, peaty smell of the forest…

I have always found it fascinating that the sun is actually a star. When we say 'sunlight,' we really mean 'starlight,' because there's no difference. In the daytime, the entire Earth is bathed in pure starlight, straight from the heavens. I've seen starlight, but I've never really seen the sun. This may sound a bit strange, but it's true. When I was young I remember being warned not to look at the sun or it could damage my eyes. Never being the type to question authority,

I heeded that warning and internalized it, so in all my life I've never really seen a sunset or a sunrise. While other people were enjoying them, I was averting my eyes slightly, or shielding them with my hand, so as not to harm my vision. Of course I caught brief glimpses; it's impossible not to, but I reflexively shifted my gaze. Then I'd worry for days that I'd damaged my retinas. In my adult life, that reflex hasn't subsided. To me, it represents just one of a number of ways that I've been hesitant to embrace the joys of life. Too cloistered, too careful. I wonder how much enjoyment I've missed due to perceived danger. I suppose that I developed neuroses like this very early in life. Maybe the freedom of this trip will provide me with the opportunity to lose them.

The sun at last disappears, leaving atmospheric dust to scatter its rays in orange, pink and red. I am glad I came here. I've only been here a half day and already I am beginning to relax and enjoy myself. I close my eyes and dream of the adventures to come, and drink in the elusive moment that is now.

The waitress returns to ask if I would like anything to eat. I order a steak with mushrooms and it is served with fluffy white rice and hot corn tortillas. I ask for another beer and enjoy my dinner. The steak is slightly tough, but a little hot sauce makes it perfect. A black-and-white stray cat, doubtless a frequent visitor to these outdoor tables, meanders up to me, and I drop a few pieces of steak for it, remembering to pat off as much hot sauce as possible with my napkin first. Its eyes widen like it has just won the lottery. I think I have a new best friend.

By the time I finish eating, it has become so dark that I can no longer read the menu card, even with the candlelight. It has been a very pleasant day, but I am tired, so I walk alongside the canal back toward the hotel, with only the starlight and the bouncing reflections from the boats and buoys to guide me. I notice that the evening has brought with it mosquitoes, since I sport several of the telltale itching bumps around my ankles, strategically located between fire ant stings for maximum discomfort, and one particularly annoying bite on the base of my neck. But once I'm back in my room, it doesn't take long to drift off into a long, satisfying and peaceful sleep.

Morning comes and the sky is clear and blue as a fly's eye. It is already scorching hot and it's only nine o'clock. I notice that my mosquito bites and fire ant stings from the previous evening have swelled to various diameters, and the one bite on my neck leaves a speck of blood on my finger when I scratch at it. I have to force myself to leave it alone, and when I have to give in and scratch, I try to scratch only the area close to the bite and not the bite itself. I find that if I use two fingers, I can place one on each side of the bite and scratch fiercely as long as I am careful not to hit the bite itself. The itching is so intense, that to scratch it is almost orgasmic. I cover it and the fire ant stings liberally with layers of hydrocortisone cream. This provides me some temporary relief, but I really need to pick up some insect lotion to prevent future annoyances, and I hope the bite doesn't become infected.

Panama City is a very modern city. Ironically, I make this observation during a taxi ride to the *Casco Viejo*, the old quarter of the city. From my hotel, the taxi ride takes me through the city center, a beehive of endless construction activity crisscrossed by a new, but heavily trafficked, highway system. The lines of cars flow like thick syrup through a funnel as we pass through the center of town, allowing me a lingering view of the sleek, shiny high-rise condominiums, hotels, office skyscrapers and business complexes.

When we reach the Casco Viejo, I direct the driver to pull over in front of a main plaza so I can continue on foot. I spend a very pleasant afternoon giving myself a walking tour of the cathedrals, monuments and domed colonial architecture that the Spanish thoughtfully left behind. Not only is it as beautiful as anything I've seen in Europe, but it's also free and practically devoid of other tourists. Let the ovine masses wait in Europe's lengthy queues, I think, cordoned off by red velvet ropes; I'll enjoy the magnificent historical cities of Latin America, ponder their stories in peaceful solitude, and save my money for things of greater consequence.

In the evening, I return to the dockside restaurant where I had dinner the previous night, looking forward to another night of watching the ships and the lights dancing on the water, and enjoying a good meal and some beer. I sit at a table near where I sat last night, but I am careful not to sit at the same table, as I want to be sure not to fall into a routine; the purpose of this trip is to break my routines. I feel a twinge of guilt for eating at the same restaurant, but in truth there are few, if any, other restaurants of this caliber along this part of the canal. At the next table there is a group that I recognize from last night. They look like a fun crew, talking loudly and laughing a lot. There are four of them, and at least two of them are quite obviously not locals. One of them is telling a story in English with a strong Scottish accent.

"…Soo mai waife and I were at our friends' hoose, staying overnaight. Our son Scotty was just a wee bairn at the time, so he was already up in the guest bedroom asleep, and we had brought one of those baby monitors so we could hear him if he woke up. Well, the evening wore on and mai waife and I were ready tae go tae bed, so we said goodnaight tae our hosts and went up tae the guest bedroom. Scotty was asleep, and we were both feeling a bit frisky, so we desaided tae get a little nookie in before our kip. Things got a little waild and we were a little loud tae put it maildly. Afterwards it struck us with a sudden shock that we had never turned the baby monitor off and our hosts were still doonstairs! They'd been able tae listen tae the entaire performance!" They all laugh with the lubricated ease provided by several drinks.

I can't help but chuckle out loud at the story I overhear. The storyteller notices. "You laike my story, eh? Hey, you were in here last naight, weren't you? Come on over here; you don't need tae drink beer on your oon; you can drink tequila with us!" The others are smiling. They wave me over and pull up an extra chair.

I shrug my shoulders, get up and move over to their table. They are obviously yachters, and they seem to have known each other for a long time. Judging by the size of the yachts swaying in the harbor, they are not struggling for money.

"Are you a tequila drinker?" one of them asks me.

"I don't mind drinking a few margaritas now and then," I answer, "I'm Doug Roth, by the way."

"Hi Doug, we're the United Nations. I'm Paco, from here; this is Ramiro— he's from Mexico. Over there's Hendrik- he's Dutch, and that one with the silly accent is Ross from Scotland."

"Wow, you guys *are* the United Nations. How do you all know each other?"

"We were all in prison together!" Hendrik says, and they all laugh.

"Here, try this, Doug," says Paco, "He's just kidding. We just got back from the Cayman Islands."

"…for money laundering!" yells Hendrik, to another round of laughs.

"I've got tae race laike a piss horse!" says Ross, "I'll be back in a second. Doug, don't listen tae anythung they say!"

"Ross and Hendrik just crossed the Atlantic," continues Paco, "…in that souped-up bathtub over there, and Ramiro and I sailed up to the Caymans to meet them." Paco's English is excellent and it's obvious that he's spent a lot of time in the USA. He also seems to be the leader of the group.

I look at the shot of tequila in front of me, as golden as the sunlight reflecting off the canal.

"Isn't there supposed to be a lime and salt?" I ask.

"So you *are* a tequila drinker!" says Paco. "You are right, my friend. Here is the salt, and a fresh bowl of limes is on the way."

"That's really just one way to drink tequila," says Ramiro, "There's many more." This brings sly smiles to the faces of the others. They have heard this routine before.

"You'd better listen to him," says Paco, "He's from Mexico, so he knows all about tequila."

"Tonight I'll teach you the Mexican way to drink tequila!" says Ramiro, and the four of them raise their glasses and yell, "Salud!" We all clink glasses. The tequila is incredibly smooth, which is good for me, as I rarely drink anything stronger than beer.

"Here, now take a sip of this," says Ramiro, offering me a small glass filled with what looks like a bloody Mary.

"What is it?' I ask.

"It's called *sangrita*," he says, "It means almost like 'a little bit of blood'. In Mexico, we drink it with tequila. You try it. You will like it!" Surprisingly, the sangrita doesn't seem to be alcoholic; it tastes more like spicy tomato juice.

"Did you ever hear of a tequila moonrise?" asks Ramiro. They all chuckle.

"Tequila *moon*rise?" I ask, "Is that like a tequila sunrise that you drink at night?"

"You're close… when I was young I used to drink tequila moonrises all the time. A tequila moonrise is any drink made with moonshine tequila!" They all laugh as if I have been set up for a big joke. As the evening progresses, the guys show me many different ways to drink tequila, most of which, I later figure, had been developed just at that moment, in my honor. It is a fantastically fun evening however, and I spend much of it rolling in sidesplitting laughter. This is exactly the sort of therapy I need.

I am invited to join the group for horseback riding on Paco's farm the following day. I have always been a 'landlubber' as far as horses are concerned; I prefer a mode of transport which I can control, such as my own two feet, rather than being subject to the whims of another being with its own agenda. I am not comfortable putting my life in the hands (or hooves) of an animal ten times my size, and with, being generous I hope, one-tenth of my IQ. But it promises to be a great social occasion and a great way to see Panama, and my head is throbbing a bit too much to resist the thought of having another creature do the walking for me.

Hendrik and Ross pick me up at the hotel the next morning and it takes us a little over an hour to reach Paco's place. We cross over the Panama Canal on a huge iron bridge that passes high over the puttering ships below. The three of us pass the time by telling jokes, talking about our families and discussing the idiosyncrasies of our different cultures: the liberality of Dutch tolerance, the maniacal fascination of Europeans for soccer and the general cluelessness of

Americans on matters of world geography. Hendrik jokes that he regards Brits and Americans as two sides of the same coin, due to our sharing of a language. I reply that, like most Dutchmen, Hendrik probably speaks better English than both Ross and I, and I use the old adage to explain the main difference between us: An American is someone who thinks a hundred years is a long time, and a Brit is someone who thinks a hundred miles is a long way!

After about half an hour, Hendrik asks, "Doug, are you hungry? We have hot dogs cooking."

"Hot dogs cooking! What are you talking about? Have you got a barbecue in the car?" It must be some kind of joke.

"Well, kind of…" he laughs.

We pull over along the side of the road and Ross pulls out a plastic bag with three hot dog buns in it. He hands one to me and one to Hendrik, and keeps one for himself. Then he reaches into the trunk again and grabs bottles of ketchup, mustard and relish and sets them up on the roof of the car, while I stand there baffled, holding an empty hot dog bun in my hand, next to a car pulled over alongside the Pan-American Highway in Nowheresville, Panama.

"You know," I say, "In the States we usually cook our hot dogs before eating them. Cold hot dogs are not only unappetizing, but they're also a horrific oxymoron!"

"Who said anythung aboot them being cold?" says Ross, and he reaches over and unlatches the hood of the car. There, nestled in the hot engine block is what looks like a soda-bottle-sized wad of aluminum foil. Ross carefully plucks it out, unwraps it, and there in front of me are three steaming hot dogs.

"Choose yer weapon!" says Ross.

In fact, the hot dogs are cooked through, and any hint of motor oil or engine exhaust in my nose must be my imagination, right?

After our quick but dubious snack, we are soon testing the car's suspension system by bouncing along the dusty dirt road that leads to Paco's farm. Some of the ruts in the road are so deep that I can't help but forcibly exhale as we wobble through them. At last we reach the modest but comfortable-looking farmhouse, white with a red-tiled roof and shaded from the sun by several high trees. I imagine that the dust we raised during our slow, bumpy journey up the drive long ago alerted Paco and Ramiro of our approach, and they are standing outside the house, ready to ride.

Rana Reilona is a crazy horse. When all of the other horses go right, he goes left. When they go left, he stands still, or turns around, or does whatever he wants to do. This is why I don't ride horses, I think. But he's an old horse, so at least he's gentle and unlikely to burst into a flying gallop with me wide-eyed and clinging to his back, my arms wrapped in sheer terror around his quivering, muscular neck, my teeth clenched tightly enough to chomp through the bit. He's too mature for those sorts of horsy shenanigans, and for this I am thankful. He patiently tolerates my amateurish attempts to guide him, and I get the feeling that if he could, he'd roll his eyes at me each time I tugged the rein one way or the other, much like my daughters do whenever I ask them to do something. Just what I need, I think, a sassy, four-legged 'neigh-sayer.'

We ride across Paco's beautiful, sun-dappled farm, past prolific rows of shimmering orange trees, their branches sagging with luxurious fruit, vast fields of pithy sugarcane, and the occasional austere wooden shed or hut. Shirtless farm hands, their skin baked chestnut-brown, fill bushel baskets with ripe vegetables. A gentle breeze provides periodic respite from the omnipresent sun. At the last moment it had crossed my mind to bring along my baseball cap, and I'm glad I did. I'm sweating profusely and my T-shirt is soaked, but I feel great. There is only a slight remnant of this morning's hangover.

The rest of the group is circled together in the distance; Rana Reilona and I, as usual, are several hundred yards away. I begin to suspect that Rana Reilona has some unresolved social issues with the other horses. Paco gives me a whistle and waves his arm. He points back toward the farmhouse. It's time to turn around. Rana Reilona and I take a different route as I try to guide him over to the others. After a while, I realize that somehow, we've lost our way a bit, because we're away from the cultivated area and tromping through high grass and scrub. I'm a bit concerned now because Paco warned us to steer clear of this type of area, which could hide the aptly named bushmaster or its cousin the fer-de-lance, two types of large poisonous snakes endemic to this region.

Rana Reilona's feet are getting caught up in loose vines. By now, the others are nowhere in sight. A little further along, my eyes widen like saucers. Rana Reilona, with me his reluctant passenger, is perched on the lip of a miniature Grand Canyon, a forty-foot-wide, twenty-foot-deep crack in the earth that slices through the land like a waterless echo of the Panama Canal, its red, earthy walls containing a moat of scrubby cactus, large rocks and, no doubt, a few fer-de-lances. Thank goodness Rana Reilona has the good sense to stop. He's not the brightest of horses, but, then again, I'm not the brightest of riders either. I concentrate and try to summon up all my knowledge of horse riding. I don't know which way to go, but I know which way *not* to go. I pull the rein to the right, since that is the direction in which I last saw the others. Rana Reilona does a complete 360 and that solves nothing. I try it again, with the same result. I pull the rein to the left, and he does another 360 in the opposite direction. Worse, he now seems to think that I want him to jump the ravine, for some reason. He bends his knees slightly, and looks hesitantly out over the crevice.

'This can't be real,' I think. I'm sitting seven feet off the ground, petrified, on the back of a socially-challenged, smart-aleck stallion as he flexes his tired old legs to attempt to broad-jump a forty-foot-wide death pit. What on earth is there to do? I try to remember every useful bit of information I have heard about horses, which, having grown up in New Jersey, is not much. Finally, I hit on a golden nugget, something I remember from summer camp, eons ago: You have to let the horse know who's boss. It seems to make sense. I've got to try something. Throughout the whole duration of this ride, I have to admit, it's been pretty ambiguous who's in charge. Let the horse know who's boss.

"OK, Rana Reilona," I say, "You're the boss." I drop the rein and just sit, leaving Rana Reilona to decide what to do. His dim horse mind considers our predicament for a few minutes. And then, as if a great revelation has reached him from the heavens, he turns and walks away from the ravine. In fact, it seems he knew the way home the whole time. When we arrive back at the farmhouse, a bit weary, quite sunburned, and very sweaty, the others greet us with a round of sarcastic applause.

"You made it!" says Paco, "My little Rana kept you out of trouble! Now, I hope you remember your lessons from last night. Because Señor Tequila is going to visit us again!"

"Oh, not tonight, guys; my head is still thumping from yesterday."

"Just one or two. Three at the most. Not more than four. We have a nice dinner on the way. I just have to set up the barbecue."

"Heat up the car engine, Ross!" yells Hendrik, and for a moment I believe him.

A collection of shot glasses appears on the table, along with an unopened bottle of tequila and a bottle of single-malt Scotch.

"Who drinks the Scotch?" I ask without thinking.

"Three guesses. Ross only drinks that brown swill from his home country. That's a capital crime in Mexico!" says Ramiro.

"Aye, the nectar of the gods! Miles better than that cactus juice you drink!" Ross counters.

"Hah! He likes his Scotch like his marriage— on the rocks!" says Hendrik.

"And they laike their tequila laike their women— cold, aged and bitter!"

I sink into my seat for another spirited evening.

All in all, it has been a fun and interesting day, but the next morning, my legs and back are stiff. When I lean down to pick my trousers up off the floor, I groan like I've been shot in the chest. I can't believe it; a horse did all the walking and *I'm* stiff from it. Getting older is ridiculous. I do less and less and suffer from it more and more.

I spend several more days in Panama, walking the footpath alongside the canal, enjoying every minute of the omnipresent heat and humidity, and admiring nature and its endless variety of greens. One day, I am invited to join Paco and the gang for a ride on one of the yachts, and it is a blissful afternoon, riding the winds and waves through the southern end of the canal and along the Pacific Coast. It is a magnificent experience.

I am looking forward to beginning my bus journey, and though the guys give me a bit of a hard time ("You crazy Yank! Why don't you just fly, like everyone else?"), we say our goodbyes. I promise to e-mail them all upon my return to the States, to regale them with tales of my continuing adventures. They in turn promise to invite me to their next gathering, in the Azores next year. That evening, I take a taxi from my hotel to the bus station, which is situated only about ten minutes away.

The bus station is a large, modern terminal with lots of glass, adjacent to a suburban shopping mall like any other. Any reservations I had about hanging around the station late at night evaporate as I enter the busy, brightly lit premises. Travelers of all genres mill about the terminal-- families with small children in tow, loaded down with luggage and packages of all sorts, openly affectionate young couples, intrepid students, stiff, suited businessmen and youthful foreign backpackers. I wheel my suitcase down a long, open passageway and find a window that lists Costa Rica on its destination board. I pay about $35 for an 'executive class' ticket, present my passport, and am handed a paper ticket with an assigned seat scribbled on it. I have arrived early, half-expecting that I would run into some kind of problem, but so far it has all gone smoothly. I am directed to a waiting area until the bus is ready for boarding.

Through a broad, rectangular window in the waiting lounge, smudged with the greasy fingerprints of scores of impatient children and bored, sweaty travelers, I can see numerous 'chicken buses' lined up, some ready to depart and crowded with passengers jostling for seats. These are the default transportation method throughout Central America, mainly for short domestic journeys. They are referred to as chicken buses (only by foreigners) due to the fact that on board, at least some of the fellow riders are likely to be of the feathered variety. The chicken buses are artistically and painstakingly painted head-to-tail in the most amazing variety of colors, as if only a small sample of each color of paint were available and the artists had to make do. They roar and spew noxious clouds of thick black smoke with each touch of the accelerator, of which there are many. The international bus that I will be boarding is clearly different, as is readily apparent. It is sleek and modern, rides about three feet higher than the other buses, and looks very comfortable, almost luxurious. It has long, tinted windows with adjustable linen shades. I am particularly glad to see this, as the trip to Costa Rica is scheduled to take sixteen hours overnight. It crosses my mind that sixteen hours seems an extraordinarily long time for such a journey, but I am content knowing that at least I will get a good night's sleep on the way.

The man at the gate signals that the Costa Rica bus is now ready to board and I follow the other passengers to the door. Once I reach the front of the line, I notice that there is a turnstile in front of me that requires a five-cent fee to enter. The only coin I have is a dime. Nobody has change. I'd happily give up the dime, but annoyingly, only nickels fit in the turnstile. I have to get out of line, leave the boarding area, return to the main concourse of the terminal, and seek out a friendly sales clerk at one of the shops just to give me two nickels for my dime. Luckily, finding a friendly sales clerk is not too difficult. It is also fortunate, as far as I am concerned, that I haven't had to change money to this point. Panama uses the US dollar as its currency, as does El Salvador, I am told. This saves me the trouble and cost of converting dollars, and eliminates the possibility of being left with useless Panamanian currency after I enter Costa Rica.

We pull out of the station almost exactly on time, and in minutes we are out of Panama City. Outside the bus, heat lightning flickers like a strobe light on the horizon. One thing I hadn't reckoned on before arriving here is darkness coming so early. This means that for any bus ride continuing past 5:00 PM, I will need to have a plan for my time after it is too dark to view the landscape. The best plan I can think of is to talk to other passengers. Hopefully I can meet other travelers or interesting locals with stories to share, and who are willing to tolerate my rudimentary Spanish. It was great to spend time with Paco and the gang. I really feel like I connected with that group, like I have friends here already. I wonder if they will still remember me in a year.

Why are people who snore always the first to fall asleep? And why do they always end up next to me? My wife snores and she's always asleep before me. My best friend Ted snores like a chain saw on our annual camping trip and he's asleep before his head hits the pillow. The extra-large, balding Panamanian sitting next to me is a snorer of epic proportions. As with a crying baby, his brief silent moments are the worst. Then my blood pressure soars, because this is when he catches his breath and gathers his energy to deliver an earth-shattering honk. When I can tolerate no more, I 'accidentally' thrust my elbow into his ribcage. He wakes for an instant, turns his head and looks at me. I don't know the Spanish word for 'snore'. I just shrug. He immediately slips back into the land of Nod. We pass through a series of winding S-turns and now he's leaning into my shoulder. Will he start drooling on me next? SKNXXX! I reason that my gut reaction to yell, "Shut the fuck up!" would probably not be helpful, especially since I'm not sure I could translate it. Can't I just once have a cute girl seated next to me? Oh, how I yearn for the uninterrupted, blissfully unaware sleep of the chronic snorer.

It's 4:30 AM. The bus rolls to a stop at the Panamanian side of the border with Costa Rica. I am a red-eyed, sleepless mess. For half an hour, the bus just sits, motionless. Passengers sleep; my seatmate's snoring swells to an extraordinary crescendo. Stray dogs snooze in the station. Finally, all of the passengers are filed out of the bus and the luggage is removed from the bins below. We each claim our luggage and pile into a small room furnished with several long tables. Drug-sniffing dogs take their time sampling the olfactory quality of each bag. The bags are then opened on the tables, and their contents are examined in detail by uniformed Customs agents. One by one, the inspected bags are closed and their owners quietly step outside. The process is almost interminable.

Then, we wait again. Everybody waits. Salsa music blares faintly in the distance; I can hear little more than its thumping beat. Every song sounds the same. Buses, cars and trucks gently idle; dogs nap; salsa thumps. Nothing is moving. Nobody seems to notice or care. Time stands still and so do I. Even the sun seems to have paused for a rest in its slow rise, and the clouds maintain an eerie twilight glow overhead. There have been a few moments in my life when I have wished that time would stand still; I consider that perhaps those wishes have finally come true, just at the wrong time.

Out of nowhere, a fistfight breaks out between five or six local toughs. Beer bottles are smashed on the street; tumbling bodies fall to the sidewalk. The bus passengers eye the goings-on warily, quietly inching in the opposite direction. Minutes later, four soldiers dressed in camouflage rush out and surround the thugs, truncheons at the ready, and the troublemakers are quickly led away, their hands twisted behind their backs.

Eventually we receive the coveted Panamanian exit stamps in our passports and the luggage is returned to the bus. The baggage rides to the Costa Rican side while the passengers are left to walk, and the whole search-and-wait scenario is repeated ten minutes later in Costa Rica. I find myself hoping that sixteen hours are sufficient to reach San Jose.

Back on the bus, my seatmate is at it again. It sounds like someone is strangling him, for which they could hardly be blamed. I diagnose sleep apnea, although my only qualification is a bachelor's degree in computer science. Annoyed, helpless, exhausted and warmed by the newly-risen sun, I manage a few fleeting moments of well-earned sleep as we continue our trek into the Costa Rican hinterlands.

CHAPTER 5

The Bestial Chorus

The smooth, flat farmlands and rolling hills of Panama have crumpled and folded like cardboard to become the rippling green Costa Rican mountains. We traverse a series of winding switch-backs on the road, and it is obvious that we have gained a significant amount of altitude since crossing the border. Billowing, smoky clouds collect around the jagged mountain summits and hover above the deep verdant valleys. Some clouds appear to be less than a hundred feet above the ground. They float like wispy ghosts, semi-transparent and slowly mutating in form, some breaking apart, others joining together. Larger clouds envelop acre-sized tracts of forest, shrouding them in misty cloaks. When the sun breaks through, it is like a beacon from heaven. One beam illuminates a tree with orange flowers so bright it looks like they are on fire. The clouds drift for a moment, and more light spills through, giving birth to more colors than I could imagine. Crimson, butter, cinnamon, hints of tangerine- all the colors of heaven and earth burst out of the treetops in a spray of light. Eventually the mist subsides, the mountains spread out, and we roll through a suburban sprawl of gas stations, tire stores, farm supply shops and the like, and into the bustle of San Jose.

San Jose is not at all what I expected. In fact, I am quite disappointed. I had heard a lot about Costa Rica through the Internet, magazine articles and travel advertisements- how developed it was, how peaceful, green and economically thriving. Costa Rica may well be, but San Jose, its chaotic capital, is none of these. It is an unattractive jumble of decaying, utilitarian wood-and-cement buildings crowded against each other. There are shopping malls with the same stores as back home, and there are the same fast food restaurants as everywhere else. How can the world have become so much the same? What is the point of traveling anymore when San Jose looks like Denver and Berlin and Shanghai? I imagine what it must have been like decades ago, before globalization boiled down the disparate restaurants and shops of the world until only about fifty brands remain, sprinkled across the entire Earth like so many grains of sand, so that every town and village, no matter how remote, has its own random array. The only difference between any two cities in the world is the placement and juxtaposition of these fifty or so brands. The broad selection of products that the heady days of capitalism promised us seems to have evaporated and left us with few choices anymore of what to buy or where to buy it.

I can see that I am not going to pick up any cultural awareness or international insight by remaining here in San Jose. The beauty of Costa Rica is clearly located outside of the city. I begin to consider other options of where to stay. One of my friends who had previously visited Costa Rica on a rafting trip had recommended Manuel Antonio National Park on the west coast. It is an easy bus ride of only a few hours, so after spending one night in San Jose, I head to the domestic bus station for a daytime trip, feeling unlikely to be disturbed by any sonorous Panamanians.

I settle myself into a lumpy bus seat and slide the checkered fabric blind to one side of the window until bright sunshine pours in. Thinking that I may end up with a bad sunburn on the right side of my face, I slide the blind halfway back so the sun spills its rays on the back of the seat in front of me, leaving about half of the pane open for me to drink in the scenery.

The sun is an essential regulator of our well-being. Not only does it stimulate the photochemical synthesis of Vitamin D in the epidermis, it also stabilizes our moods. There is a condition known as Seasonal Affective Disorder, whimsically referred to by its initials, SAD, in which a decreased exposure to sunlight during the winter season adversely affects the disposition of the sufferer. People living in northern parts of the world, which experience markedly diminished sunlight in the winter, both in duration and in angle, are more susceptible to this condition. One of the methods of treatment for this depressed emotional state is light therapy. With so many factors outside of my control, from brain chemistry to the angle of the sun, how much responsibility for my happiness can possibly rest within me? If a violent criminal can shift the blame for his actions away from himself due to the circumstances of his upbringing, don't I have the same right to blame my dour disposition on the weather?

Local people file into the bus in groups of two and three, some with large bags of candy or snacks that they must intend on selling. An American backpacker in his early twenties, easily identifiable with his overstuffed blue pack and pale skin (not to mention the fact that, at about six feet, he towers over most of the locals) works his way through the crowd. Judging from the way he is dressed, he is one of the many 'surfer dudes' that come to Central America for its low cost and excellent waves. As I turn to resume my view out the window, I hear him sit down with a heavy sigh in the seat next to me. Almost immediately, he asks, "You American?"

It is amazing that in other countries, Americans have an almost magnetic pull for each other. People who would never notice you on an American street will shake your hand like an old friend and spill their guts to you. "Yeah, I'm American," I respond, and thence begins the usual routine of where-you-froms and what-you-doing-heres, and the like. I try not to get too heavily involved in conversation as it would keep me from my intended plan of watching the daily life of Costa Rica roll past my window, but I don't want to be impolite. I wonder if it is some ingrained social rule deep in my brain, too powerful to resist, that compels me to forego my ringside seat to the Costa Rican wilderness just to avoid being impolite to a stranger.

His next question catches me off guard.

"Aren't you a little old to be doing this?"

"Old to be doing what? Riding a bus?"

"You know, backpacking around in a place like Costa Rica. Most of the American guys I meet here are just graduated from college, like me. You don't see many older dudes backpacking down here."

"Well, I don't know. Am I? Is there an age limit? Maybe I'm a little old to be doing just about anything. But I have to do something. What do you think I should be doing? What do you think you'll be doing when you're my age?"

He looks at me with a curious expression on his face. Perhaps my answer was a bit defensive.

"Hey, don't take it the wrong way," he says. "I think it's cool that some older people still can get out and around in the world. Why not, you know? As long as you're still healthy!" He reaches over and pulls back the window shade, and blinding sunlight floods in. I split the difference with him and just draw the shade halfway back to its original position. I flip my sunglasses down from the top of my head to counter the increased brightness.

"Hey, those are some awesome sunglasses," says the surfer dude. "Where did you get them? I didn't know they still made sunglasses like that!"

"I don't remember where I got them, but I've had them for years. The only thing that matters to me is that they fulfill their intended purpose and protect my eyes from the sun. That's all I need. I'm not wearing them as any sort of fashion statement or anything."

"Well, that's pretty obvious," he says with a smirk. It seems more youthful sarcasm than animosity, so I let it slide.

"Thanks for your honesty," I say, returning the smirk and the sarcasm. He snorts, which I take to be a stifled laugh.

In fact, I walk a fashion tightrope. I've never given much thought to my style of dress. Not until Celeste became a teenager, anyway. Then suddenly I was blessed with my own in-house fashion critic, taking great pains to ensure that I made a good impression (or, more accurately, didn't make a bad impression) because I hadn't put the appropriate amount of thought into what I was wearing. "Dad, you're *not* going to wear that, are you?" became one of the top ten most frequently-asked questions in my home, even though to me that answer seemed obvious to me, since most of the times when it was asked, I was already fully dressed. When Celeste was a young child, I always used to wonder at what point she would know more than I did about a particular subject, and at what age I could begin to learn things from her, or receive her valuable advice. I was blindsided when she taught me that the intricacies involved in choosing a shirt and trousers for the day were extremely complicated. I had never realized how important it is that a delicate balance be struck between not looking too old-fashioned, and not looking too stylish (for my age), too colorful or too bland, too mismatched or too contrived. Sure, you can wear two red things together, as long as they're the *same* red. Or almost the same. Or am I wrong again? Who makes these rules? How did my daughters learn them, while I didn't? The sunglasses, apparently of a style popular during the Jurassic period, had been a point of contention long before the trip- functional to me, a fashion train wreck to my daughter.

With slightly less measured patience than I have for my daughters when they make the same type of comment, I ask the surfer dude, "So, what's wrong with my sunglasses?"

"Nothing," he says. "But you know, they're, like, really out of fashion. Sunglasses should look like this." He takes his sunglasses out of his pocket. They are like a thousand other pairs I have seen. "This is what people are wearing these days."

"So you think everybody should wear the same sunglasses?" I ask.

He slips back into his seat and pulls the bill of his baseball cap down to shield his eyes.

"No, not the same. Just, like, the same style. Something more contemporary."

"You know, that's the philosophy that's sold to us by the marketing people because it's easier for the suppliers and it helps move inventory— people think that a perfectly good article of clothing is no longer wearable after a few years, because it's out of style. Why do people accept this philosophy that the marketers push on us?"

"Yeah, I know what you mean. I don't like the big corporations telling people how to live," he says.

"But you do follow fashion…" I point out.

"No, that's my own choice," he says. "I just happen to like this style."

In my mind I doubt that his 'choice' coincidentally follows the line of fashion. I consider whether a large number of people can be manipulated without realizing it. I wonder to what extent I myself am unwittingly manipulated.

"Maybe I'm setting a new fashion," I say. "Somebody has to. Better me than the 'big, evil corporations!' "

"Hey, why not? If they work for you, keep 'em. They're part of your persona."

"Naw, it doesn't have anything to do with the sunglasses. It's just that I try to think for myself. I have no problem with corporations or anything, but to me, people just follow along with what they're told to do and don't even think about it. I've been doing that too much in my life. I decided to stop. *That's* why I'm here."

"I respect that," he says. "Me, I'm taking a gap year from school. Just going up and down the coast, me and my surfboard."

"That sounds great," I say. "I wish I could've done that a long time ago. When you get to my age, the thing is, is that…"

Suddenly he interrupts me. "Wait. Why did you say that? Why does everybody say that?"

"Say what?"

"You just said, 'the thing is, is that.' You said 'is' twice." The dude's whole disposition has changed.

"I did?" I ask reflexively. "I don't know. Probably just a stutter."

"No it's not a stutter. You know how I know that? Because everybody says that. It drives me crazy. Can't you just say, 'The thing is,' and then say what the thing is? You don't need to say 'is' twice. Doesn't anybody actually think about what they're saying? If you thought about it, you'd realize it doesn't make sense. You say it like that just because everyone else does. It's like when people say, 'I could care less', when they really mean, 'I *couldn't* care less.' It drives me crazy."

I look at the dude out of the corner of my eye. Is he serious, or just playing some kind of game with me? "Sorry," I say with feigned repentance, my hands raised as if in capitulation, "It's just the way I speak. I didn't mean to offend you."

He sits back in his seat for a moment, facing straight ahead, not really looking at anything. "Sorry. Asperger's," he finally says.

"Huh? Asperger's? Oh, I've heard of that. It's something you're born with, right?" The realization sinks in… loudly plopping into the seat, the window shade… that explains it.

"Well, you know, it's really just that my brain is wired differently than yours, that's all," he says.

"A communication disorder, or something like that?"

"Something like that. It's a disability that affects social skills. It's like a double-whammy, since I have the disability and I'm also intelligent enough to realize it. I've learned to deal with it for the most part, but it comes out sometimes when something bugs me, like what you just said. It sucks, really. I went to school and they taught me these rules of grammar, and then just because I followed them so well, they told me I had some kind of syndrome. I try to talk like other people, but when they say something like 'foreseeable future' for example, I have to grit my teeth to keep from yelling, 'There is no such thing!'"

"It's good you've learned to compensate. I had no idea until just now that you were… that you had…"

"It's hard sometimes," he continues. "I had to learn what most people just seem to know naturally. How not to talk too much or too little. That sometimes people aren't interested in the things I talk about. When it's all right to state the obvious."

"What do you mean, 'to state the obvious'?" I ask.

"Well, for example, in the middle of winter on a snowy day, you can say, 'Wow, it's cold!' and it's a good way to start a conversation. But if you say something like 'The sky is blue' or 'The snow is white,' people will look at you like there's something wrong with you. It's like there's some unwritten code or instruction manual that other people have, that I've never seen. It's very frustrating. You have to act in a certain way that's been mapped out over the centuries. If you deviate from this format, you're considered an oddball."

The surfer dude and I talk a little more as the bus continues, and at other times we are silent for long stretches. But in the back of my mind I cannot help thinking how right this dude is. There are strong constraints on how we must act and speak, if we want to be able to interact with others. Not just the obvious ones, but tiny, almost imperceptible nuances that we dare not violate. Ways that we speak and act that don't make sense, and that we don't even think about, that have become the social norm and therefore part of our personalities. How can I possibly distill the real me from this collection of built-up habits, conditioned responses and social reflexes that I have become?

The bus rolls to a stop and my thoughts coalesce back into the immediate and present. I am surrounded by green and beauty, and I want to enjoy it.

Manuel Antonio is a fairly well developed, but still heavily forested, national park on Costa Rica's Pacific coast. The seacoast is spectacular and rocky, and the beach is interspersed with coconut palms. Scattered rocky islands speckle the bay and, as in Panama, green is everywhere. I find an adequate one-room cabin for rent by the beach and book it for a few nights. After I pick up my keys from the reception desk in the office, I stroll along the wooded path to my cabin to drop off my bags. The maid is already there, sweeping out the room. From the looks of the pile of dust she has gathered, it has been a while since the last time this occurred. Among the detritus is a bleached, desiccated frog. I point it out to her and she just laughs, not of embarrassment, but more of a childish giggle, as if to say, "How did that get there?"

The cabin is pleasant, if Spartan accommodation. I have decided to downgrade my level of lodging with the hope of getting a little more in touch with the environment and the cultures of the countries I am visiting. It doesn't hurt that I will save a little money in the process. The only things I really need are a mattress to sleep on and a lock on the door. Everything else is unnecessary luxury. Besides, feeling the salty spray of the sea on the wind when I open my door in the morning is a priceless bonus.

I love the beauty of this forest. Though I pass quite a few other people tromping along its various wooded paths, there is much of nature within easy view. Playful black-and-white monkeys swing and bounce in the tree branches as scarlet macaws squawk and chatter with alarm. A tempest of bright blue butterflies swirls over a leaf-filled mud puddle, casting fluttering shadows over its sunny surface, and then suddenly scatters into the woods. I hear a dull thumping next to the path, like someone dragging a bag of potatoes, and it turns out to be a large lizard scampering through the underbrush.

I could spend weeks here. The shopping malls and other similarities to New Jersey ended when I left San Jose, and now I am in another world— an Eden— a world of color so bright it hurts my eyes and air so fresh that I feel reborn. The Central American outdoors has lifted my spirits far more than any pharmaceutical brain-balancing ever could.

The daylight disappears very quickly, but the night air remains just as refreshing, and a swathe of stars, uncompromised by earthly light or pollution, is a brilliant spray of fire opals in the black velvet sky. I never want to go inside again!

After a satisfying dinner of chicken and rice with the customary corn tortillas, I sit on the rugged stone wall in front of my cabin, just listening to the sounds of the forest by night, accompanied by the intermittent thundering crash of ocean waves, and watch for shooting stars. The monkeys, frogs and insects join in a wondrous chorus. The variety of sounds is incredible. I can't identify with any precision what type of animal is making which sound, and my imagination runs wild. A vaguely rhythmic rasping noise sounds like someone scraping a pencil across a radiator vent. A high-pitched pinging, which must be some type of frog, reminds me of a fork hitting a crystal wine glass. Assorted chirps and whistles and the occasional screech of a howler monkey, sometimes alarmingly loud, leap out from the buzzing white-noise background of a nearly infinite variety of insects.

A shuffling sound in the tall grass startles me, and in the darkness I can make out the striped tail and lean silhouette of a coati mundi. Within minutes, I hear the same sound again and I see a moonlit opossum sneaking through the undergrowth. I've seen more wildlife in this one day than I have in the past several years at home. But nature is not finished with my night. Returning to my cabin,

I see that a small crab has taken up residence between the peeling wicker shelves and the cracked wooden wall. I briefly wonder what else might wander through the two-inch gap under my front door during the night.

My dreams take me back outside again. I soar soundlessly above the roaring Pacific, while moonlight gathers in pools on the rippling sea below me. The coconut palms gently sway to the music of the forest. All my worries are gone and I am a happy man— free at last from the weight of the world.

Sunlight caresses my face as morning arrives, and I awaken truly refreshed. No commuter traffic this morning, no malfunctioning computer systems to deal with, only a world of nature to see. I lie still for a while, savoring the feeling, then I throw on a pair of shorts, put in my contact lenses, and I am ready for the day.

There is a lively local restaurant by the side of the road, on the edge of the Costa Rican rain forest, and I find myself there for lunch one day on the recommendation of a Canadian guy I met while walking the trails. It's not a fancy place; it's more of an open-air lunchtime café and bar, with two or three whirling blenders going most of the time, churning out a rainbow of piña coladas, daiquiris, margaritas and the like.

I settle myself into a seat in front of a small wicker table, and soon a waitress appears with a laminated plastic menu. I order a piña colada to sip while I browse the menu, which boasts the quintessential international and Mexican food such as coconut shrimp and nachos, along with the customary Costa Rican fare. I do my best to blend world cuisines and choose beef fajitas with a Caesar salad.

It is a friendly place, busy but not rushed, and the staff seems to take extra time to speak with the clientele. I ask my waitress about the age of the building, since it appears to have a mix of both old and new styles. The original structure, she informs me, is about fifty years old, but it was rebuilt after a fire partially destroyed it about ten years ago.

Having no dining companion to converse with, I entertain myself by surveying the interior while I eat, trying to determine which parts of the building are new and which are original. I glance up at the ceiling, a thatched structure with hanging ceiling fans; it must be over forty feet high. Obviously this would have to be new, I conclude, as it would be unlikely to survive a fire. My eyes settle on a curious spot of white near the very peak of the ceiling, and after looking it over for a few seconds, I realize that it is a playing card, somehow attached to the thatching, well above the level at which the ceiling fans are hung. When the waitress returns, I ask her about it. She looks a bit unsure.

"That," she says, "Has been there a very long time. Much longer than I've worked here, and that's over twelve years."

"You mean… that the roof was part of the original structure?" I ask incredulously.

"Oh, yes. The fire started back in the kitchen area, and took out most of the building, but the thatched roof stayed."

"You've got to be kidding!" I reply. "How is that possible?"

"Nobody knows," she says.

"Well, what about the playing card— how did that get up there?"

"I'm not sure I should talk about this, señor— I think it might be bad luck!"

"Bad luck?"

"Excuse me, sir; I have to serve these other guests," she says and hurriedly walks off. She returns sometime later with the bill, and I leave her enough colones to cover the meal and a nice tip. As I am departing, I ask the bartender whether I can speak with the manager.

"Certainly, sir," he says, "One moment."

A minute or two later, a tall, mustachioed man with a serious face approaches me.

"Sir, was everything OK with your meal?"

"Oh, yes, the meal was very good and the waitress was very good too," I answer. "I just had a question for you about the building. I asked the waitress and she seemed a bit disturbed by the question."

"What did you ask her?"

"Well, I was just asking about that playing card on the ceiling way up there, how it got there."

"Oh, I see. You will have to excuse the waitress, sir; some of the people here, they are very superstitious. It is a rather peculiar story, in fact, and even I feel a little funny about it, if you know what I mean, although it did happen many years ago.

"I was just a boy at the time, but I still remember it. My father owned the restaurant in those days. It was a lot smaller then, because we did not have many tourists and it was mostly the local people who would eat here. One night, it was raining very heavily. On such nights, very few people come here. My father was just about to close the restaurant early and let the staff go home, when a poor man walked in. He was dressed in very dirty clothing, and it looked like he had been living outdoors for some time. There are many people like this in our country. The man asked my father for something to eat, and my father told him the restaurant was closing for the night. The stranger pleaded for just a small meal, and told us he hadn't had anything to eat for several days. Unfortunately, he didn't have any money. My father had a good heart, however, and asked him what he would be willing to do in payment for a meal. The man asked my father if he had a deck of cards. My parents used to play cards a lot on slow nights. It was one of their favorite hobbies. So my father pulled out a deck of cards from behind the counter and handed it to the stranger. The stranger shuffled the deck and asked my father to pick out one card, remember which one it was, and then replace it. My father did as he requested and shuffled the cards again afterward. Then the man picked up the deck again and handed it to him. 'Now, find your card,' he said. My father looked through the entire deck of cards, but could not find the card he had just replaced. My father had seen lots of card tricks before, so he was certain that the man had slipped the card into his raggedy clothing somehow. Well, you can guess the rest; when my father asked where the card was, the man simply pointed up. It was there, twelve meters above, on the roof. We were so amazed, we could not speak at first. Of course, the stranger earned his dinner. When he departed, he thanked us heartily, and said that the room was now 'protected by spirits.' Many years later when we had the fire, this whole area was untouched, and the card remains there to this day."

"Which card is it, by the way?"

"I believe it is the king of hearts, sir."

It is an incredible story. I can't help smiling to myself as I walk away, giving the owner a wave. There are so many things about this world that we will never understand. That's what makes life so inter-esting- if we had it all figured out, our minds would be unable to experience the magical feeling of wonder that we should feel each day. How uninteresting the world would be if there were no mys-teries to ponder, no secrets to be told, no unseen places to explore. Contemplating the enigmas of this universe, I imagine, brings us closer back to our childhood than anything else can. I return to my hotel instilled with a keen desire to explore.

A small cardboard sign thumb-tacked into the wooden wall in the hotel office advertises a 'Caiman Watching Tour.' It sounds like it could be interesting; I would love to see this local version of the alligator, but that is the complete text of the sign. I inquire at the desk about it; the price sounds reasonable, so I sign up. The pickup time is 8:00 PM, which is ideal, I am told, as caimans are easy to spot at night. At the designated time, or soon afterward, a nondescript white minivan arrives at the hotel entrance. The driver, a colorfully-dressed young man with slicked-back hair hops down from the driver's seat. He appears to be barely out of his teens. "Mr. Roth?" he asks, and doesn't wait for my answer, presumably because I am the only one waiting here, and of the few other people in sight, none of them appear likely to answer to the surname Roth. "I'm Miguel," he says in almost perfect English, "I'm your guide."

Miguel directs me into the front passenger seat. I am the only other person in the vehicle, and by his manner, it becomes obvious fairly quickly that I am the only one who has signed up for tonight's tour.

After about a half-hour of driving, most of it on winding, pot-holed roads, Miguel pulls the van up to the shore of a small lake. Another young man, even smaller than Miguel's miniscule frame, though not nearly as young, stands by the darkened lakeshore, holding onto the end of a canoe that rests half in, and half out of, the obsidian water.

Working by just the headlights from the car and the light of the moon above, Miguel and the other young man ready the canoe for our expedition. They throw in two paddles, a plastic flashlight and some other gear, and slide the canoe further into the water, so only the stern remains onshore. Miguel gets in first, after turning off the headlights and locking the car doors. Then he directs me to board. Finally the other man, who I by now have gathered is the boatman or chief paddler, barefoot but wearing long, faded jeans, scrapes the stern through the gritty muck of the lakeshore until we are floating freely. Swiftly and gracefully, he leaps aboard from the knee-deep water, simultaneously giving the canoe a good shove away from the shore. Miguel pushes a paddle to him across the bottom of the boat with his foot, and we are on our way.

The canoe slips soundlessly across the shimmering moonlit lake. The air is moist and heavy with the scents of wet grass, aromatic flowers and rotting leaves. The sounds of the frogs, birds and creatures of the night proliferate here, and as they echo off the water, the effect is almost unearthly. I have no idea how we are going to locate caimans at night like this, but the very fact that they are here somewhere in this same lake, perhaps gliding beneath us even now as we course through the water in this wobbly canoe, gives me the shivers, albeit in a pleasant, horror-movie sense.

Miguel holds up his hand, his fingers spread, his palm toward the boatman, in a gesture that I interpret to mean 'stop.' It seems my interpretation is correct, as the boatman pulls his paddle onboard and lays it to rest across the gunwales. Miguel retrieves the flashlight from the deck and another from a sack on the bottom of the boat and turns one of them on. The beam is powerful, cutting like a knife through the darkness into a patch of tall grass by the shore. He holds the light in both hands and directs the beam across the surface of the water, so the cone of light intersects with the plane of the water, producing a wedge-shaped shaft of light that he slowly sweeps back and forth across the lake. He hands the other flashlight to me.

"Look!" he suddenly yells, "Look over there!" I look in the direction of the flashlight's beam, and I see nothing but a tiny red light shining on the surface of the water about a hundred feet away. "Luis! *Por alla!*" I soon realize that the tiny red light is the reflection of the eye of a caiman floating in the water.

The boatman, Luis, dips the paddle in the water and gives it an incredible heave that I find amazing for his small size. A few more small strokes and we glide to within twenty feet of the floating reptile, which I can now see clearly in the flashlight beam. Suddenly, there is a loud splash and it disappears underwater. Within minutes, we catch the shimmering reflection that indicates another floating predator. Like a pair of flaming golf balls levitating above the surface of the water, the two deep red, miniature sunsets sink into the murky depths. I am excited at seeing these creatures, but Miguel is over the top, like a little boy seeing his first puppy. He jumps from his knees to a crouched position and leans out over the bow of the canoe, pointing maniacally. The canoe rocks like a seesaw in a tornado.

"Do you see him? Do you see how big he is? Look at that!" yells Miguel, gesturing wildly.

"Haven't you ever given this tour before?" I ask, and even I am not sure whether I am being sarcastic or truly bewildered. He ignores me or doesn't hear me.

"Look at that!" he yells again, "He must be ten feet long!"

A growing concern for my situation starts to overtake me. A ten-foot man-eater is not fifteen feet away and there is nothing but the thin skin of a canoe between me and this watery blackness teeming with hungry gator mouths, and this mad teenager is jumping up and down like a rabbit on amphetamines. The silhouetted creature suddenly bolts into the blackness, no doubt displacing more water with one powerful swish of its mighty tail than Luis could in a month of paddling. Luis sits in the back of the canoe totally unconcerned, as if he were only a casual observer, rather than a participant, in this potentially ill-fated adventure.

Amazingly, Miguel's over-the-top enthusiasm doesn't wane at all during the hour-and-a-half-long expedition. We spot caimans about twenty times over the course of the evening, though how many different ones we sight I am less sure of; I think it is likely that we have spotted the same animals several times. I have to admit that it's a fairly entertaining experience, although my excitement level doesn't come close to that of Miguel. Luis maintains his quiet, stone-faced expression the entire time. Most important, the canoe never does tip over, although several times I swear that it is only the hand of God that intervenes. By 11:00, I am safely back at the hotel.

I walk to the reception desk to pick up my key. The desk attendant greets me. "Ah, *Señor* Roth! How was the caiman hunting?"

"Very good, thanks. A lot of fun and, I think, a little dangerous! But I'd definitely recommend it."

"*Magnifico*. There are many animals here in Costa Rica. But remember, the most dangerous animals travel on two legs!"

"I'll remember," I promise, "Thanks and good night."

Within minutes, I am in my cabin listening to the bestial chorus once again, marveling at the splendor of nature I am experiencing and happier than ever that I planned this trip.

After a few days in paradise, I am ready to move on. Costa Rica has been an amazing experience for me. I never imagined that it was possible to get this close to so much nature in such a small country. But it has been too easy. I feel like I haven't earned the reward. I look forward to my adventures in Nicaragua and beyond, well off the heavily-trodden tourist trail. Who knows, maybe I'll have a real adventure. I make my way back to San Jose brimming with enthusiasm for the trip ahead.

CHAPTER 6
Blue Sunshine

The bus terminal in San Jose turns out to be nothing like its spacious counterpart in Panama City. It is a small, cramped and unremarkable station in the city center, enclosed by a fence of upright, spear-tipped metal bars. This station serves only the one particular bus line that I am taking to Nicaragua, and the other bus lines have their own stations. Though well protected, it doesn't seem any more dangerous to me than any other place I've been in either city. The passengers are mostly local people carrying large bags, off to visit friends or relatives, I imagine. The ticket purchase proceeds without event, and we line up to board the bus about ten minutes prior to the scheduled departure time. Two men are busy washing the bus with a hose and buckets of detergent, and they give the greasy wheels a good wiping. The bus is modern, shiny and comfortable. The so-called developed world has nothing on this.

My bus is scheduled to arrive in Managua at ten o'clock at night after an eight-hour journey. Most of that journey will be after sunset, so I need to find an interesting seatmate to talk to after dark. Looking around, I see an older man with a clipped white beard sitting alone about halfway along the aisle. He seems friendly and approachable; he also looks American. I am still not comfortable carrying on a lengthy conversation in my halting Spanish, and after my experience with the surfer dude, an older American seems just the ticket. Who would have thought I'd meet someone even older than me on this voyage? For a moment I'm half tempted to ask him if he isn't a bit old for this, but that's most likely a non-starter.

I stow my water bottle in the pouch on the back of the seat in front of me and settle into the surprisingly comfortable seat. I don't mind having the aisle seat, since if we're going to have a conversation, I will still be able to steal glances out the window. It doesn't take long for the old man to realize that I am American and to start speaking.

"I love this ride," he says, turning his head to face me, "The Costa Rican forest is incredible."

"Oh, yeah, it's amazing," I agree. "Do you take this bus a lot?"

"I've traveled all over by bus and train. I'm not much for flying," he adds, shifting toward me in his seat. "I pass through this way every so often. I live in Honduras, so it's not so far away for me."

"But, you're American, yeah?"

"Oh, yeah, from way back. Dexter, Missouri is my home town. Or *was* my home town, I should say."

"How did you end up living in Honduras?"

"It's cheaper— that's the main reason. Costs me about a tenth of what it would cost me to live in the U.S. Also, it's more interesting." He smiles as if he were just now appreciating his adopted home for the first time.

"Interesting in what way?" I ask.

"Well, I can do whatever I want to, basically. None of the modern annoyances to worry about. Unless I *want* them, of course. There's also a sense of community that I was missing in the States."

He is outgoing, but not forward, and very quickly I am at ease with him. He is bright and sensible, intelligent in a homey sort of way, with a disarming smile and a dry, but uplifting sense of humor. It's obvious that he is very much at ease speaking with other people. He looks a bit like Ernest Hemingway with his closely cropped white beard and stocky build. His smooth but weathered face is sunburned around the cheekbones. His clothes are a bit worn but not ragged, and he wears a khaki fishing vest with loads of pockets, unbuttoned in the front, revealing a modest, T-shirted beer belly.

"Yeah," he continues, "If anyone would have told me when I was a young boy in Missouri that one day I'd be living in Honduras, I would have thought they were crazy. It's amazing what life throws at you. Life is a miracle— you've got to enjoy it."

"Mine hasn't thrown much good at me these days, unfortunately, and now it's pretty much over." I'm not sure why I am saying this. I'm not feeling the depression so much since I came to Central America. Maybe it's because this guy seems so easy to talk to, and he's obviously lived through his forties.

"What's over?" he asks, knitting his brow slightly.

"My life," I reply.

He regards me curiously. "What do you mean? You got some kind of disease?"

"No, I just mean all the important things are over— the interesting part. I graduated from college, got married, had kids, raised them, you know. All of that stuff is done. I feel like I've gone through life's checklist and ticked all the major boxes. Then I got sick of just watching television at night, mowing the lawn on weekends..."

"So you came to Costa Rica to stir up the sauce a bit?"

"Actually I came to Panama first. I took the bus here. I'm crossing Central America by bus."

"That sounds like a great trip," he says without hesitation, and in doing so, he becomes the first person I've come across who's told me my trip was a good idea. I feel somewhat validated. I like this old guy.

"So how old are you," he says, "If you don't mind my asking... late forties, early fifties?"

"Well, somewhere in there, you know- on the lower end..." I reply with a grin.

"Pretty young for your life to be over. So what does your wife think about you running off?"

"She didn't mind too much. I think she's kind of tired of me anyway," I laugh. "No, I'm joking. Really, we have a pretty good relationship. She doesn't mind. I think she also knew that I was going a bit stir-crazy."

"Well, you're going to find this hard to believe, but I started out in the same way, sans the understanding wife. Came here 20 years ago when I was about the same age as you, in my mid-forties. Found a place in Honduras that I love and I've been there ever since, when I'm not traveling. I'm Blue Sunshine- that's what everybody calls me."

"Blue Sunshine! What the heck kind of a name is that?"

"I sort of made it up myself. My real name never seemed to fit me. Earl Mitchell— too bland. Too pedestrian. I chose Sunshine because I've always loved the outdoors. Can't get enough sunshine. Then I thought, well, that sounds too happy, and maybe a little too childish. I'm not always that happy; sometimes I'm even downright miserable, so I added the 'Blue' part. Blue Sunshine describes me pretty well."

"It sounds like an old hippie sort of name. A bit dated."

"Well, then I guess it fits me pretty well, because I'm an old hippie. And I'm a bit dated, too."

"I see. Well, I'm Doug Roth. I don't have any explanation for that name. I never really thought about it, so I'm not sure whether it fits me or not."

"Well, let's see… two syllables— quick and easy to say. Sort of average, middle-American, nondescript. Is that you?"

"That's pretty much me. I guess it does fit."

"Might as well hang onto it, then." He smiles.

The bus takes a slight turn, and the reddening rays of the sun slide through the window on the opposite side, settling their warm caresses on my bare arms. It reminds me of all the time I spent playing outdoors when I was a kid. Blue Sunshine… it does have a pleasant, poetic ring to it.

"You're right about the sunshine part," I say. "It's a strange thing, but when I think back to my younger days, it seems that the sun was brighter, much brighter, but brighter in a way that didn't hurt my eyes. And I remember the chirping of the birds, so loud and clear and pleasant. I never hear the birds now. At least… I never notice them. But I always remember being outside in bright sunshine. It's like it never rained or got dark. Then later, once I started working, being outside on a sunny day was a rarity, and when I was outside there was always yard work to be done or something, and the days seemed to slip away before I could grab them. That's one thing I was hoping to do here— spend some more time outside in the sun."

"That's *one* thing you need to do. The other is to stop thinking about your past, and talking about your life as if it was over. If *your* life is over, where does that leave *me*?"

This unshaven old character is right, I think. This trip is good for me. It's a real change of pace from my same old rut. Maybe it will change my attitude.

I'm not sure what to say next, so I glance around the bus, looking at the other passengers on board. The seat backs are rather high, but not so high as those on a plane, so I can at least see something of the passengers in front of me. All appear to be locals, and some are chatting quietly amongst themselves, while others are eating packaged snacks, reading or looking out the window. I've always found it relaxing to travel on a bus or train, watching life up close, having it roll past me on an asphalt conveyor belt, never knowing what might lie just a bit further ahead.

I've got nothing to read, and from the look of it, neither does Blue. I know we both realize there's a long way to go, it's getting darker and there's nothing else to do, so our conversation will resume, one way or another. Besides, he doesn't seem like the kind of guy who's accustomed to being quiet for long stretches of time, and I could use someone to talk to at the moment, anyway.

Blue breaks the silence. "Got your chloroquine, I hope?"

"What do you mean?" I ask.

"Chloroquine tablets. For malaria. You've got some, right?"

"I haven't got malaria."

"No, it's a preventative," he explains. "Didn't you get any before you came here? Didn't you see your doctor?"

"No, I had no idea," I tell him. "I've never been down this way before. There's malaria here?"

"Not so much, but we've got some. It was one of the things that held up building the Panama Canal. You better stop at a pharmacy when you get a chance. Better to be prepared, especially if you'll be in the low, hot places. You got bug repellent?"

"No... but I do have some bug *bites!*" I say, pulling down the collar of my T-shirt with my finger to reveal the half-inch-wide red welt that still graces my neck. I guess I didn't plan very well. I just sort of decided to come, got some frequent-flyer tickets, and jumped on a plane."

"You must have really needed to stir things up pretty bad. Here, take some of mine. You can keep this." He pulls a tube of insect repellent out of one of his many vest pockets. "Make sure you cover all exposed skin areas real good, especially if you're planning to be outside around sunset. You don't need to worry about it in the higher altitudes, but once we hit the flatlands of Nicaragua, it makes good sense."

"Anything else I should know?"

"Plenty. This ain't Ohio, you know."

"Like what, for example?"

"Well, like your wallet, for one. Even I can tell where it is, so you know that the people who are really interested will know it immediately. Put it in your front pocket instead of the back, and spread your money around a little. That way if you get robbed, first, you'll at least know about it, and second, you may still end up with some money the thieves overlooked."

"Spread it around where?" I ask.

"Keep a little bit in your wallet. If your wallet's empty it looks mighty suspicious. Put some into your pocket on the other side, loose, and put some more in your socks. And if your watch is worth more than 25 bucks, which it looks like it is, I wouldn't wear it. I'd carry it in your pocket or your bag. It's already painfully obvious that you're North American. Don't reinforce the stereotype by looking rich too."

It seems like good advice. It sounds like this old character has been around enough to know. I've never met anyone like him in the States before. I'm sure there's a lot of things about Central American travel I can learn from a guy like this.

"This international bus network they have down here is pretty sophisticated," I remark to Blue. "I really didn't expect that it would be this easy to get around and that the buses would be so nice. It's amazing that things like this exist down here when the reputation of these countries in the US is so bad."

"Yeah, this is one thing they really do well down here. There are still a number of things that they don't do well, but they can certainly provide people with a relatively high level of comfort— if you have the money. And the money you need is very low compared to what you'd pay up north."

"Panama City seems pretty modern, too. The city skyline looks almost like Miami's, from a distance."

"I know what you mean, but you have to be careful how you use that word 'modern.'"

"What do you mean?" I ask.

Blue turns slightly toward me in his seat again, so he can gesture freely with both of his hands while he speaks. His thick, hairy forearms accentuate his gestures. "Well, for many people, the word 'modernizing' has become synonymous with 'Americanizing.' I don't mean just for Americans, but for leaders and even the general public in other countries as well. They seem to believe that the American way is the modern way, the example... the *only* way, and they take on American ways of doing things without really evaluating them, or questioning whether they're appropriate or not, for their particular country. Take the whole notion of 'developed' and 'developing' countries. Who decides when, if ever, a country becomes developed? Has any developing country ever made the transition to become a developed country in the history of the use of those terms? Who decides which countries are developed and which are not, and by what criteria is it decided? Why are there only these two categories and not a 'development scale' of, say, one to ten? These are things that I think about when I hear about developing and modernizing countries. I hear people say things like, 'That country still hasn't entered the twenty-first century,' which is an absurd statement, of course, since all countries entered the twenty-first century on exactly the same day. What they really mean is, that country isn't doing things the same way that America does them in the twenty-first century. Again, who makes the decision about whose twenty-first century is the 'real' one- the exemplary one?"

I sit silently for a moment, stunned by the change I've just witnessed in my seatmate.

"Wow, you must have been a university professor in your earlier life," I remark.

"Why do you say that?" he asks.

"Well, just the way you spoke right then, when you were explaining your ideas on developing countries. That would have been a perfect explanation for a college international relations course. You delivered it so clearly and you raised a lot of good points." Indeed his whole demeanor had transitioned from that of a vacationing country retiree to one of a seasoned lecturer, wanting for only the tweed jacket and elbow patches.

"Well, thank you for that, I guess," he says, and he's right back to his 'Aw, shucks' country-boy voice. "I do have a tendency to go a bit overboard. You're not the first person to point that out, in fact. Used to drive my ex-wife Caroline crazy."

I laugh. "Well, it's no problem for me. I've often been accused myself of using the longest words available to make my point. Why use a one-syllable word when a three-syllable word will do?" We both laugh. "It's not like there's a shortage of syllables floating around or anything!"

"Where are you headed in Nicaragua?" asks Blue.

"Well, I've never been to Central America before and I don't know too much about the countries. I figured I'd head to Managua and have a look around, then find a way to get down to the lakes. The map showed some pretty big lakes and I thought they'd be an interesting thing to see."

"You mean Lake Managua and Lake Nicaragua. Lake Nicaragua is much bigger and more remote than Lake Managua. There's also an island in Lake Nicaragua with a village on it. I'm not sure you realize how big that lake is. These countries are small, but they're not tiny."

"I've seen the lakes on the maps; they look pretty big."

"Very big. Lake Nicaragua's also one of the only lakes in the world to have sharks."

I turn my head to look him in the eyes. "Sharks in a lake?" I wonder if he's kidding me.

"You bet," he confirms. "Bull sharks. Most likely they come in through the river that leads from the lake to the sea, but a lot of people, including me, think there's a breeding population living in the lake."

"I'll be sure not to set foot in that lake!" I insist.

"…But it is something to see," he continues, "The lake, that is. And there are better places to go than the capital. In fact in many of these countries, *most* places are better than the capitals. Why don't you try Granada? It's right on the lake and this bus actually makes a stop there on the way to Managua. It would be much more interesting for you. It's an old, well-preserved colonial town, and it's much safer than wandering the streets of Managua."

"Colonial, yeah?"

"Yeah, it's quite a nice little place. I've stopped there a few times. Easy to find your way around, easy to find a hotel, and a great place for a good long walk. You'll get to know the country and the people much better there."

"Sold. All right, I'll check out Granada. Any particular place you'd recommend to stay?"

"When you get off the bus, take a right and keep walking until you get to the main square. There's hotels on all the streets around the plaza. You won't have to walk far, and nobody will bother you. Nobody you need to worry about, anyway."

"So you've obviously traveled around a lot," I surmise.

"A bit, I do like to travel. And I like people who travel. They look at life in a different way. I'm not talking about tourists. I'm talking about *travelers*."

"What's the difference?" I ask.

"Tourists are the people who go on cruises, sign up for package tours, and stay at beach resorts. They don't have the time or the inclination to seek out what's really going on in a place. They're not coming into contact with the local people, except those that serve the tourist industry. A traveler is someone with a genuine interest in the culture of the places he goes… the real, gritty, unpolished truth… someone who really gets out on the road, like we are now."

"I suppose this is a bit different from having the ayurvedic massage at the Costa Rica Spa & Resort, isn't it? Not that I've ever been one for that. This trip is much more my speed."

"I can ask someone just one question," says Blue, "and from their answer to that question, I can tell how well-traveled they are."

"What question is that— how many different countries have you visited?"

"No, no. It's much more telling than that. The question is— Are you rich?"

I stare at him, wondering whether I am missing something. "Are you rich? That's the question? Because you presume that only wealthy people can travel widely? I don't think that's necessarily so."

"No, that's not it at all. It has to do with how you answer the question. You see, most people, even most rich people, will answer no, on the basis that, either they're not as rich as they would *like* to be, or as rich as someone else is, or whatever. In our society, it's not typical for people to admit to being rich. First, the definition of 'rich' changes according to how much money you have. It's like that carrot on a stick they used to use to get a donkey to pull a cart. It's always a little bit out of reach. We tend to think that if we only had a certain amount of money, we'd be rich, and then we get that amount of money and we see that it's just an illusion— our expenses go up, our standard of living goes up, and the bills keep on coming, just higher and higher. The other reason is that it is considered impolite to flaunt one's wealth— overtly— since we don't want to create envy or bad feelings among our friends."

"What's all this got to do with travel?"

"Well, the more you travel around the world, the more you see that our standard of living is not typical, and that a large percentage of the earth's population has difficulty even finding enough food or fresh water to get themselves through the day. The fact is that most people in this world live day by day just as far as the basics of food and water are concerned, never mind the other things that we'd consider necessities: shelter, clothing, medical care... Most people in the world would be far more familiar with the style of life in the slums you see by the side of the road here, than with our lifestyles in the States. My point is that anyone who has the resources to travel for leisure is far wealthier than this, orders of magnitude wealthier, and if you're truly well-traveled, if you've really had a good look around the world, and somebody asks you if you are rich, how can you not immediately and without hesitation respond 'yes?' And that's the test that I use to see how well traveled a person is."

Upon concluding this discourse, he adds almost as an afterthought, "So then, I'll ask you... are you rich?"

"I hate to blow your theory," I answer, "But yes, I'm rich in the relative, worldwide sense, and affluent in the American sense, but no, I'm not well traveled."

"You will be, after this trip. And it sounds to me like you've got the makings of a good traveler in you already. It's great to know that there are people with enough interest in the world around them to plan a trip like you're taking."

"Well, to be honest, my interest in taking this trip is more in the world inside me than the world around me. I needed to do something bold, something new, something I've never done before. Like you said, 'to stir the sauce.'"

"Going through a rough patch at home?"

"No, just in my head. I've been thinking lately that the only major event of my life that hasn't already happened is death."

"You're starting to depress me, and I just met you. Is this what you're always like?"

"I'm not trying to be depressing. I'm just stating the fact. I've accepted it."

"Look, this mid-life thing— it's kind of like a second adolescence, you know?"

"Third, in my case. I went back to college in my mid-twenties and acted the part."

"OK, third. Maybe adolescence never ends. Or maybe it just recurs at various points of your life. It's always a little awkward, except this time it's not as exciting when you find hair growing in new places— like in your ears, for example. The point is, I remember feeling the same way as you twenty years ago, and I haven't died. I did and still do interesting things. Moving to Honduras, for example. I'd barely been out of the States before.

"Anything else? I mean, that's pretty interesting, but that happened about twenty years ago, you said."

"Well, my life is a lot different now. I fish; the money I've got is what I've got... I don't go chasing money anymore. That's an American thing. I'm very happy with my life in Honduras, and I spend as much time as I can doing things that I enjoy. That's what you should do— focus on the things that make you happy, and try to spend as much time as possible doing those things. One thing you have to keep in mind is that life is… well, *bizarre*. You make certain goals for yourself, you struggle in a particular direction, trying to end up in a certain place… but eventually you end up in another place… a place so far from the original goal that it's almost as if there was a different fate waiting for you all along. During the course of your life, you can end up breaking all the rules you set for yourself, and find yourself looking at every issue with an opinion that is diametrically opposed to the one you had at an earlier point in life, and yet you swear that you haven't changed. Life is bizarre… always remember that. Just ride the waves and enjoy it as much as you can."

"What are you trying to be, my sensei or guru or something?"

"I'm just trying to help. As I said, you remind me of myself twenty years ago."

"You know, one of the things that bugs me is that I find that there's not an awful lot of things to do for enjoyment anymore, at my age." I tell Blue. "At least it seems that way."

"Let me tell you something I discovered since I retired and came down here. Here's the dirty little secret of life: There are only eight things that you can do."

His statement catches me by surprise and I wonder if I've misunderstood him. "Eight things? What are you talking about? I've done more than eight things since breakfast this morning!" I had expected him to disagree with my contention and go on to list a wide variety of activities I might enjoy, but instead he's limiting all possible activities to only eight?

"No, I mean broadly classified. Everything you can do in your spare time can be broadly grouped into eight categories. You could say that there's only eight things to do in all of life, other than the necessary bodily functions like breathing and so forth, which I'm not counting. In other words, there's only eight ways to enjoy yourself in your spare time. Now, the categories have big overlaps, so you frequently find yourself doing things that fall into several categories at once."

"I'm not sure I follow you."

"OK, let's take an example… travel, since we were just talking about it. Travel really runs a wide spectrum from passive to active. What you're doing right now, riding a bus, is really about the most passive way you can travel. It's not much different than watching a movie about Costa Rica, only in real time. But once you get off this bus and get yourself a hotel, or even when you take a walk on the street, well then you're into active travel. The mountain climbers, polar explorers and jungle trekkers are involved in the most active kinds of travel. All of their senses are involved— they see, hear, smell, feel and taste their environment. I really admire those guys."

"Did you ever do those things?" I ask.

"No, I never had the time, or the money, or the energy— not all at the same time, anyway. And maybe, I didn't have the guts. But you never know. I'm not dead yet. But anyway, everything I just mentioned is a type of travel."

"OK, so travel is one of the eight things."

"It's one of the eight things; in fact, for me, it's the most enjoyable if the eight."

"Well, what are the others?"

"Hold on now. Let's take them one at a time. Eating and drinking— consuming, you might say, for pleasure, is another. If you're just eating and drinking anything because you're hungry, just to fill that empty space in your gut, then it's just survival, a bodily function, and doesn't count as a free-time activity. I try never to do that. Food is wonderful. It's simple, and it's scientific. I used to do a lot of cooking, so believe me, I know. And, in fact, there's only a certain number of tastes that can be created."

"Now don't tell me you have a list of those, too! There's a word for this sort of thing— keeping numerical track of all the activities and all the tastes in the world— OCD. Obsessive-Compulsive Disorder."

"No, it's nothing like that. Food is much simpler. There's only three basic tastes your body craves— sugar, fat and salt. You don't have to be OCD to recognize that." He pauses for a moment. "Well, on second thought, maybe it helps," he says with a sly grin. "Anyway, all good cooking involves the selective use of these three ingredients; I mean using them to enhance the basic dish being served— meat, fish, vegetables, bread or whatever. In unhealthy foods, they're the main ingredients rather than enhancers. I'm digressing here. My point isn't about preparing the food, just eating it. Consuming is one of the greatest pleasures in life, if we don't take it for granted. It can be a learning experience, a new taste sensation, a deeper sojourn into a new culture…"

"A social interaction…"

"Well, that's actually another of the eight things. Like I said, many times, in fact, more often than not, we are doing more than one of these things at a time. Like, for example, we are traveling and we are also interacting socially. If we were eating, too…"

"So, socializing is a third thing."

"It is. It's another great thing about life. Interacting with your family and friends and other people in a positive manner. In fact, that leads up to the fourth thing, which is sex."

"That's a social interaction, in a way."

"It is, but it's significant and unique enough that it deserves its own special category, don't you think?"

"I guess so. It's your theory, not mine; I'm just listening."

"You know, you *must* be depressed. You didn't jump on that sex one. Most people would have made some kind of joke."

"I can't think of one. I'm not that quick on my feet with jokes."

"You're not surprised that it's not my favorite of the eight things? That I told you travel is my favorite?"

"I actually admire you for that. You're like me. You're not a sheep. You don't follow the herd. American pop culture dictates that sex is the most important thing in life, just like they push beauty, money, youth, and whatever else... especially anything they're trying to sell. Most people would think there's no other option than to put sex first on the list."

"Well, I didn't say the list was in any order. It certainly is something I enjoy, especially since I got remarried when I moved to Honduras."

"You have a Honduran wife?" I am somewhat surprised, as he hasn't mentioned this fact before.

"I do, and she's great. She's quite a bit younger than me; in fact, she's younger than you."

"Wow, and sex isn't your number one? What's wrong with you?"

"Now *there's* the joke I was waiting for. That took a long time."

"I told you I was slow," I said. Blue smiled broadly. Whenever he smiled, his sunburned cheeks and white stubble lent him a silly Kris-Kringly aspect that I found comical, and I couldn't help but smile with him.

"Well, what about you?"

"I have a wife. Only ever had the one... and she's enough trouble!" I joke. "No, I'm just kidding; she's great. I told you she let me take this trip with no problem."

"I mean as far as sex is concerned."

"You're asking about my sex life? Well, I don't want to get too kiss-and-tell about it, I mean, I did just meet you today. But OK, I will tell you that by my age I've been through its whole life cycle, from its awkward, innocent birth to its... well I guess it never really dies, it just..."

"...It just decays?"

"Well-put. In a way, I guess. You know what I mean. But don't get me wrong; it's still the best two minutes of my week."

"Gotcha. I know where you are, man; I was in the same place with my first marriage. That's one of the reasons I got out. Well, that and the fact that she couldn't stand me. I was going through some crap; I lost my job, and that was it. I came down to Honduras and never looked back."

I smile to myself as I am reminded of my friend Cal, who recently, during an unguarded moment in an all-guy conversation about the decline of sex in middle age, let slip the comment, "I love my wife, but not in *that way*," before quickly realizing the ridiculousness of his statement. Another friend chimed in by claiming that he and his wife had become 'spouses without benefits.'

The bus pulls up to a roadside restaurant for a quick dinner stop. Although rather isolated, the restaurant is large, clean and efficient. The passengers line up at the cafeteria-style counter, choose their entrees, side orders and drinks, and sit down to eat at wooden tables on a wide concrete porch. I choose the *gallo pinto* with fried chicken and freshly cooked corn tortillas. The smell of the tortillas is heavenly. The plastic chairs outside the restaurant have been bleached by years of sunlight to a pale red, despite the fact that the tables are protected beneath a wooden sunshade. It is too dark to see much past the braided trunks of the palm trees just outside the eating area, but where we are sitting it is well lit. Insects zip aimlessly around the fluorescent bulbs like comets in miniature solar systems. We choose a table and Blue sits directly across from me.

"All right," I say, "So the first four of the things you can do in your life are traveling, consuming food and drink, interacting socially and having sex. What are the other four?"

"Let's take them one at a time, like we have been. Passive entertainment is another one. This would include going to shows, watching the street entertainers, listening to music, watching television... things like that."

"It seems like a lot of people back home think there's only that *one* type of thing to do, and nothing else!" I unwrap my stack of steaming tortillas and carefully remove one, then spoon some rice and beans onto it and roll it up with my fingers.

"A lot of people do fall into that trap," says Blue. "It's an easy thing to do. Especially at our ages, you almost have to actively resist it. Like we've obviously both done. I don't even have a television in my home. Of course, that's mostly because I can't afford one, but I understand what you mean. I don't miss it."

"I'm afraid I'm a newcomer to the resistance movement. I didn't fight my way out of that one until recently. I just saw myself getting old and sitting in front of the TV until I died— not a very encouraging prospect. Coming on this trip was one way out, but I'm not sure I'm rich enough, or energetic enough, to make this a full-time lifestyle."

"I did it, and I wasn't rich by any means," Blue says between sips of his soft drink.

"I'm sure you've got more money than me. My ex-wife got almost everything in the divorce. I'm living on peanuts!"

"But you said you travel a lot."

"I said I *like* to travel," he explains. "And I do it when I can, but very cheaply. This bus ride is what, twenty bucks? Besides, I don't travel that often— I've just been around a lot because I've done it over the course of many years. But we're getting off the subject. There's also what I call *active* entertainment. This is doing creative things— making art, making music, as opposed to just listening to it. Learning a new language or skill, playing cards, or even creative thinking, are all active entertainment."

"Thinking as active entertainment..." I ponder the concept. "I wonder if there's a way to make money from that!"

"In my case, I view this in a much more positive light than I do the passive entertainment that the masses seem to prefer," he adds. "Better exercise for your brain!"

Most of the passengers have finished their meals and are beginning to board the bus again; Blue and I discard our trash, join them and return to our previous seats. The bus continues its journey toward the Nicaraguan border.

"So what else is there?" I ask Blue.

He turns his face toward me and searches my expression. He lowers his voice and I sense just a hint of embarrassment on his face. "Well, there are entheogens— you know, mind-expanding plants."

He's caught me completely off guard. "Drugs?" I whisper, my eyes widening. "I *knew* there was something funny about you! Was this whole conversation a setup for offering me drugs? Is that how you support yourself down here? Forget it. I'm not interested in that. I'm just trying to have a look around at something other than a video screen or my backyard. I'm not a dropout from society!"

"Calm down, man; I'm not offering you drugs; I'm just telling you my theory about the eight things, remember? I'm not trying to morally justify them or anything else— we can talk about that later. I'm just saying what there is. Now listen. I did not say 'drugs.' I said entheogens— mind-expanding plants. There's a big difference."

"Not to the law, there's not."

"No; you're exactly right— not to the law. And I have an issue with that. The drugs you are thinking about— the ones you hear about in the news— heroin, cocaine, crack, meth— they are *not* mind-expanding. They are mind-contracting. They are addictive, dangerous substances. People who use those substances start on a negative track and their lives go nowhere but downhill. They don't learn anything from the experience. I've seen it. It's all about feeling good, and when it stops, they just want that good feeling again. They'll pay anything to get it, sacrifice their health, and all the other parts of their life atrophy. This is not what I am talking about at all. In fact, let me make it clear— I am strongly opposed to drugs. What I am talking about is the controlled and occasional recreational use of marijuana, magic mushrooms, peyote and other plants that the good lord has put here."

"He's also put poison ivy here, and hemlock, and arsenic," I interject.

"After living for 20 years here in Central America, I think I know a little about it," says Blue. "Marijuana has never killed anyone, but the fact that it is illegal in much of the world has killed many, and continues to do so. Where a market for a product exists, it will be served. Leaving it in the hands of organized crime is absurd and dangerous. It brings them fabulous wealth, supports their violent means, and develops smuggling channels that are used for dangerous drugs, weapons, human trafficking and so on."

"But surely there's a market for all drugs, even the dangerous ones. That blows a hole in your logic."

"I'm not saying that we should legalize everything. There's a market for hired murder, too, but I'm not suggesting we should legalize it. Hired murder isn't harmless. Mind-expanding plants are harmless, at least much more so than their illegality is. The only rational reason for a government to consider regulating these things is to minimize their overall harm to society, is it not?

"It's really a matter of semantics with these substances. The US government calls them all 'drugs,' so they're tarred with the same brush, even though the differences between marijuana and heroin, for example, are as great as those between chocolate and motor oil. If they had always called marijuana and magic mushrooms 'entheogens' and the other substances 'drugs,' you would look at them as completely different things. It's all words. People don't normally call alcohol a drug, except when someone's trying to make some kind of point. If they did, I'm sure you'd look at alcohol the same way, or worse, you'd look at those substances the same way you look at alcohol. Because, as you know, alcohol is a drug."

"So say all the druggies. We're just going to have to agree to disagree on this one. I'm not quite so liberal as you are on the subject."

"That's fine; we each have our own opinions. That's how it should be. We're thinking people. For me, the mushrooms, especially, help me understand. They've gotten me through some rough patches in my life."

"You *think* they help you understand. It's really just some drug-induced delusions that you're having."

"How can you say that, never having experienced it yourself? What if… can't you just concede the remotest possibility that I might be right? How will you ever know?"

"Like I say, we will never agree on that. But I really enjoy talking to you, and I mean that."

"Thanks. You're a pretty bright guy. Of course we won't agree on everything, but I like a person who thinks. Again, I'm just saying they're one of the eight things, whether you partake of them or not. I do happen to agree with their occasional use, but that's just an aside. Even if I didn't agree, I'd have to include them in the eight things. An interesting side question is, why do these plants produce psychoactive substances? There has to be a reason. They're not toxic, so it can't be a defense mechanism— what creatures eat mushrooms anyway, besides people?"

"Pigs," I reply.

"What?"

"Pigs eat mushrooms. That's how they find truffles in France. They tie a rope around a pig…"

"All right, I know," says Blue. "But you're sidetracking the conversation."

"You asked the question," I reply. "All right, so anyway, that's how many of the eight things, now? Or, as far as I'm concerned, the seven things."

"That's... let's see, seven out of the eight."

"What's the eighth one? Any more crimes in there?"

"No, the eighth one is pretty straightforward. Probably no controversy with this one. Physical activity, exercise. This includes playing sports, running, working out and that sort of thing. Sorry to disappoint you."

"You know, I'm not really sure I agree with you about any of this. The whole thing seems a bit silly. I see what you mean in a way, but your categories are pretty broad. Broadly defined, there may only be eight things to do, but when you look at the sub-categories, the number of possibilities is almost infinite."

"So *you're* telling *me* that there's an infinite variety of things to do in life?"

I'm suddenly stuck for something to say. I can only manage "Ack..." He's got me. My mouth hangs open for a minute before I say, "I see your point. That's pretty good. Did you plan that whole thing out?"

"Didn't have to," says Blue, "You knew it all along."

With that, almost as if on cue, the bus rolls to a stop at Granada. I say goodbye to Blue and retrieve my bag from the luggage bin aside the bus. Blue hands me a card with his address and phone number in Honduras on it and welcomes me to call if I run into any trouble. I thank him and trudge off into the sultry darkness.

CHAPTER 7
Magnificent Chaos

How can you tell when you've crossed the border from Costa
Rica to Nicaragua? Go into a café and order *gallo pinto* (mixed
rice and beans). If the beans are black, you are in Costa Rica. If they
are red, you're in Nicaragua. This simple fact delineates the border
better than any barbed wire fence or surveyed imaginary line can.
My own entrance to Nicaragua, however, is more perfunctory than
culinary; bored immigration agents hastily leaf through my passport, stamp it, and return it to me without even the most fleeting eye
contact.

Moneychangers swarm like locusts, waving stacks of Nicaraguan
cordobas, or possibly counterfeit copies thereof. The usual array of
vendors, only slightly less aggressive than the moneychangers, is
lined up at their tables, hawking soft drinks, bottled water, packaged snacks and unidentifiable fried foods dripping with cooking oil
from their flame-heated basins. Travelers clamor through the churning mass, passports in hand; buses and cars spew their exhaust; the
occasional dog or goat wanders through. I derive an unlikely and

inexplicable sense of calm from this crazy scene. Everything is as it should be. This is exactly the sort of street drama that I envisioned prior to my travels. I wonder if the other passengers find it strange that I remain outside the bus, deliberately immersing myself deep in this chaos and smiling broadly, rather than returning to my seat like the others to await departure from the border zone. They must think me half-crazed myself, an alien cog fitting seamlessly into the gears of this lunatic human machine.

I'm a little unsure of myself wandering through the mostly unlit streets of Granada. Groups of young people are hanging around along the sides of the buildings, talking and laughing loudly. Not surprisingly, I'm the only one wheeling a suitcase along behind me, the other few passengers that disembarked in Granada having departed in the taxis that had queued up adjacent to the bus stop. But I trust Blue; in spite of his druggie inclinations, he seems a decent guy and I'm sure he wouldn't steer me wrong. Take a right off the bus… keep walking till I get to the main square… and there it is! Blue was right; there are several hotels around the main square, some basic and some quite fancy. I walk into one of the fancy hotels and inquire at the desk about nightly rates and the types of rooms available. The rooms are almost shockingly inexpensive. I pull out my passport and credit card immediately and register for a single room. After photocopying my passport, the desk clerk hands me a key and directs me through the small lobby to a stairway at the back of an indoor courtyard containing a very small swimming pool. The hotel is luxuriously decorated in blue tile and the walls are artistically accented with oil paintings of local scenes and people. There are a fountain and a restaurant that looks enticing, but there is no elevator. It is a tastefully elegant and clean hotel, but not ostentatious. I am very happy with it. Relieved of the burden of my luggage, I take a short walk along the streets again and they do not seem nearly as threatening as I had thought. I return to my room ready for a good night's sleep and eager to explore again in the morning light.

An amazing sight greets me in the morning, the like of which I have never seen before. It seems that the entire population of the town is outside, sweeping up the sidewalks and streets, and even the bare ground in the main plaza. Trash is collected and emptied into bins and bags, or simply piled next to the road. The town looks beautiful and well cared-for. I am almost embarrassed to step on the freshly swept ground with my dirty sneakers.

A bit seedy but a beautiful colonial town, it doesn't take long for Granada to cast its spell on me. It's a friendly place, clean, cheap and charming in a down-to-earth kind of way. There is a smattering of other Americans here, though many of them don't fit the profile of the cultural-minded explorer. A number of them are about my age, though they only seem to amble between the hotels and the American-style bars, of which there are quite a few. I peek into one or two and they are all the same and of no interest to me. They serve American beers and chicken wings, and American football is the staple on the prominent televisions. They look just like a thousand sports bars back home. Why would these men (and they are all men) take the trouble to come to a somewhat isolated backwater in what most Americans would consider a no-go country, and then ignore the fascinating beauty that it offers them? It doesn't take long to see that they are after a different kind of beauty, one that can be found in the young Nicaraguan girls that populate the nearby street corners.

A short walk from the town center is Lake Nicaragua. Though the waters of the lake are far from clear, it is a spectacularly beautiful sight, a vast inland sea ringed by mountains and volcanoes. Stretching far beyond the horizon, it appears more like an ocean than a lake, with small windswept waves breaking as they approach the stony shore. A ferry lies moored at the end of the lone dock, which reaches thirty yards into the lake. Only a few people are anywhere to be seen, and they are playing in the surf, washing away the heat of the day and seemingly oblivious to the 'no swimming' signs in front of them. I see no evidence of the sharks that Blue mentioned, and I hope they are not near the swimmers.

I inhale deeply as I gaze out over the lake. The air is warm, but it smells fresh. There is but a faint whiff of engine oil and rotting vegetation. As bits of plants that were once living drift aimlessly in the ripples of the lake, so my own thoughts drift back home to Dawn, Celeste and Estelle. I miss them intensely, although I've been gone just less than two weeks and I haven't even made any attempt to contact them so far. There are several reasons for this, one of which is circumstances- I simply haven't had access to a telephone or computer in many of the places I've been. But I have to admit, the main reason is that I want this time to myself, to work out my own issues. Perhaps by backing away from them a bit, I can gain the perspective I need to get a truly accurate picture of where I am in my relationships with them, who I am, and who they are.

The easiest one is Dawn. I think back to our earliest days. I first met Dawn when we both worked for the same company after I graduated from college. The economy was going through a rocky patch at the time, and the best job I could manage to get was working in the warehouse of a local department store chain, in spite of my newly-minted university computer science degree. My colleagues in the warehouse were all male and we had a great time laughing and joking around with each other all day. Dawn worked in the adjacent office keeping files of something or other, but she may as well have worked a hundred miles away, for all I got to see her. However, she certainly did catch my eye on the unusual occasion on which she had to come into the warehouse. When she did, all work would virtually stop, as any guys in the vicinity would gather around her to see what she wanted, and to try to interest her in their various forms of well-rehearsed flirtatious chitchat. The one guy, Pete, had devised a special whistle that he would give whenever an attractive girl walked into the area, in order to alert the other guys covertly to her presence. Dawn was the inspiration for many of his whistles.

I don't remember the first time I saw Dawn, but I do remember that whenever she walked into the warehouse it was like a breath of fresh air washing all over me. After joking around with the guys all day, it was always a pleasure to see her flutter in to drop off a paper or pick up a file, like a rare and stunningly colorful hummingbird flitting to a flower for just a moment, then flying away all too soon, as if it has better things to do and better places to be. Afterward, my mind would be fixated on her for the rest of the day, and I would look forward to my next fleeting glimpse of her.

But what's happened to Dawn and me over the last twenty years or so to change this? Well, we've just gotten older, haven't we? Things are bound to cool off after twenty odd years (and those twenty years were, in fact, *quite* odd). Still, I wonder if our interests haven't drifted apart too much these days. She seems to have developed an unnatural attachment to the television. An *obsession*, as my daughters would call it, with their generation's penchant for overstatement. Would Dawn ever be interested in joining me on a trip like this? When we were young I could have imagined it; today I'm not so sure. Anyway, she does make a good roommate, and overall we seem reasonably compatible.

Celeste's got one foot out the door. She's *always* got one foot out the door, if not two. She's spreading her wings, and I'm sure she'll be fine. I just don't understand the tattoo thing, though. It's a fashion, obviously. Tattoos have been around for generations, yet in middle-class America, a relatively small percentage of people got them until recently, and a lot of the people who did get them in the past were in the military. Why should this have changed? If the appeal of a tattoo is limited, shouldn't the rough proportion of people they appeal to stay constant over time? I believe it should. If you could somehow keep people isolated from one another for the first eighteen years of their lives, I would bet a year's salary that the proportion of people who think a tattoo is attractive would stay the same from one generation to the next. The change in popularity lately is, in my opinion, solely due to the influence of other people in our lives. Celeste likes tattoos because other people like them, most likely (unless, of course, she happens to belong to the original small percentage of people who they appeal to by nature- but I consider this to be unlikely). Like certain types of sunglasses, tattoos happen to be fashionable in the current era. Unlike sunglasses, however, it is extremely difficult to remove or replace tattoos. Therefore, Celeste will essentially be forever marked as a member of the "millennial generation," appearing to later generations as out-of-place as an old man with an eternal ducktail or permanent hippie beads would to her. I wish her luck in the strange, weird future. I hope she remembers me when she becomes a successful professional fashion critic.

And that brings me to Estelle, if I remember her name correctly. It's been so long since we've had a decent conversation, I can't even be sure of that anymore. I have to be very careful what I say to Estelle when I do see her, lest I set off the hair trigger that sends her stomping away to slam herself behind the nearest door. Estelle's emotional sine wave has an amplitude that is off the charts. Lately it seems like she is always angry with me. I have scanned my memories thoroughly many times for clues to the source of this anger- some long-forgotten slight perhaps, or some unrealized misunderstanding or mistake, but I have always come up empty-handed. I don't recall her having been born angry; she must have picked it up somewhere along the way. She even gets angry with me for things that *she* does. Once I asked her whether she'd seen the book I'd been reading. I had laid it on the table and had gotten up to make a sandwich, and when I returned, the book was gone. The complete disappearance of any small object in my house is nothing unusual; in fact, it is a routine event that happens most days. However, I really wanted to continue with my book as I was enjoying it, and it was one of those very rare days when I didn't have anything else more pressing to do. It was also one of those even rarer days when Estelle happened to be wandering through the land of the living, so I asked her whether she'd seen my book. She said 'no' and went back to whatever she was doing. I spent about half an hour searching for my missing book, and then gave up. Two days later, I noticed the door to Estelle's room was slightly ajar, and glancing in, I spied my book lying splayed in the middle of her floor. The next time I saw Estelle, I asked her why she had my book, and why she had originally denied having any knowledge of where it was. Predictably, I suppose, she became angry with me for not trusting her, and stomped off into her room, with my book now an unintentional hostage. This situation obviously required me to invoke my disciplinary responsibilities, and the whole issue became highly unpleasant for both of us. Unfortunately, the only lesson learned may have been on my side, as I have learned to tread carefully, and to keep any conversational matters light and upbeat, in order to avoid future negative experiences.

I wonder if, in her own way, Estelle is going through something similar to what I'm experiencing. I don't recall having a particularly angst-filled teenage era, but now the emotions are bursting through in a different way. The display of emotion seems to differ by sex; for women, their expression is a lifelong phenomenon, blossoming with astonishing hyperbole in the teenage years, while men are more staid through most of life but for a few wildly unpredictable years buried somewhere in middle age. But perhaps these episodes are born of the same seed, the eccentric years of midlife doubling back on the crazy teen years, connected by some unseen metaphysical thread in the same way that an acupuncture meridian might connect the foot to the heart. Or maybe it's more than a connection; perhaps they *are* the same, but if the emotional release valve is not vented in the teens, these feelings percolate around in the mind until the next weak seam is found sometime in one's forties. Then the sequestered emotions burst through in an altered manifestation, in the same way that youthful chicken pox might show up later in an older, more virulent form as shingles. In this way, maybe I can understand what Estelle is going through. Maybe we have more in common than I think. Or maybe I am just kidding myself. The worst part of it all is that I feel I have completely lost my relationship with her. I don't understand where it went. But I do realize that this will be an ongoing challenge of my life.

Then, finally, there is me. What was my problem again? Oh, yes, depression. Well, aside from the ongoing parade of family issues, there is the job thing. Somehow, I'm going to have to make peace with the fact that I've probably risen up the career totem pole about as far as I'm going to. That shouldn't be too hard to handle- I haven't done badly. For years, working my way up to be corporate Vice President was my overarching, hard-driving goal. But looking at it from my perspective now, one level below, I would say that Vice Presidents aren't, in fact, any happier as a group than anyone else.

And the work, and the stress, well, they don't stop there. It just gets worse. So maybe I'll take my sour grapes story to heart and just stick to my Director position for a while. Except that now even that seems to be slipping out of my grasp. The management decision to bypass 4mul8er really put a twist in my briefs. Should I look for a new job? Lose all of my years of experience and seniority to bet my bankroll on an unknown? Probably not. I stare out at the lake, my mind reflecting on these troublesome issues as much as the light-dappled water reflects the mid-afternoon sun.

As the swimmers below me retreat from the water, I notice that one of them has lost part of his leg below the knee. Not to a shark-this was obviously a surgical amputation from a number of years ago. The amputee barely seems to notice it as he hobbles around adeptly between stones on the grassy shore. He is probably in his late twenties, quite a bit younger than me, and he seems to be enjoying himself a great deal playing around with his friends. I look back at myself less than a month ago, with all of my limbs intact, a great family, a decent-paying job with good benefits, a big house in the sterile, status-conscious suburban infinity of America, and try to fathom how it is possible for someone living in those circumstances to be depressed, while this young man, disabled and with only a cut tree branch for a crutch, most likely living in filthy squalor in one of the poorest countries in the Western hemisphere, can be so utterly happy. Is it because he is living in the moment, while I live in a bizarre mélange of past disappointments and future worries, like a temporally-twisted Schrödinger's cat? Or is it the chemical imbalance my doctor described, my brain seasoned with the wrong cocktail of herbs and spices, and doomed to simmer in a stew of melancholy until the magic of medication sweetens the sauce and reveals for me once and for all the bright side of life? Perhaps it is a bit of both, though there is a lot to be said for sunshine, fresh air, and stepping off the million-dollar treadmill once in a while. Maybe by focusing less on obtaining, retaining and maintaining possessions, I can share a bit in these people's energetic *joie de vivre*.

What's that ringing? Just my ears. One of the strangest afflictions of middle age has to be tinnitus, those sudden and inexplicable buzzing or ringing sounds you occasionally hear for no reason whatsoever. Tinnitus is the UFO sighting of the auditory sense- you are absolutely certain that you hear the sound, but nobody else does. You know better than to ask the person next to you whether they heard it, for if you do, you will only receive that look, the same look a person would give you if you asked whether he just saw that flying saucer. So you are left to contemplate your own auditory hallucination, and to wonder whether highly-intelligent aliens have singled you out as an earthly guinea pig to receive the test tone of their galactic emergency broadcast system. After a brief interception of their transmission, the expression on my face must register the acknowledgement that the alien race is looking for, and they break off their communication secure in the knowledge that they have reached me, and then return to their conquest of distant galaxies until it is time to resume their system verifications and interrupt my peaceful ponderings once again.

Back here on earth, a swarm of tiny bugs is dive-bombing my eyes, so it is time to move on.

I spend the remainder of the day getting acquainted with Granada, with its ornate but decaying churches, spontaneous street entertainment, sidewalk cafes and colonial grandeur. My hotel room, though not extravagant, is pleasant and comfortable, and I sleep through the night without waking, until the persistent beams of dust-filled sunlight poke through between the pleated curtains.

The old men and women arrive early in the morning to the central plaza. Overdressed for the weather, they take their usual places on the benches that line the open grassy area. Every day they take the same places, the same seats. Sometimes they talk amongst each other, but most of the time they sit silently, admiring the gardens, watching the children play. At their age, there is no more to be done; life has gone by. There is time only for a final review of events passed, and shared reminiscence among old friends. How long will it be before I become one of them? Have I got enough memories stored up to last me through those years? Will I be satisfied? Have I done enough?

The city map that I pick up in the hotel lobby shows a large marketplace within a reasonable walking distance. It seems like a great place to spend the morning. As I stroll in the direction of the market, the streets become more congested, and it is obvious that the market is a cornerstone feature of the town. This is the place that everyone goes to meet, mingle, shop, browse, ogle and dine. I find it fascinating.

I exalt in the magnificent chaos of the market. The jumble of aromas that fade in and out jars the senses: the smell of meat that has been at room temperature for far too long, wood smoke, sweaty bodies, fresh fruit, powdered laundry detergent. A dog stops to urinate in front of me. A baby sleeps in a wooden crate, a man does likewise on a shelf, his feet propped up on some boxes. Hawkers yell repetitively to advertise their bargains: *"Frutas!" "Carne!" "Papas!"* A smorgasbord of fruits, clothing, personal items, rice, corn, meat, fish and every other commodity that could be needed or wanted appears in front of me as I gradually pass my way through the crowded, cavernous passages.

I realize how obvious it is that I am American by how easily I recognize the few other Americans that pass by in the crowded market. We may as well have American flags stamped on our fore-heads. We are all wearing sunglasses (although none are as unique as mine); none of the locals wear them. Our skin glistens with the glossy sheen of sun block. I am also the only one here wearing shorts, and my skinny legs are a sight, but that is a difference that I am happy for in this heat. All of the hawkers and touts can tell who is American, and they logarithmically increase the intensity of their sales pitches, sometimes switching to English, when I walk by. The taxi drivers know it and give me a loud honk on their horns when they see me. Even the children can tell, and they wave and say "hello" (and in the case of one confused youngster, "goodbye") to me. And of course, we Americans can recognize each other, giving a quick nod or a longer-than-usual glance to our fellow travelers, secure in the notion that others of our feather are here. I have no feeling of danger. I figure I must be either stupider, crazier or smarter than most other Americans, for I can see no reason why this insane carnival would not interest more couch-bound Yanks. Although I have a few linger-ing doubts, I decide to settle on 'smarter', and smugly walk on.

I remember seeing so many stray dogs the previous evening that I decide to buy a bag of dog food at the market. I have always had a soft spot for dogs. Perhaps it is because dogs are so uncomplicated. You can completely read a dog within five minutes. You will know everything you need to know about the dog in that time, whereas it would take years, even decades, to know a person as well, if, in fact, you ever can. Dogs don't carry baggage from the past. A dog's emotions are right there on the surface, unconcealed, for anyone to see: playfulness, anger, confusion, excitement, fear, love… they're all displayed at face value with no shame, through highly expres-sive eyes, ears and tails. Dogs may be animals, but they are no more like wild animals than we are, most likely having been domesticated and socialized to humans from the earliest days that people lived in groups. The ancestors of today's dogs were most likely wolves that learned that being non-aggressive toward humans could lead to desirable rewards in terms of food handouts, and humans learned at the same time that, in exchange for a few scraps, canines could be valuable early warning systems of intruders and predators, and later, useful hunting companions. The millennia of camaraderie between my ancestors and those of dogs have not been lost on me.

My plan is to carry a bag of dog food with me on my wanderings so I can distribute healthy handfuls whenever I spy a hungry hound. For a moment I envision myself as a sort of Johnny Appleseed for canines, spreading the seeds of good cheer to dogs far and wide, in the form of nutritional sustenance. A few cordobas procure me a heaping bag. I exit the market and keep an eye out for straggly four-legged creatures. Where have they all gone? Now that I have dog food, not a single stray dog comes into my sight. As I continue to meander through the dogless streets, the thin plastic bag begins to rip in several places and I have to balance the bag on top of my hand to keep the kibble inside.

By midday, the heat has risen to a blistering crescendo. Sweat washes the sunscreen from my face into my eyes, and my contact lenses become coated with it. I become a ridiculous figure: a squinting, ostrich-legged gringo inexplicably toting a bulging, spilling bag of dry dog food. I note with irony that my skin is turning nut-brown, which seems an appropriate shade at the moment.

T-shirts don't last long in this heat. If I wear the same shirt for a whole day, the resulting stink becomes overpowering. Although I have no company to offend, I head back to my hotel anyway, to take my second shower of the day, and to change my shirt. Alas, it proves a useless exercise, as fifteen minutes later, I am just as sweaty as I was before the shower.

There are some creative minds at work in the street entertainment department here. One of the routines, adopted by several groups of young boys, consists of a large wooden frame dressed up in traditional styles to look like a nine-foot-tall woman. The 'head' is a tightly-stuffed burlap sack with a painted face and long black strands of yarn meant to look like hair. The frame is made to sit on one boy's shoulders, and the long drape of the skirt covers the boy, so that all that can be seen by observers is the absurdly tall, elaborately decorated woman. Since it is obviously very difficult for the encumbered lad to see through the costume and maneuver it through the streets, another boy acts as the guide and leads him to outdoor restaurants and similar gathering places where they are likely to encounter a generous, and presumably captive, audience. A third boy serves as drummer. Once the group identifies an appropriate spot at which to commence the show, the drummer begins playing a rapid staccato beat, and the boy in costume spins wildly, sending stuffed arms flailing, long skirt swirling, and yarn hair flying. The guide boy yells, "*Baile! Baile!*" (Dance, dance!) while the drumbeat grows more frantic and the giant dancing woman twists even more crazily in a dizzying frenzy. Inevitably, the boy beneath the wooden figure becomes winded and no doubt saturated in sweat from the sweltering heat, and the group collects whatever offerings the audience sees fit to bestow on them. They then move on to find the next suitable venue. A delightful display at first, the routine becomes rather predictable after the fifth or sixth viewing.

Granada is a small place. After a day or so of walking the main streets and the central plaza, I begin to recognize people. "That's the guy that was in front of the church earlier," or "There's that same couple that I saw eating at the restaurant across the street," I think. Within three or four days, many of the people in town look familiar, and I develop a level of comfort with them. I practice my Spanish with the street entertainers and the souvenir-sellers. So it goes with the tourist touts, the drug sellers and the prostitutes.

Every time I walk past the prostitutes, they hit on me. "*Te acompaño?*" (May I join you?), or "*Quieres chica?*" (Do you want a girl?) Though assertive, they are not too aggressive. Often one will walk next to me along the street for a stretch, hoping I'll buy. They seem harmless and even kind of sweet. I joke with them. Some of the girls are so young looking, they remind me of my own daughters' friends. They seem to have a lot going for them: beauty and youth-- two of the things our culture values the most. What they are missing, of course, is the third thing, money.

"I owe someone a lot of money," Maria tells me in Spanish. She is a beautiful young girl with dark doe eyes and a smooth, youthful complexion. She is alone on the main street and has just hit on me for about the fifth time tonight, so I sit down next to her on a bench to talk to her. "I'm in some trouble," she says, "so I have to do this, at least until I can pay him back."

"Do you live around here?" I ask her.

"Not really. I live pretty far away. It takes nearly an hour to get there and it's much more dangerous there than here." She goes on to explain that she works until at least midnight every night, unless she gets an offer to stay overnight. Although she opens up to me in conversation, she never stops rubbing my shoulders and asking me if I would like a massage or something more. To be completely honest, I don't mind the attention. It's been a long time since I've received advances from a pretty young girl, so I don't fight them so hard. But

I feel quite sorry for her. I decide to let her get on with her night, as I am unlikely to rescue her, as much as I might want to. I reach into my wallet and hand her 200 cordobas for her time, hoping it will at least help her a little with her money troubles. Such a little bit of money for me can really mean a lot to people here. An American man standing next to us, taking a photograph of his female companion with a cell phone, startles me. As I go to get up from the bench, Maria kisses me. Suddenly, the American with the cell phone turns and snaps our picture.

"Gotcha, you pervert! You're going to jail!"

"What?" I exclaim, my eyes widening.

"You heard me. That's an underage prostitute you're with, as if you didn't know. My wife and I are working to help these girls. We know all these girls, every prostitute in Granada, and that girl's only seventeen."

"I was only talking to her!" I protest, my voice now quivering.

"Nice try. I saw you give her money and I saw you kissing her. She had her hands all over you!" He walks away, looking back at me and shaking his fist. "You're going to jail, either here or back in the States. Wait and see! Get used to the idea! Your face will be all over the Internet by tomorrow! There's only a couple of hotels in this town! You can't hide!"

I look around. Maria has disappeared. I stand alone on the darkened street, my heart thumping, my world swirling. My smugness from earlier in the day has dissipated. I am not so smart after all.

The peacefulness of the evening is destroyed. I sleep fitfully that night, my mind running through all kinds of scenarios of what might happen to me. Riding on a wave of adrenaline, I get up early in the morning, have a shower, order breakfast and go for a walk. The same streets that were bustling last night are now empty and the sun is already baking one side of the street. The walk doesn't relax me, so I return to the hotel. It's time to move on. I decide to ask at reception the best way to get to Managua. The person at the desk is speaking with a police officer and looking at the guest list. I hear her mention my name. It feels like a bolt of lightning has hit me. A surge rushes through my body; my already sweaty face now sweats even more profusely, dripping down my shirt collar. They haven't seen me. I quickly step outside and make my way to the lake. I don't want anyone to see me on the streets of the town until I figure out what I'm going to do. I think about how ridiculous my story sounds. I wonder what 'evidence' they will find in my hotel room. My God! They will find two wet bath towels! It's going to look like someone stayed overnight in my room, when in fact I myself took two showers. I'm not a gambler, but I don't like the looks of my chances in this situation. Am I just being paranoid? Does this make sense? Should I just speak to them and try to clear up the misunderstanding? Sometimes you just have to go with your gut. I don't want to risk it.

I decide to leave immediately for Managua, and then leave the country for Honduras, as soon as possible. I sneak back into the hotel when the girl at the desk is not looking, and collect only my small, high-value belongings: my passport, wallet, camera, etc. I leave the larger bag with all my clothing and other articles in the hotel room, and steal quietly outside. The large bag would be too obvious to sneak out of the hotel and would hinder a quick getaway. I'll just have to buy more clothes elsewhere. I jump into the first taxi I find and give the driver $40 to take me to Managua.

The taxi looks like it can hardly make it out of town. There is a huge serpentine crack in the windshield and sunlight glints off its edges. The engine makes a loud, sputtering sound every time the driver steps on the accelerator. We take off through the Nicaraguan countryside, past farms and fields of sugar cane, and about 45 minutes later, we reach the outskirts of Managua. The streets are as much a circus as any place I have seen. A long-horned white bull with a swinging dewlap plods aimlessly across the road in front of us. A man cruises by on a bicycle, pedaling madly through the bustle, a small goat slung over his shoulder like a baby.

A beggar wearing nothing but an extremely dirty pair of pants bangs on the car window. The driver ignores him. He has seen too many such people to notice one more. I wonder whether I should roll down my window and hand him some cordobas, but before I can retrieve my wallet, the traffic light turns green and the driver pulls out. I briefly consider that regardless of how desperate my situation seems to be, there are still plenty of people in the world who would happily change places with me.

Managua is a collection of rather nondescript buildings, some modern and some crumbling, the vast majority in some intermediate phase along that scale, spread out and strewn haphazardly and seemingly without plan along the shore of Lake Managua. I recall reading many years ago about a devastating earthquake that nearly leveled the city, and it seems to me as if urban planning ceased at that point, if indeed it ever did exist. Still, I notice few signs of debris, and business has obviously been rebuilt. The city oozes a pleasant tropical ambience that San Jose, being at a higher altitude, cannot match.

Unfortunately, I have no time to deepen my cultural understanding of Managua. I am desperate to get out of this country. I must put a border between me and the Nicaraguan police, and the sooner, the better.

Again I find myself, sooner than expected, at yet another bus station, this time without my luggage. Where will I purchase my replacement clothing? I consider the brutal irony that barely twenty-four hours ago I was strolling through a huge market with a world of things on offer, with money in my pocket and precious few things that I needed to buy.

CHAPTER 8
Painted Flowers

C rossing into Honduras, the mountains become wilder, higher and much more jagged. Ridge after undulating ridge of corrugated earth is visible as I stare into the distance, each one taller, darker and mistier than its predecessor, until the most distant row of peaks becomes a hazy, purple, barely-discernable silhouette. A smattering of browns and tans of assorted hues joins the innumerable shades of green in the landscape's palette, particularly in the places where erosion and rocky outcrops have overtaken the steepest slopes. Menacing shadows in the resulting crags add an air of mystery and depth to the rugged scenery.

The bus passes through swathes of brilliant sun-blasted green-and-brown countryside and magnificent valleys. An extremely violent American film, dubbed into Spanish, plays on the video screen. My quiet contemplation is heavily punctuated by on-screen explosions, gunshots, beatings and stabbings. There are only about a dozen passengers on this bus, so I have a double seat to myself. A few of the passengers talk quietly amongst themselves; others distractedly watch the video. A few seats in front of me, a woman is crunching loudly on *chicharrones*. It sounds like a bag of bolts being dropped into a garbage disposer. For a moment the sound of the munched chicharrones blends with that of the movie's machine-gun fire and gives me the feeling of being in an actual war zone.

I'm glad to be out of Nicaragua, but what do I do now? To make matters worse, the bus pulls over without warning at a military checkpoint and we are directed to disembark; then we are all lined up against a wall with the blazing afternoon sun pouring down on us like molten steel. With the sun in our eyes the jackbooted soldiers request our passports. Just what I need. A rush of anxiety washes over me like a rogue wave. Are they looking at me? Will they notice that my heart is thumping like a discotheque? Do they already have my name, and will they arrest me on the spot? Will I pass out in this intense heat?

I continue standing in the sun for several minutes, struggling to shield my eyes from the light. I still have this nagging worry about my retinas, and it irritates me that I do, but it's way too bright to look at the sun anyway. On top of all this, the insect bite on my neck, an unintended souvenir from my first night in Panama, has started bothering me again. It seemed never to really heal right, and now I could swear it is swelling up again. It doesn't hurt so much as itch, but the itching is intense. When I go to scratch it the skin depresses, almost as if there is some kind of cavernous space under my skin. It strikes me that I never picked up the malaria preventative. What if I have malaria? I make a mental note to see a doctor, whenever and if ever I get the chance.

I survive the brief encounter with the military police, which is never explained, but which I take to be a routine part of life here. But

I am badly shaken up. I can't just nonchalantly continue my touring in this condition. I need a break. I need to get my stress level down.

There is only one place to go where I might find some comfort. That old hippie from the bus, Blue Sunshine, had handed me his address and phone number and said I could contact him if I had any trouble. Well if this isn't trouble, then what is? He said he lives here in Honduras. I just hope he meant the invitation. He seems pretty knowledgeable about this region and I'm sure he's had to deal with all kinds of catastrophes in twenty years of living here.

I pull out the card that Blue gave me. I am glad I put it in my wallet rather than just loose in my pocket, or it might have been left back in Granada with most of my clothes. He has his address on the card, and in parentheses, he has scribbled the words 'La Ceiba.' I inquire of the bus conductor, and he informs me that yes, the bus line does serve that location.

It's quite a journey to La Ceiba, the nearest city to Blue's house. But, I figure, the more distance I cover and the more obscure the location, the less likely I am to be found. This journey involves a rambling route through Honduras, first to Tegucigalpa, the capital, then on to San Pedro Sula, in the northwest of the country, then finally to La Ceiba, back toward the east. Talk about a circuitous route! I remember reading that San Pedro Sula is one of the most dangerous cities in the world. I don't think I will be spending much time there.

Unlike the other capital cities of Central America, Tegucigalpa does not lie on the Pan-American Highway. It is located about two hours to the north on another road, and it is necessary to change buses in a very small town at the junction of the highway and the road to Tegucigalpa.

Despite its name, the Pan-American Highway, which has provided the main route for my trip thus far and is the primary artery of regional travel and trade, in many places does not seem to fit the classification of 'highway'. It seems more like a secondary rural road, not for lack of traffic by any means, but because much of it is a winding two-lane street with switchbacks and traffic lights, traversing the hearts of cities and towns rather than skirting them. These factors can stretch a fifty-mile journey to several hours.

In any case, my bus from Managua displays San Salvador as its final destination, and to get to Tegucigalpa I need to leave the bus in a dimly lit village parking lot, with only a one-star hotel and a closed bus company information office to justify its existence. I wait with several other passengers, all locals, for the connecting bus to Tegucigalpa. By now it is quite dark and there is relatively little traffic on the road that passes in front of the parking lot. The other riders seem tired and sit down on top of their suitcases or on the paved area along the front of the hotel, but my mind is still racing and I can't relax. I take a brisk walk around the parking lot to try to dissipate the energy I feel. I pass a recreational vehicle with Mexican license plates and a rough map painted on the back, depicting a circular route that stretches from Mexico City down to Tierra del Fuego, then all the way up to Fairbanks, Alaska and back to Mexico City. There are some ambitious travelers around here, and I've got to meet them. Maybe it will help clear my head.

There is a light on inside the cabin of the RV, and an electrical cord snakes from an outlet near the RV's door, along the ground and into the hotel. It seems I have plenty of time to kill, and as luck would have it, within minutes the door opens and a slight, bearded man in his mid-fifties exits. He's wearing a thin, long-sleeved gray sweater with broad red stripes. It looks terribly warm for the weather and from the looks of it, he's been wearing it with some frequency.

"I see you're doing a bit of traveling," I say to him in Spanish. I am feeling more comfortable with my language skills after using Spanish almost exclusively in Nicaragua.

"Yes," he answers, "We've come quite a long way." He stoops to check something on the underside of the vehicle with his hand.

"I'm traveling across Central America myself, by bus." I tell him. "Looks like your trip is a bit more extensive. Which direction are you heading now, north or south?"

"North." I follow him as he walks around to the map painted on the back of his vehicle and traces the route with his finger. "We started in Mexico and drove as far as southern Argentina. Now we're on our way back to Mexico."

"Wow, so you're passing this way for the second time? And you drove the whole way?" I find this amazing and wonder what it would be like to take such a trip.

"The whole way as much as it's possible to drive. The road ends in southern Panama at a place called the Darien Gap." He places his finger on the map of Panama, close to the Colombian border. "So we had to ship the car from Panama City to Colombia, and my wife and I took a plane. That little detour cost us a few thousand dollars altogether, and we had to do it in both directions. Otherwise, we drove the whole way."

"Hmmm. And I thought *I* was adventurous. How long have you been traveling?" I ask.

"A little over a year. Once we get back to Mexico, we'll stay there for a couple of months, spend the Christmas holidays there with the family, then start the northern part of the trip."

I pause to ponder the immense journey detailed on his map. "Man, that's a lot of driving!"

"It is a long way," he agrees, "But it's worth every mile." He bites his lip as he grins.

"I can't imagine that too many people ever take a trip like that in their lives. How are you able to do it?" I ask.

"Well, I saw that a lot of my friends and neighbors would work very hard to buy *things*. But as for myself, once I had all the important stuff, the *canasta basica*, I didn't need any more *things*," he explains. "Buying more things didn't make me happier. Now my friends, they are all still working and saving so they can have more things. I don't save money so I can *have*; I save so I can *do*. To do is much more important than to have. For me, anyway."

"What's the best thing about driving across the Americas?" I wonder aloud, trying to imagine myself in his place. "What is your favorite part?"

"The best thing? I'd say the different cultures, the scenery along the way, all the people we meet… I love everything about it. What's not to love? Everybody has to do something with their life. This is what my wife and I decided. Really, what else is there to do? What else does one need?"

I know the answer to that. There are only seven other things to do. I find myself envying this man. My brief Central American sojourn has only covered a tiny portion of his journey. He has turned it into a lifestyle… a passion. At least for these several years, travel is the core of his existence. Sure, my trip has taken a bad turn, but it certainly has been an enjoyable and interesting alternative from my repetitive and uninspiring day-to-day existence. And now if I could get past this dark patch I'm going through, I may see a rising sun of optimism for my future. Who knows, maybe Dawn and I will drive the length of the Americas one day.

The groaning of a bus coming around the corner into the parking lot snaps me back into the reality of my situation. Central America may be a beautiful and fascinating place, but it's no place to be on the run from the law.

It's too dark to see anything out the windows of the Tegucigalpa bus, and there are very few electric lights in the area. Most of the time we are cruising through utter blackness. Occasionally we pass a small, whitewashed farmhouse and its lights illuminate a petite world of thick emerald vegetation. I've got nothing to read and nobody next to me to talk to, so I try to catch some sleep. I barely slept at all last night and I've been stressed out all day. I feel a little calmer after speaking with the Mexican traveler, as it helped me focus on what this trip is all about. I've got about ten days left until my plane departs for home and I want to enjoy them as much as possible. Whatever consequences the future holds in store for me, I cannot prevent. More than ever before, I must live in the moment.

By the time we reach Tegucigalpa, I have slept for about an hour. It's getting late now, so I ask the bus conductor for a hotel recommendation. He tells me about a cheap but clean local hotel a few minutes' taxi ride from the bus station. I find it a good option as I plan to continue my journey as early as possible the next morning.

The hotel is indeed cheap and it may well be clean, but I can't tell since the electricity is only working on the ground floor and my room is on the second floor. It's dark and sparsely furnished, but it has a bed, and once I lie down, I don't wake until the sun is streaming through the dirty windows. With the morning light I notice that the room has no shower, nor even a sink. I wash up as well as I can in the

Spartan communal bathroom in the hallway, which is a challenging task, considering that there is no soap and no towels.

It's after ten o'clock by the time I make it back to the bus station the next day. The five o'clock AM bus for San Pedro Sula is long gone, but there's another one at one o'clock, so I putter around the station for a few hours. I haven't eaten anything since midday yesterday in Managua, so I ask at the counter where I can get some food. The lady directs me to a local fast-food chicken restaurant a few blocks away and I eat enough for two people. On the way back to the station I buy a bottle of soda pop for the trip.

As we drive toward San Pedro Sula, the landscape slowly transforms from tropical to arid, eventually becoming almost desert-like. Brown overtakes green as the dominant color. Vegetation becomes sparse, and stocky, prickly cacti become common along the roadside. The terrain also smooths out a bit; the mountains become less jagged, their silhouettes less stark. The land takes on a stony, gritty texture, and a fine coating of dust becomes visible on the bus window.

After a few hours, I change buses in San Pedro Sula and the bus gets a much-needed washing. On board yet another bus, my journey takes me back toward the east, parallel to the Caribbean coast, to the city of La Ceiba.

By the time I get to La Ceiba, I feel like I've spent my entire life on a bus. The sun is already on its way down and I have to shield my eyes with my hand. I'd better hurry, I think, because I got the impression that Blue lives a ways out of town, and I don't want to find myself lost in the darkness, trying to find an unmarked house that I've never seen before, on an unmarked street in the middle of rural nowhere in Honduras. I also don't want to startle Blue and his wife with an unexpected knock on the door too long past sunset.

I disembark from the bus and scan the streets for an available taxi. I always try to have a good look at the driver, preferring an honest face and an older man if possible, the kind that looks like he's been driving a taxi for many years. If he's made a career out of it, I feel he's more likely to know his way around and less likely to take advantage of a naïve, vulnerable Yankee who doesn't have enough sense to stay home. I also prefer if he looks like I could take him in a fight if I had to, in case my intuitive decision is mistaken.

I find the perfect driver, a white-haired, nearly toothless man with leathery brown skin and a warm smile. He squints briefly when I show him the card Blue handed me with his address, seems a bit unsure, then nods his head slightly a few times, and opens the door of his taxi, motioning for me to get in.

"*Cuanto cuesta?*" I ask him.

"Twenty dollars," he replies. He's obviously realized that I'm American. I have no idea how far, or even in which direction, Blue's place is, so I am unable to determine whether the fare is appropriate or not. From this point onward, I'm completely dependent on this man, since even if he were to drive me twenty miles in the wrong direction, I would never know it.

Fifteen minutes later he waves down a passing driver in a flatbed truck loaded with bushels of splattered, muddy vegetables and shows him Blue's address card. I sigh with both exasperation and relief. Even though he isn't entirely sure where Blue's house is, it's also obvious that he really is trying to find it. My driver gets his directions, does a quick U-turn without bothering to check for oncoming traffic, and speeds off in the direction from which we came, sending tremendous clouds of dust billowing into the darkening sky. Within ten minutes, we're turning into a long dirt driveway marked by rounded stones on either side. Chickens and dogs are going crazy with the excitement of our arrival. Moments later, a light goes on outside, and soon after, the silhouetted figures of a man and a woman are standing just outside the front door. I open the taxi door and stand up.

"Blue? Blue, is that you?"

A moment's silence, then, "Doug? Doug from New Jersey?"

"Yes, yes, it's me. I'm sorry to just drop in on you like this. But I've had a bit of trouble and I wasn't sure where else I could go. When I left you on the bus you said…"

"Of course, of course, come on in. Bring your bags. We've got an extra bed you can stay in tonight. Here, let me give you a hand… What, don't you have any bags?"

"Not really." I hold up my empty hands and shrug.

"Well, what the hell happened?" he asks, "Did you get robbed?"

I give him the usual answer of someone who doesn't feel like explaining something. "It's a long story. What I need now is just to get settled. I've had a bit of a rough couple of days."

"Of course, no problem… This is my wife, Luz. She only speaks a little bit of English." He indicates the woman standing next to him, a mature but petite and very attractive Latina. Luz flashes me a warm smile and gazes down toward the ground like a shy child.

"That's OK; I've been practicing my Spanish… *Mucho gusto en conocerle, Luz. Me llamo* Doug Roth."

"*Mucho gusto,*" Luz replies, "*Su español es perfecto!*"

I pay the taxi driver the agreed amount and he rumbles off into the dusty distance. The chickens and dogs begin to settle down and I am struck by the isolation of this place, the near total silence when we are not speaking, and the brilliant canopy of stars overhead.

We walk into the house. It is petite and cozy, and well decorated with local arts and crafts. It is exactly as I had pictured Blue's house to be. Inside the small foyer, Blue points to a particularly colorful painting.

"Take a look at this painting," he says. "A neighbor of mine down the street did it. He's a painter— that's his favorite of the eight things— creating, active entertainment."

"Do we have to talk about the eight things again?" I protest, "Are there only eight things to talk about, too?"

"Just listen; I'm trying to explain something to you. Look at these flowers in the painting. These are the flowers in my garden right out here in the courtyard. What do you think?"

"I guess it's a pretty good job. They look pretty realistic."

"Which do you think are more beautiful?"

"Which of what?" I ask, confused.

"The flowers in the painting, or the flowers in the garden."

"Well the flowers in the garden, obviously," I answer.

"Why do you say that?" he asks.

"Well, because they're real, and the ones in the painting aren't."

"I would say that that is a conditioned response. You answered without thinking or considering it. Is the beauty of the flowers in their reality, or is it in their shapes and colors? Isn't it possible that the shapes and colors of the flowers in the painting are even more beautiful than the shapes and colors of the real flowers? And if you take a look at the real flowers, you can see they have little brown spots and holes where bugs have eaten at them, while the painted flowers are flawless." Almost before I've even entered the house, Blue has already begun his intellectual analysis.

"I have to hand it to you, Blue; nobody has ever asked me a question like that before. I'm stunned and I really don't know how to answer it."

"There's no right or wrong answer," he assures me, "I'm just asking your opinion. But I want your real opinion and not the stock, reflex answer."

I smile as I recall from our first meeting on the bus Blue's tendency to lose his folksy drawl and take on a professorial tone when sharing his outlook on life. In my view, it's one of his most endearing characteristics.

"My real opinion is that I could really use a beer right now, if you don't mind."

"Well sure, come on in; have a seat. You don't mind the local brew, I hope… 'cause that's all I've got. It's actually pretty good. I like it better than the imports. Used to drink American beers all the time when I first came down here. Then someone gave me one of these and I've never looked back. Realized I had spent a fortune drinking foreign beer when they make great stuff right here."

"Anything's good for me. I'm not sure I could even tell the difference, anyway." I sit down on a cane and wicker chair facing a rustic bar that Blue has obviously built himself out of aged, blond wood. The room is full of fishing paraphernalia- lures, reels, a fly-tying bench. Along one wall is a row of various lengths and gauges of fly rods and casting rods, and the numerous tables and shelves around the room display baskets, antique tackle, and fishing books in English and Spanish. Tastefully interspersed throughout this fishing motif are more examples of local artwork. Colorful paintings of fruit, tidy tropical villages and beautiful, dark-skinned, ebony-haired young Latinas hang on the walls (obviously a preference of

Blue's), handmade pitchers and ceramic bowls rest on the tables, and somehow, *somehow*, all of this works— with such simple décor from two wildly divergent themes, Blue and Luz have created a decorating masterpiece in which I feel instantly at home, yet never lose sight of the fact that I am in Honduras.

Blue comes around the bar holding two bottles of beer. The beer is not exactly cold, but I don't mind— it's cooler than the stiflingly humid air, which is good enough for me. Luz has obviously retreated to the kitchen or some other distant locale. I get the feeling that she is accustomed to leaving 'the men' alone at the bar. I can imagine that Luz's culturally traditional view of marriage roles probably meshes perfectly with Blue's philosophy. They seem like a happy couple.

"This is a great house, Blue," I tell him, "And Luz is a great woman. You're a lucky man. What's it like living down here, anyway? Don't you miss home?"

"I don't miss home, because here I am. This *is* home for me, and it has been for the last twenty years. Luz's parents, brothers and sisters all live nearby, so I have a built-in social network. And it's a real small town, anyway, so I know almost everyone around here. They're good people, really."

"I've always been treated well down here." With one exception, I add to myself, and that was a misguided American. "It's amazing the difference between the perception back in the States and the reality of this place."

"Let's keep it that way," he says. "I like being one of the few gringos in town!" As we speak, I am absent-mindedly rubbing the insect bite on my neck. "What's that you've got there?" asks Blue.

"This thing on my neck is getting weird. I got this bug bite in Panama when I first came here. Really stung. Itched like crazy. A little bit of blood came out at first. It swelled up a little bit, but a couple of days later, it seemed fine. Now it's getting all soft and squishy."

"Let me take a look…" He leans over me and pulls a pair of wire-rimmed glassed from his vest pocket. "Yeah, that's a botfly."

"Botfly?"

"Yeah, you got a botfly in there."

"What do you mean, 'in there?'" These are the kind of statements that worry me.

"A botfly lays its eggs in an open wound. Doesn't matter if it bit you or something else did. If it finds an opening in your skin, it lays its eggs in there. The larva hatches, and that's what you've got— a botfly larva under your skin." He removes a sheath knife from his pocket and begins heating the blade with a lighter.

"What the hell are you doing?" I ask, rising from my chair.

"You want it out, don't you?"

"Well, yeah, but… shouldn't I see a doctor?"

"A doctor'll do the same thing and charge you for it, and it'll take ten times as long," he reasons, "Besides, where are you going to find a doctor around here? Now, this won't hurt— much; I've sterilized the blade and I'll let it cool off. These little buggers are tough as hell to get out. They have these little barbs on them, like on a fishhook. Here, drink this." He hands me a shot of tequila. I recall my night of tequila-drinking lessons by the Panama Canal, and drink it straight down. It's not nearly as smooth as the Panamanian tequila, and I reflexively wince from its bitter aftertaste.

"But at least a doctor would use a cleaner pocket knife- I would hope, anyway!" Blue looks more like a half-drunken, slightly unwashed sea captain than a surgeon. "Have you done this before?" I ask.

"A few times," he says, "Only ever lost one or two patients, though." I involuntarily raise my eyebrows. "I'm kidding!" he adds, as if I had doubts.

The procedure is more unnerving than painful; the skin around the bite seems to be dead so I can't feel much. But the spectacle of Blue's thinning, white hair in front of me, his brow knitted in concentration, his sky-blue eyes squinting through silver-rimmed half-bifocals, and the thought of his ancient pocket knife, no doubt well used from scaling a few thousand bass in its days, now skimming my jugular, give me the willies. Or maybe it's the thought of him playing tug-of-war with a live insect larva with fishhook barbs, anchored in its burrow within my very own neck.

"Where's that tequila?" I groan while trying desperately not to move my throat, "Hang on a sec...!" I draw deeply of the golden nectar, bitterness be damned.

Ten minutes later I am half-drunk, washed up, bandaged, and bug-free. We're sitting in front of Blue's bar, and this time, my tongue unglued by alcohol, it is I that am lecturing him, complaining about one of my many pet peeves.

"In the past, at least the way I imagine it, people used to look up to intellectuals. It was really an honor to be a famous scientist. People like Edison and Einstein were almost celebrities. But it wasn't that way when I was in school, and it certainly isn't that way now. Describe a high school student as 'intellectual' or 'smart' these days and watch what happens. Words like that have almost become insults, and marks of social rejection. I had to become a 'closet intellectual' in school."

"'Closet intellectual?'" asks Blue.

"Yeah, I had to pretend I was less smart than I was, in order not to be socially excluded. Kept my test scores down to a 'B' level, didn't participate too much in class, you know. There are lots of ways to be socially excluded in high school, but I would say that being smart is one of the worst."

"It's a shame. I kind of felt the same pressure, too. Can't imagine that aspect of our culture is too good for the country. Can you imagine what it might be like if it were the other way around? If intellectuals were popular and kids in school were competing with each other intellectually, as it's supposed to be in theory? But I think it's always been the other way to some extent."

"Now it's worse, though," I continue, "There's been a serious dumbing-down of the world. Just look at what's happened to the news media in our lifetime. It's all become entertainment-based pop-culture gossip, or strange stories about odd people doing odd things. Nobody can tell you what's going on in the world with any accuracy. I'll bet more than 90 percent of Americans couldn't even name the Prime Minister of Canada, yet they would all know all the arcane life details about this celebrity or that, singers, sports stars, actors and those sorts of people. That's where the interest is. And who are the top scientists of today? Nobody knows or cares. Why go into science, when all the money, fame and sex appeal is in the entertainment field?"

"Yeah, you're probably right. It's not something I think about too much now, since I don't have a TV. Haven't had one since Caroline and I split."

"You're lucky. I should have chucked mine a long time ago. The news is all celebrity gossip, the shows are all sex-crazed situation comedies or soap-opera-type workplace dramas, and the kids' movies are all burp-and-fart humor. The glory days of television are long over."

"Didn't you tell me before that you watched a lot of TV? It sounds like you hate it."

"I guess I do. It's just a waste of time, but my family likes it, and I like to spend time with my family, so…"

"Well, a man needs to answer his own call. I can't say I understand people's fixation with celebrities. What do they do in their spare time? They eat crackers, scratch themselves and go to the bathroom, like everyone else. There— I just saved you the cost of a year's subscription to the world's most intrusive gossip magazine. Not too fascinating for me. I don't know what people are expecting to find out that's so interesting. What bearing do these people have on our lives? None. Would they have any interest in our lives? Probably not. And they shouldn't. We've each got our own lives and our families' and friends' lives to concentrate on."

"The newspapers and the Internet news are almost as bad. There seem to be two types of headlines these days: Lists of things, like '12 reasons you should do this or that' or '10 signs of whatever'; or, questions, like 'Can Stuffed Animals Give You Rabies?' or 'Is Oxygen Bad for You?' To me, the headline should answer a question, not raise one. If oxygen is bad for you, then for sure that's news and the headline should be the conclusion: Oxygen is Bad for You. If it's not bad for you, then it's not news. How can a question be news? How can a list be news?

"What's happened is that the news has gradually shifted over the last few decades from being a form of information to being a form of entertainment," I continue. Now the weather is headed that way, too."

"The weather? How do you mean?"

"Yeah. The media industry has realized that people like to be shocked, and they hate to be bored. Whenever they give a once-in-a-century storm warning, which seems to be about twice a year these days, people glue themselves to the TV. So one of their problems has been, how can you exaggerate the weather so it sounds shocking rather than boring? Well one easy way is to exaggerate the temperature readings. First they came up with the idea of a 'wind-chill factor' for winter temperatures. The wind-chill factor allows them to quote significantly lower temperature figures when it's cold than a regular straight reading would. Sure a higher wind velocity makes it feel colder than a lower wind or no wind, but when is there ever no wind in the winter? And who exposes themselves to the full-on force of the wind, anyway? But my main question is, where does the wind-chill factor go in the summer, when they're citing those high temperatures? It disappears and is replaced by the 'heat index,' which allows them to say things like, 'It's ninety degrees, but it feels like ninety-eight!' How can one temperature feel like another? How can ninety degrees feel like ninety-eight when ninety-eight feels like a hundred and four? And of course the heat index, which is based on humidity, disappears in the winter. Humidity doesn't disappear; just the heat index does. But now, for the most part, they've given up the boring actual temperature figures and the weather reporters will simply say, 'It feels like ninety-eight degrees in New York today.' Pretty soon, I imagine, we will have temperature reading inflation, and ninety-eight will no longer sound hot enough to excite people. Then some new factor will have to be invented to exaggerate the figures even more."

"Well, as I've said before," says Blue, "I don't get my news, or weather forecasts, from the television. I read the Honduran *prensa* occasionally and the international news reviews when I can. I, for one, would rather be informed than shocked. I hope you're not too shocked to be informed of this!"

I laugh and tilt my bottle to finish the dregs of my beer. It feels good to have a healthy rant once in a while. I smile, lean my head back and close my eyes.

"Let's get some sleep," Blue says. "I know you're probably tired after your trip out here, and I know that whatever you have on your mind is pretty heavy. So I suggest we call it a night. We can talk more tomorrow. One thing you never did mention, though… do you like to fish?"

I have to admit, it has been quite an eventful day, traveling across Honduras on a series of buses, dropping in unexpectedly on an acquaintance I've met only once before when I have no luggage and no plans, and having a drunken fisherman perform surgery on my neck to remove a live insect. Whatever will tomorrow hold?

"I've never been much of a fisherman, but I do love the out-doors," I tell him. "Are you thinking of going out tomorrow?"

"I was going to, because, hell, I go out almost every day. But if you're not interested, we can do something else. This is a nice little part of the world to have a look around."

"I'd love to go out fishing," I say. "That's something I haven't done in a long time. What time do you usually go out?"

"Well, I'm usually up and out by five. The way the daylight works around here, you're better off getting up early, even if you're not going to fish. Once the sun goes down, there's not much going on around these parts other than eating and drinking beer. Come to think of it, that's about all that goes on when the sun's up, too!"

"Five's fine for me, Blue. Give me a shout when you get up, so I can have a few minutes to get ready."

"Great. Here, let me show you where you'll be staying. Guest rooms are kind of in short supply around here. This sofa actually pulls out into a bed." Blue pulls off the cushions and stacks them in the corner, then I help him pull a folding cot out of the bottom section of the sofa. It is already made up with sheets, though they look well used, a bit threadbare and somewhat dusty, as if they have been there a long time. The cot is a little lumpy; it squeaks when I turn, and the demons in my mind taunt me for a while, but exhaustion eventually wins out, the demons call it a night, and sound sleep overtakes me.

CHAPTER 9
An Unexpected Trip

B lue's boat is about what I expected, an old wooden skiff about twelve feet long, painted quite a few years ago, it seems, white with red trim, and fitted with a coughing, wheezing engine. I am surprised, however, to note the name of the craft: Caroline, obviously named after his ex-wife. I ask Blue whether Luz minds this.

"No, Luz doesn't mind at all," he says, then with a crooked smile, he adds out of the corner of his mouth, "Course, she doesn't know about it, so it would be odd if she *did* mind."

"You mean Luz has never seen your boat?"

"No, she never has. Luz doesn't have any interest in fishing. I'd love to have her out here with me some day. She's a great woman and a good wife, and cooks up a hell of a fried catfish. But no, fishing just isn't her thing."

"Did you ever think about naming the boat *Luz*?"

"I'm sure I did, but for some reason, Caroline's the name that came out when I started painting, so Caroline she is."

It's a beautiful day, as usual, with billowing cumulus clouds piled up over the land, and clear blue over the coast and the sea in the distance. Blue is sitting at the back of the boat, steering it by directing the propeller of the sputtering engine one way, then the other. He guides us carefully down a shallow, silt-bottomed creek, into a marshy area half-choked with tall green sea grass. He's obviously been this route so many times before that he's effectively cut his own channel through the brackish swamp.

"You keep a lookout for caimans, OK?" he says with a smile and a wink.

We continue along silently for a while, aside from the chugging motor. Then Blue asks, "So what is this big problem you've had? How can I help?"

"Aw, you know, sometimes I think all of my problems boil down to the same old thing."

"And what thing is that?"

"I don't know, Blue... I just feel like I'm in the autumn of my life already. I don't know what I did with all that time. It seems like I missed about ten years somewhere."

"Don't worry about that. Autumn can be one of the most beautiful seasons of the year. And so can winter, by the way. Each season has its own unique beauty. You can't think that way about your life, son. When September comes, you should be taking walks in the crisp fall air, squeezing a few more barbecues in, and cutting some firewood for winter, not sitting there fretting about how June is gone. Now come on- we're gonna catch ourselves some fish. This here's a great spot I'm taking you to. We'll get us some flounder or sole today. I've got chunks of cut squid for bait. They love that."

"Great!" I reply. As he baits his hook, I notice a 2-inch scar below his left shoulder.

"What's that scar?" I ask without thinking.

"Oh. That's just a little bit of nature. Too much sun, you know. I had a touch of skin cancer that I had to get removed a few years back."

"Oh, sorry. Was it bad?"

"Bad enough to be removed, not bad enough to worry about now. One day at a time, my friend. It's just a reminder that the sun, the giver of life in this world, can also take it away just as easily." As if I needed a reminder to be wary of the sun.

"Not in your case, I hope!" I reply.

"Not this time. Not worth the worry. It's the scars you can't see that hurt the most." I am left wondering what he meant by that.

A few hours and a couple of flatfish later, we reel in our lines and rinse our hands in the warm salty water. "Hungry?" asks Blue, and I can't help but respond, "You bet!"

Blue has packed us a fantastic lunch— a thick wedge of creamy cheese; a bunch of tiny, sweet bananas; some small orange-and-green oranges (are they still called oranges when they are green?). He's also brought along quite a few bottles of Honduran beer, which are by now well on the warm side. Although they are in a cooler, it's doubtful to me that they were ever more than slightly chilled. It's no matter; they still go down great in the sun. Finally, there are fried corn tortillas to top it off.

"So what do you think of Central America so far?" asks Blue between swigs of warm beer.

"Well, to borrow an expression from my daughters, it's awesome," I say. "But I mean 'awesome' in its original meaning, not the latter-day, watered-down version."

"I gotcha," he says. "I love this place. That was a great idea of yours to see the whole string of countries together, by bus."

"This trip was going great," I admit. "But now I've done something to really blow it."

"Well, what is it that you've done?" he asks. "Are you ever going to tell me?"

"I don't want to think about it. I'm a bit of a mess right now; I have to apologize for that. I've been really frustrated with my life and I'm not really sure what to do. That's kind of the reason for this whole trip."

"You're circling back on yourself, son. The reason you took this trip was because your life was getting rough, and now something bad happened to you on the trip, but it's really just your life that's bad. You're really not making sense. But let's look at it one step at a time— it sounds like you've got a great life… an understanding wife that lets you run off to Central America, a decent job, a nice house, no doubt, and a couple of kids. Compared to a lot of other people…"

"I'm not comparing myself to others. I'm comparing my real life to my dreams of what I would like my life to be."

"…And there's a big difference between the two… Well, one of them's got to be revised then. So, what's wrong? What more do you want?"

"That's what everybody says, Blue, and it's even what I tell myself in my head. Those are all the things that everybody's supposed to want, and when they have them, they're supposed to be happy. The trouble is, I'm not even sure I ever really wanted those things… a big house, being locked into a mortgage for thirty years, a job that just goes on and on as I get older and older... I wonder how much of that stuff were things that society told me I wanted. I don't think I ever even evaluated what *I* really wanted. I was just like a sheep, following the others. And now here I am in the middle of my life, waking up, finally. Now I'm trying to think for myself— to make my own decisions— and to not be a sheep."

"But do you really make your own decisions?" he asks. "Aren't we all sheep in some ways?"

"True... it's very hard not to be one. But I do try to think through every decision logically and make sensible, rational choices rather than following the crowd."

"But think about it. Really, how much of what you do is not because you want to do it, but because you think you *should* do it? How many things do you do just because they're what other people expect or would like you to do?"

"Well... just about everything, I guess!"

"Right, and we're all that way, to some extent. You have to follow social norms, for example. Regardless of what you really feel like doing, or how you feel like acting, you will be socially isolated if you do not behave in certain ways. When I was young, my friends and I were a really tight group. There was no real definitive list of who was in the group and who was out, but there was kind of a central group and a slew of satellite members on the periphery who hung around with us occasionally. Anyhow, the group set the moral standards for the individuals within it. Not explicitly in any kind of code of conduct or anything, but in more of a subtle understanding that developed over time of how the group expected its members to act. Since we were young, certain types of behavior that might be considered antisocial to adults, or even to the same people as adults, were toler-ated and even expected then. If an individual member strayed too far from what was considered acceptable behavior, either going too far or not going far enough, the group would push or pull that member in a subtle manner, generally without anyone even realizing that it was happening. For example, at that age, in our upper teens, under-age drinking was considered normal and acceptable within our group. Anyone who did not want to participate in that activity was goaded and prodded until, as usually happened, they gave in and had a few drinks. On the other hand, if the group believed that any one member was drinking too much, or too often, or getting drunk alone, the group would sense a potential problem and would use its influence to drag that person back to the center line. This sort of group psychology or crowd behavior is normal, and different groups obviously have different core sets of values. Those core values may be different than those of any individual within the group. That's why angry mobs of people are dangerous. But back to my point, which is that even as young and free teenagers, rebelling against authority, people do not think for themselves."

"Teenagers less so than anyone else, from my experience." I think about Celeste and her tattoos. "They think they're free minded, but they're much *more* likely to follow a crowd, not less."

"The crowd, yes, but just because you are not following the crowd doesn't mean you are free of other people's influence. This is what I'm saying. How many things do you do, or not do, to make that inner voice of your parents happy, even though you haven't lived with them for over twenty years? Or to please your wife, who's not here and will never know what you're doing? Or not to disappoint your kids, who also won't know and probably don't care? What would you be like if you could really free yourself from other people's expectations and do what you really wanted to do? I'll bet you wouldn't even *know* what to do. Because what are we besides bundles of other people's expectations of what we should be?"

"Wow. I need another beer after that."

"Here you go… grab one." The bottles slide over each other in the cooler water, making a loud 'clink' as I do.

"So you think it's like that all through life, in society in general?" I ask.

"In a lot of ways. Although society claims to be tolerant of different points of view, the fact is that even the 'different' point of view must be within the normal range of 'acceptable' points-of-view in the opinion of others, and within the timeframe and the cultural context of the group in which it is expressed."

"Wow, that's a mouthful!"

"But it's true… think about it. You can't espouse an opinion that is not at least somewhere on the normal spectrum of opinions, without being ostracized by society. For example, let's take slavery. Slavery is obviously an atrocity, and anyone who speaks in favor of it is not likely to find many friends— and rightly so, in my opinion. But that is the philosophy of this age. Throughout most of ancient times, in ancient Egypt and Rome, I would imagine that the opposite viewpoint would have been the most prevalent (except among the slaves themselves, obviously), and that we would have been the ones to be ostracized, for not supporting it. How would we have thought about slavery if we had lived then, rather than now? The same thing will probably happen with monarchists in countries like Britain in the future, since modern society has acknowledged that privilege by birthright is wrong in terms of racism and so forth, and that very easily carries over to the ridiculous vestiges of monarchy that still exist in the world today." He pauses for a moment to think. "But let's take a less politically-charged issue to illustrate my point. In US society, our culture dictates that there are three meals in a day, not two, not four: breakfast, lunch and dinner. I find it amazing that just about the entire population accepts this premise as absolute gospel. You never hear anybody say otherwise. Oh, some people may not eat three meals a day, but they all acknowledge that they are there. You'll hear people say, 'I don't eat breakfast,' or 'I skip lunch,' but just by stating it in that way, they are acquiescing to the indisputable doctrine of three meals per day, and accepting that it is they who deviate from the established societal standard. I'm just mentioning this as an example of how difficult it is for people to really think outside of the cultural box that they have been born into.

"There's even a specific word in English that describes this whole situation: the word 'should.' When you tell someone that you *should* do something, it is an acknowledgement of other people's expectations for you. Using the word *should* demonstrates that you are aware that other people expect you to do something, when most likely at that moment you are not doing it; you are deviating from the world's expectations. But by acknowledging this deviation with the word *should*, we are requesting to be at least temporarily excused from the obligation. Who decides what *should* be? Not ourselves- it is not any individual. Society as a whole determines what is appropriate and what *should* be done. We have little choice but to do it, or to meekly acknowledge our awareness of it and excuse ourselves with the word *should*."

We continue our conversations and our fishing until the heat and intensity of the sun become too much to handle. The cooler is now empty of beer and full of fish, so we make our way back to the tie-up point, and walk from there back to Blue's house, a distance of about a mile. The combination of beer, sun and exhaustion overtakes us, and we both fall asleep sitting on opposite ends of Blue's sofa. Luz is saddled with the unenviable duty of cleaning and preparing the fish for dinner.

Hours later, we are well rested and resume our discussions by Blue's bar.

"Everything around me has changed, and keeps changing." I'm trying to relate to Blue my sense of being left behind by time. "I graduated from high school, and then there was the five-year reunion, then the tenth and then the twentieth. I thought I had really gotten old. But then more years passed, and then it was the five-year anniversary of my twenty-year reunion and the whole thing started over again. It's getting crazy. Just as I'm comfortable and happy in a new phase of life, like being the father of young children, a valve somewhere opens up in the sky and a big chunk of time slips through, and then my kids are teenagers and I'm adrift. I'm not comfortable with the steady, onward march of time. I can't find a stationary point to cling to, an anchor in the sea of time, and I'm afraid I'm being swept away to God knows where. Why can't things just stay the same, at some point when I'm happy?"

"Why can't they? I think you know the answer to that. Because that's not the way things work. You have to work within the confines of the system that you're in. We can't redesign it, I'm afraid, although it does make for a fun daydream. Are you afraid of turning fifty?"

"Not so much of turning fifty… that amount of time is finite, and it will pass. But it's soaring through the empty space of post-fifty nothingness after that, that scares me."

Blue stretches his arms and settles back into his chair. "Let me tell you a story," he says. "You're going through so much the same type of thing that I did when I was about your age that I find it… well, I find it just unbelievable. I've often wished I could go back in time and talk to my younger self from that time… well, obviously I can't, but talking to you is almost like the same thing.

"I told you before," he continues, "That I was married back in the States and I got frustrated, moved down here to Honduras and married Luz. Well all that's true, but that's the simplified version. Very simplified. The real story was a bit more complicated, like all real stories are. You know, I thought I'd pretty much blown it when Caroline and I split, and I still wonder about it, to tell you the truth. Don't get me wrong; Luz is a great woman; she's a lot of fun, a wonderful cook, and I do love her dearly, but… well by my way of thinking, you only have one love of your life, and for me it was Caroline.

"Caroline and I met in college. Well, *I* was in college anyway, and she was a waitress in this fancy-schmantzy restaurant. Sometimes my friends and I would walk through the town at night, making our way from bar to bar, as all good students do. I remember seeing her through the restaurant window for the first time. The customer at her table must have said something funny, 'cause she broke out in this huge smile and the whole room lit up. I know that's an old saying, but with Caroline it really was true. She could light up a room. When she smiled at that moment I instinctively just stopped walking and stared at her through the window. She must have noticed that someone was looking at her, because all of a sudden she looked over at me, still beaming like the sun, just for a second. That was it for me. I knew I had to meet her. But I was just a poor college student, scraping nickels together just to buy a few beers. There was no way I could afford to eat at a place like that. Even if I could, who would I go with? It would be ridiculous to eat in a place like that alone. I certainly couldn't take another girl, and what one of my friends would want to sit through an awkward, posh dinner with me just so I could meet a girl? It became an obsession- how would I meet her? I used to find any excuse I could think of to walk past that restaurant, just to look in the window and see if she was there. If she was, I would sit on the grass in the park across the street so she couldn't see me, and just watch her, sometimes for an hour. She was absolutely amazing- golden-brown hair, hourglass figure- the whole works. She was a perfect ten out of ten. How many times in your lifetime do you see one of those? I developed this plan to meet her.

"Now the easy way, you would think, would be for me to get a job at the restaurant where she was working, right? Well, unfortunately things don't always work out the easy way. The restaurant wasn't hiring at the time, so I had to find some other way in. But I put my college mind to it. Turns out there *was* a job for a delivery boy open at the fruit wholesaler they used, and the wholesaler had a soft spot for local college students. The problem was, the fruit wholesaler was all the way across town, and even though I had a driver's license and could drive the delivery truck they had, I had no other way to get to and from work than to walk several miles each way. And between the work and the walking, I was cutting it pretty tight, being a full-time college student. And then it turned out that the deliveries to the restaurant were made during the day, and not in the evening, when Caroline worked. If I'd have looked a bit closer, I would have realized that ahead of time, and looked for some other way to meet her. But now I was going to school, working and walking every day, and I rarely had time to even look at Caroline any more. Then one day, a crazy thing happened. I was rushing through town on the way to work, and suddenly, out of nowhere, Caroline is right in front of me. She must have turned a corner while I was looking somewhere else, because all of a sudden, there she was. I looked at her for a moment, and my jaw must have dropped to the sidewalk. But it was she who first spoke to me—'Hey, you're that guy from the park!' she said. I could barely even speak, I was so flabbergasted, but I think I managed, 'What park?' Turns out that all those nights I sat in the park watching her through the restaurant window, she actually *could* see me. Man, was I embarrassed. But at least we had finally met, and best of all, we clicked right away.

"I lived for her after that. She was my world. We spent every moment together that we possibly could. After college…well, it was just natural that we would get married. We rented this little place outside of St. Louis. I worked all day as a junior clerk in the Accounts Receivable department of a small contracting company; she worked mostly nights and weekends, waitressing in the city. Not the ideal schedule for a couple of newlyweds, but we made it work. Whenever we were together, we were on fire. She used to come home after midnight some nights, and I'd be asleep on the sofa with the TV on, but I'll tell you, it didn't take long to get *this* boy woken up. I was one happy guy back then; that's for sure. Well, the years went by as they do, and my daughter and two sons were born; then the next thing I knew, they were mostly grown up. I was in my forties at the time, which is a rough decade under any circumstances, and I was feeling kind of…lost, you know? Whereas before, everything came along pretty naturally: graduation, job, marriage, kids… the map kind of ended after that. There was no clear progression to the next level. I began to try new things, just for lack of anything else to do, and to keep me from being bored, like cooking. I started making all kinds of exotic foods. Trouble was, after all those years in the restaurant, Caroline wasn't particularly interested in fancy food, and the kids just didn't seem to care. I got really into fishing for a while, but that just took me away from the family, and when I was alone, I would get all these weird thoughts. I thought about how big the world is and how I'd never really been out of the Midwest. I'd see all these places in the news and wonder if they really existed. I became fixated on India— it seemed so exotic, so utterly foreign, so colorful... women in multihued saris, the smell of incense in the air, the dirt, the earthiness... the reality. I knew I loved Indian food since I had cooked it many times. I did some research and found an ashram, a Hindu holy place, in Rishikesh in the north, where you could go to meditate, focus on the simple things... flowers, breathing. A spiritual leader was there to guide people. I felt that was something that could help me. It was a way to find a deeper meaning to life than chasing past-due invoices and trimming the hedges.

"I brought it up to Caroline at dinner one night when the kids were out," Blue continues. "She thought I was crazy. 'We have a mortgage,' she said, 'We have the kids' college to save for. How could we afford a trip to India?' She went on about how she didn't like bugs, and dirt, and not having a clean bed and a flushing toilet, and air-conditioning... and I began to detect these subtle nuances that a husband can, that she really wasn't interested in going to India. Well, I felt her rejection like a load of bricks on my chest. Looking back, there was no way she could have known or understood what I was going through at the time, or how important this was to me. Sometimes you think these things are painfully apparent, but they're really apparent only to you. Anyway, I knew my dream of traveling to India with Caroline would never happen. 'So this is how the rest of my life will go,' I thought. 'Mowing the lawn and bringing that all-important paycheck home, as far as the eye can see, until I draw my last breath.'

"Well, I tried for a while after that; I really did. I loved my family and I knew I had a responsibility to them. I kept at it for a while, but things started getting bad a work; they had some layoffs and the rest of us had to work extra hours to make up for it. I was going in to the office on weekends and couldn't even go fishing. My daydreams about India filled all my free moments. Then one day I was called in to the head office and told that I would be part of the next round of layoffs. I received a pretty decent severance check, since I'd been working there over 25 years.

"Life has a strange sense of timing, and right about the same time, Caroline, who had been rising up through the ranks at the restaurant through the years, was offered the General Manager position for the restaurant, which was by that time one of the top restaurants in St. Louis. So there I was, with a lot of money, no job to take up my time, a wife who could pay the bills on her own, and three nearly grown kids. I could finally take the India trip. I really wanted Caroline to come, but as I said, she was never interested in the first place, and now with her new job it was out of the question. I planned a month-long trip to see all the holy sites, the Ganges at Veranasi, the Taj Mahal, the red city of Jaipur, and to top it off, two weeks at the ashram in Rishikesh. I spent all of my time planning my trip, reading about Hindu philosophy, listening to Indian music... I even bought some Indian-style clothes and started wearing them around the house. Well, Caroline was all serious and professional about her new position and didn't know what to make of me. She said I was acting silly, going through a second childhood. She reminded me that I had responsibilities now and I was still a parent, as if I'd forgotten. She didn't even want to talk about the trip. The night I left we had a hell of a blowout. We parted on bad terms for a month, which I suppose wasn't ideal.

"India was everything I'd hoped it would be. The beauty was incredible... the colors. I was instantly hooked. But alongside the spectacular beauty was heartbreaking poverty. Much more wide-spread even than here in Honduras, at least more visible. The streets were a perpetual motion machine of people, dogs, cows, goats, chickens and monkeys, all mingling and trying to survive on whatever scraps of food they could find, everything liberally and thoroughly caked with dirt and trash. You could not help but be spiritually moved.

"When I got back to the States," he continues, "I was a changed man… well, a *changing* man is a better way to put it. I was burning incense in the bedroom, which Caroline hated. I started experimenting with entheogens… psychedelics, as they were called then. I came up with the name 'Blue Sunshine' for myself, because it improved my outlook and described me a lot better than Earl Mitchell. By this time, Caroline thought I'd gone off the deep end. She barely spoke to me. I tried to get her to laugh and joke around with me, and have fun like we used to, but she had forgotten how to laugh long ago. We were strangers living in the same house, sleeping in the same bed. She had an image of me in her mind and I didn't fit it anymore. She thought that was *my* problem, when in fact, I was the real me, and it was her image of me that was wrong. How can I change myself to match someone's image of me? It's much easier for them to change the image to match the real person. But, she wasn't interested in seeing the logic of the situation; the relationship had in essence run its course, and, inconvenient as it was in terms of timing, it had to end.

"I tell you, Doug, she was the love of my life. Was, is, and always will be the love of my life." He turns and looks me in the eye, as if to underscore the sincerity of his confession. "I'm sitting here twenty years later telling you that. But somehow I lost her. I was looking for a deeper meaning to life, and the only meaning I found is that there isn't one." He pauses for a moment to collect himself, and wipes his eyes with his hand. "But the search was essential. I couldn't have missed it. Wouldn't want to have. It was part of my life experience. But it cost me the love of my life. I'm not even sure how it really happened. It's like the town you grew up in. Whether you stay in that town or whether you leave it and move somewhere else doesn't matter. After a certain number of years, one day you're there, you take a look around, and you realize it's not the town you grew up in anymore. The town that you knew and loved just isn't there anymore. Things have changed too much. It's nobody's fault. And it's the same with the woman I loved. She's just not there anymore. Hell, *I'm* not there anymore, either. And what's taken the place of Earl Mitchell the happy family man in Missouri is Blue Sunshine, the white-haired, aging hippie in Honduras. It's not a bad life—I have everything I need. After the divorce, I took whatever I had left after the lawyers got through with it, and decided to move somewhere cheap, where I could fish, think, live a simple life, and enjoy the outdoors- the real things in life. Soon after I got here, by the good grace of God, I met Luz. Luz is an angel. She puts up with me. And hell, I'm not such an easy person to live with—I know that. But for now, I'm happy to see what life's got in store for me." He draws up the corners of his mouth into a tight-lipped grin.

"That's a sad story," I tell him.

"It's not a sad story. A sad story is when someone dies or gets hurt. It's just a true story; in fact, it's only part of a story, because the story hasn't ended yet. It's the story of my life, and life goes on. Right now, I'm happy!"

"But you're obviously still in love with Caroline after all these years."

"We're still on decent terms. One of my friends insists that you can never really know your spouse until you divorce them. Well, Caroline's still OK in my book."

"Our society, for some reason, is accustomed to dealing with love as if it were a toggle switch— do you or don't you love someone? Is the switch on or off?" Blue has regained his professorial intonation, and is once again slicing the air with his open hand as he explains. "In reality, love is a sliding scale. It's a continuum. Between 'definitely not' and 'definitely yes,' there's a long gray area. When you're in the early stage of a relationship, sliding upward along that scale, at what point do you make the judgment call and say that you've arrived at love? At what point, with only twenty or twenty-five years of life under your belt, do you become certain that your feelings will last another 60 or 70 years? Nobody was more sure of this than I was with Caroline, but look at us now— divorced twenty years, living in different countries, and I speak to her maybe once every couple of months, usually about the kids. Who could have foreseen this then? How can you know?"

"But you're obviously not opposed to marriage, seeing as you married Luz."

"No, I like being married. I liked being married to Caroline. It was just the last two years or so that were difficult. I certainly don't regret marrying her in any way. I just didn't want to be nailed to her like a cross for the rest of my life after we both knew that it was time to call it quits. And I have to say that dating is much more difficult when you're middle-aged, since your looks have, shall we say, mellowed, and the complexity of your character has increased greatly. Life's a lot easier for a twenty-year-old college student than for an over-the-hill hippie."

"That's one way I've been lucky. I have to admit it. I've seen lots of my friends' marriages disintegrate, and Dawn and I are still going strong. If anything, I feel closer to her now than I did when I was young. But I do wish I understood the kids better. Those toggle switches have been maxed out on 'on' since the day they were born, but I think they tend to view me as a bit of a pain, more than anything."

"There's a lot of ways you've been lucky, son. You'll work it out."

"I know. If I pull this one off, it will be my main achievement in life. Hopefully, the kids will remember me in a positive way long after I'm gone."

"I know what you mean," says Blue. "For some reason or other, a man needs to know that he's made a difference in the world before he goes. A legacy. I think it's just part of our nature. Some build big businesses. Some countries' leaders make monuments to themselves or have their faces printed on the money. The fortunate people can leave behind a great work of literature, music or art. And of course, almost anyone can leave behind the legacy of children they've raised. But all of those things pass quickly. The genetic pool is diluted by half with each passing generation. Buildings tumble, companies fail, new leaders emerge. A few hundred years from now, very few people from our time will have left a trace, and that is only the beginning, since I imagine that the human race will continue for possibly billions of years into the future. We are nothing."

"Now *you're* sounding like the depressed one," I shoot back. "We are not nothing; we are *something*; it's just that nobody seems to know what that something is. Maybe it's part of the depression thing I was going through, or am going through, but recently I started reading through the obituary section in the newspaper."

"Wow, you really have caught the mortality bug," Blue interjects.

"Maybe so, but I noticed some things about them. First of all, everyone is described in the header only by their name and the type of work they did. Is that the most important descriptor of one's life? I personally would much rather see 'Doug Roth, Father and Family Man' than 'Doug Roth, IT Director.'"

"Why even think of that?" says Blue. "It doesn't seem likely that you'll ever get to read your own obituary."

"I'm just saying, it bugs me. The other thing is that they all seem to be put together in the same format, as if there's a form you fill out that says, 'career?, town of residence?, surviving family members?' Isn't there anything else? Like, 'Journeyed across Central America by bus'? Where does that go? I want it to say the things that were important to me, not the things that are in the newspaper's form letter."

"Look, Doug, these things don't even matter. Your obit is in the newspapers only one day and it's after you're dead. It's not like it's some damned cosmic résumé that people are going to use to evaluate you! You've got to stop reading those things!"

"Well, I have to do something! Nobody gives us a road map through life, you know!"

Blue sighs and looks pensive. His eyes gaze up at the ceiling for a moment. "It really makes you wonder about the purpose of life." I can tell he's waiting for me to reply so he can enlighten me with his views on the subject. He is a true fisherman; he has dropped the bait and is waiting for me to bite. I won't disappoint him.

"Now it's getting heavy..." I throw up my hands in mock futility. "That's just such a typical conversational topic. Nobody knows the meaning of life, and no matter how much people discuss it, nobody will ever know."

"I didn't say the *meaning* of life," he explains, "I said the *purpose*. What is it that we're supposed to be doing?"

"Why do you think there's a purpose? Maybe there's no purpose."

"If there's no purpose, then existence would be pointless. Why do we as conscious, decision-making beings exist? Without purpose, it's just a tremendous waste of energy. The universe doesn't waste energy. I don't think that's the case."

"Why not?" I find myself hoping that if I question him enough, he'll slip into one of his discourses. I find these quite entertaining, and he does, in fact, make some good points.

"Because life is a very complex system. I'm not talking about our lives, but of all life in general, the whole biosphere. You can easily see it here in Central America. Every creature has its place, its purpose, from the smallest insect to the biggest jaguar. The complexity is staggering. I just can't imagine that all of the minutest details in life have been worked out, but that at the top level, the strategic level, the overall plan is missing. I think it's more likely that we're just not seeing it."

"Well I'm certainly not seeing it. I can just imagine meeting God after I die, and Him saying to me, "Doug, what the hell were you doing down there?""

"I don't think God would say, 'hell.'" He flashes me a devilish grin.

"You know what I mean; that's how exasperated He would be with my lack of sensible direction. At least these days."

"The trouble with all religions is that they were interpreted and misinterpreted, sometimes deliberately, by people over the centuries, and if there truly is divine word in there, I'm afraid it is diluted to the point where the real divine directive is questionable, to say the least."

I sit back and smile. Here is the discourse I've been waiting for.

"I'll happily do what God tells me to do, but I won't necessarily do what another person tells me is what God wants me to do. That's one of the big problems in the world today— people telling other people what God wants them to do. If God really wanted you to do something, do you think he would spread the word second-hand? Use some go-between as a messenger? And then, there's the very nature of how the main religions are spread that really concerns me—a lot of it is by force. The force is almost inherent in the doctrine when they basically say, 'If you don't believe this story,' which is usually quite incredible and given without much real evidence, 'then you will endure an eternity of torment. If you do believe it and pass it on, then you win the prize of everlasting glory.' To me it sounds a lot like one of those e-mail spams you get, that tells you you'll get some reward for passing it on and a punishment for deleting it."

One thing I have always had great confidence in, is my belief in God. It's one of the few things I'm sure of, although it has occurred to me lately that believing in God is just the sort of thing I *would* do; it has all the necessary ingredients of the dictated, brain-washing babble from my youth that I have always embraced and believed without question. I was first introduced to religion when I was so young, I was unable to grasp the difference between my parents and God. A deity seemed superfluous in a world in which my parents were the providers of everything, and in my infantile view, the ultimate and final power of everything. Couldn't they control the weather, too? Still, I am comfortable with my unwavering belief in God, and

I believe that I am capable of parrying most intellectual challenges to my faith.

"You're a skeptic," I explain. "That's OK; I think God forgives our skepticism. In fact, I think He likes it. It shows that we're thinking about things; it shows that natural search for truth that's in all of us. It's a positive thing. I don't think He wants us to robotically accept things. He has confidence that He'll be with us, in the end."

"Well, for someone who appreciates skepticism so much, and independent thinking, I'm not hearing much skepticism from you."

"Well, I'm hearing a lot from *you*," I counter, "...who was so sure that God wants us to use entheogens!"

"OK, fair point," he concedes. "But I would say that the very fact that I'm skeptical means that I haven't decided one way or the other. If I had, I wouldn't be skeptical; I'd be certain. Religion is basically asking a person to accept, based only on hearsay, that certain incredible events occurred in the distant past. That is a lot to ask. If you believe it, you re saved. But if you believe it, are you then more likely to believe other fantastic stories based only on hearsay? Does God prefer the gullible to the skeptical? What is the point of that?"

"Hold on. Are you saying I'm gullible because I'm religious? That's what it sounds like to me. If that's the case, then about eighty-five percent of the world is gullible and you've got a superiority complex."

"That's not what I'm saying at all. I'm not insulting religious people. Like I said, I'm religious myself. I'm just analyzing the facts. God gave me intellect; I feel no shame in using it." He pauses to swallow his last sip of beer. "As I said, religion requires that a person believe in a series of remarkable events, with no evidence. By definition, a gullible person is more likely than a skeptic to believe such a thing.

Therefore, a gullible person is more likely to be saved than a skeptic, no?"

Blue continues. "One of the problems I have with religion is *purpose*. What's it for? So on earth, God separates the good people from the bad for the afterlife, but what for? Isn't it a little too late to do that after life is already over? Why not do it *before* putting people on earth? And what's the point of punishing the sinners after life is done? No rehabilitation, no forgiveness, but an eternity of pain? Why?"

"Now don't tell me you question the existence of things just because you don't understand them," I say. "I don't understand how television works, but I sure do believe that it does. And why does everything have to have a purpose? Do the rings of Saturn have a purpose? I think if you don't believe in God, you disrespect yourself. I find I have more self-respect if I think of myself as being put here for a purpose, rather than being just a lump of highly-evolved protoplasm!"

"I prefer to think of myself as highly-evolved protoplasm, because it gives me a sense of achievement!" We both laugh. "Ready for another beer?" he asks.

"Sure," I reply, "These are great!"

Blue considers my point for a moment as he retrieves two more slightly chilled bottles of beer, then adds, "If God does exist, we should all draw straws to see who is going to tell him that He should be clearer in His message about what it is we're supposed to be doing."

"You think God's communication skills are lacking?"

"Well, for one thing, look at all the different religions in the world. You'd think He could have at least been more clear about which one is correct. Especially with all the importance riding on it,

He could at least clarify that. I don't see that one sorting itself out. It also wouldn't hurt if He decided to reiterate the point that He doesn't appreciate people slaughtering each other in His name."

"Maybe He wants you to decide on your own what's right. Tell me, if you knew what He wanted you to do, would you do it, no matter what, even if it went against everything you believe in?"

"Well, not everything. Depends what it was."

"Ahh, heathen! So you only want to know the purpose of life if it's something you want to do; otherwise, you'd sooner not know so you can just keep puttering around like you are, and claim ignorance during your divine judgment! I say you either want to know or you don't, and if you want to know it, you must follow it. There'd be no excuse for missing church then, if you had a direct decree from God to attend!"

"This is my church, the outdoors. The mountains and coast of Honduras. God created it, and I love it. The flowers and trees are my altars, and fishing is my religion. And speaking of which, Luz has prepared some fine filet of sole for us. Fresh from this morning! Let's partake of this fine fish, whose purpose in life was to fill our bellies!"

"That was a wonderful meal," I tell Blue afterward, "But I'm feeling a little queasy. There was something weird about these mushrooms in the salad. They didn't seem quite right to me. They had kind of a *squeaky* texture to them; you know what I mean?"

"You'll be fine," he assures me.

"Can you ask Luz where they came from? This is one of the words that confuse me in Spanish. I know in some countries the word for mushroom is '*seta*', and in others it's '*champiñon*,' but I never know which word to use in which country. Maybe there's other words. What is it here— do you know?"

"Luz didn't prepare the mushrooms— I did," says Blue.

"You did?" I ask, surprised.

"Yes, they were from my own private stash. You can be sure they were of the highest quality."

"Stash? What are you talking about?" I feel a jolt of adrenaline hit my bloodstream as my suspicions start to rise.

"You'll see in a little while. We're gonna have ourselves a real interesting night. This'll be fun. Just what you need."

"You... you spiked my salad? With drugs?"

"Not drugs, mushrooms, Doug. Fresh, the way God created them."

I drop my fork and knife. "You've got to be kidding! I don't want this! This is not what I need! I've got enough problems; I don't need to deal with drug addiction too!"

"They are not addicting," Blue says firmly, "They are not dangerous. You cannot fatally overdose on them. You will not flip out. As long as you're sensible and don't try to drive or do something crazy, and keep yourself in a safe, comfortable place..."

"Central America! You call this safe and comfortable?" I push my chair back from the table and stand up. "What if I get arrested? Then I won't be in a safe, comfortable place, and neither will you!"

"Trust me," he says.

"Trust you! You just dosed my dinner! I'll never turn my back while you're around; that's for sure!"

"Yesterday you let me cut a bug out of your neck with a pocket knife. *Trust* me." If I was out to rob you or harm you I could have done it a thousand times by now. Listen- mushrooms, marijuana and these types of things are just plants. They are not chemically treated or extracted or concentrated or anything else. They are just plants. It's just because of the structure of the law that they are included in the same category as narcotics, chemicals and addictive substances. They really belong in a similar category to alcohol, only safer, because they aren't addictive. If you take the same precautions as when you have had a few drinks, you should be fine.

"Now, just listen," says Blue. "Remember what I told you when we met on the bus? These are not drugs. They are entheogens— 'theo' as in 'theology'— God. God-generators, literally translated." Blue has obviously decided that this is the ideal moment to deliver another one of his sermons. "They have been used for thousands of years all over the world, historically, by many different cultures. For religious rites, tribal gatherings or just for recreation. In all that time they were never illegal, until just a few decades ago. Don't confuse legality with safety. In the Netherlands, many of these same substances are legal. Does that mean they're safe there and not here? Or that the Dutch government isn't concerned about its citizens' safety? Let me tell you something. Peyote, a part of a cactus that is an entheogen, is illegal in the United States, except that it is legal for members of the Native American Church to use in their religious ceremonies, since they have historically done so since time immemorial. The US government made an exception for them."

"What does that have to do with me?" I plead, highly agitated.

"I'm just saying, think about it logically," says Blue. "If this were really a dangerous substance, would the US government make it legal for only one specific minority ethnic group to use? Imagine the liability for that! I think that, more than anything, proves that it must be safe."

I've got to calm down. There is no point in arguing with Blue. He's right; I've got to trust him at this point; there's no other option. I can't run out into the streets of some unknown town of Honduras while I'm on some sort of wild raging drug trip. I've got to stay here. At least Blue knows how I'm likely to react; he also hasn't robbed or killed me yet and that's always a good sign. And ironically, I'm the one who's already on the run from the law, not him.

I sit back in my chair and try to relax. Nothing happens for the longest time. I wonder if they will have no effect on me. I wait with some trepidation. Will I go crazy? After a time, I feel a little bit of strange confusion. Ordinary things become humorous, silly even. Colors catch my eye and appear more intense. Lights grow brighter and begin to throb and writhe. Small ripples begin pulsing through the room. When I close my eyes, geometric patterns buzz through my head, and then explode into bursts of colored light. Everything seems steeped in silliness. It's like looking at the world through a child's eyes and understanding it with a child's mind. But wait… there's something more to this. It's not all psychedelic patterns and colored lights. I can also evaluate my own life in childlike simplicity. My mind turns in on itself, examining the concept that is *me*. Who am I? Perhaps more broadly, *what* am I? I'm a body made of individual cells, each with a designated function, working together as one entity. More than this, every one of us is a *system* of life. Along with perhaps ten trillion body cells, our bodies are also home to maybe ten times as many microbes living symbiotically with us, without which we would be unable to survive. These microbes help our bodies break down food, make vitamins, and keep the 'bad' microbes at bay. So perhaps ninety percent of my body's weight is not me! But what *is* me? Does my 'ego', my 'self' the essence of my being, reside in one of these cells? No— can't be. The cells are continually dying and being replaced by others. Perhaps it is deeper than that—in the molecular structure. But the human body is composed mostly of carbon and hydrogen. Nothing special. Nothing that is not present in the nonliving world, in great quantity. Surely atoms cannot be combined in such a way to create life, much less to *think*. Or can they? I think; therefore, I am, indeed.

And *where* am I? Surely if all my limbs were to be amputated, I would still be me. A number of my organs could be removed or transplanted without changing my personality (other than adding to my depression, perhaps?) The brain, of course. Back to the brain chemistry. This is the center of one's universe. Take away the brain, and we are gone. But what is different about the brain? It is also made of cells, which in turn are composed of molecules and atoms. Am I really just the result of an ongoing chemical reaction, same as a fire or a bolt of lightning? '

A stream of wonder passes through my mind, as if doors are being opened for the very first time. And what opened these doors—some mushrooms? Strange. But it goes beyond that. Things get weirder. I consider the known fact that I exist in spite of being composed entirely of lifeless atoms. Somehow a sense of self has arisen in this clump of organic matter, and it is not at all unusual. In fact, it is routine. It has presumably happened to every one of us who has existed, since the dawn of time. But if one consciousness can develop in a brain, is it a great leap to think that there might be two? Or three? Or an infinite number? Why should such a question be absurd when it is already absurd to think that even one would exist, and yet we know that it does? Have I not debated in my mind which of several actions to take at a critical juncture in life? Is there not a cool, careful Doug who deliberates before making a move? And another Doug, quick to react, whose actions careful Doug might regret later?

Perhaps there are other Dougs who weigh in and are all controlled by the most assertive... the *alpha*-Doug!

Have I lost it? Am I schizophrenic? My thoughts go in loops: Who am I? The reply— Who's asking? It makes no sense. But yet it makes all sense. I just *am*. What if I were to stop doing everything and just *be*? What would this mean?

I receive a gentle admonishment— from the heavens? "You are wasting your time. You will never know the answers to these questions. You, and all humans, are incapable of understanding. You may ask, but you will never receive, and could never comprehend, the answers. Go back! Live your life!"

My mind swirls in a stormy sea of ideas; then it is the sea; then it is the storm. The trip starts to recede. The meandering thoughts continue, with less urgency. Eventually, my brain settles and it is as if a powerful, turbulent tempest has passed through, leaving the air breathtakingly fresh and as clear as crystal. All of the dead branches have been lopped off, the choking weeds in between cleared away. Then, I see that the landscape has changed— my internal landscape. It is as if my mind were a vast riverbed with multitudes of thoughts and sensations overflowing the riverbanks, allowing me to think and feel in different ways, and when the flood subsides, the river has slightly altered its course. The same water flows in the same direction; I am still me, but a few of the meandering curves are left dry as the river finds more efficient routes to the same place. It is refreshing, in a way, to see tired old thought patterns, which had ground their way into my being over decades, are not the only way of looking at things. Afterward, peace. I don't have to explain myself; I just am.

That night, colorful lights and crazy geometric lattices dance a panorama on the insides of my eyelids, or I imagine they do. Or maybe I am dreaming the whole thing. Who can tell? Is there a difference?

In the morning, Blue tries to explain to me that he was doing me a favor by opening up my mind, but I don't want to hear it. I have enough problems; the last thing I needed was an unexpected mushroom trip. Although the mushrooms don't seem to have done me any harm, and I have to admit that it was an interesting experience, the whole thing isn't my cup of tea, and to be surprised by it is out of the question. Blue isn't a bad guy and I have enjoyed our discussions, and I can even see myself returning some day to chat with him again, but right now I am upset with him and I just need to move on.

Luz drives me in their beat-up, ten-year-old rust bucket to La Ceiba bus station. The situation is very awkward, and I don't know what to say to Luz. I'm in no mood to make small talk, and I'm still highly irritated, so I mostly sit with my arms crossed. Luz tries to make conversation with a few pleasantries, but eventually she gives up, and we continue the ride in silence. Although Luz wasn't involved in 'the incident', she caught the gist of it, and I get the feeling that this isn't the first time this series of events has panned out at the Sunshine house. The Sunshine house…the Sunshine family. I never did ask Luz whether she goes by that name. It would be ironic; in Spanish, her name means 'light.' Once she drops me off at the station in La Ceiba, it is a four-hour wait before the next bus leaves for San Pedro Sula and Tegucigalpa.

It is late at night by the time I arrive in Tegucigalpa. There is no place to eat, but I find another passable hotel within an easy walk of the station, and this one has functioning electricity on all floors- definitely a plus. A thin veil of a curtain barely covers the tiny window in the room's cinder block wall, but I am exhausted, and sleep comes easily. I awaken once in the night to use the bathroom. I flick on the light, interrupting a party of at least a thousand roaches. It's far too late to change hotels. All I can do is close the bathroom door after using it, leaving the roaches to their festivities. In an odd way I am briefly thankful that I don't have any luggage, because I won't have to comb through it for roaches.

In the morning, I escape the roach motel and I have just enough time to scrounge a breakfast of greasy fried chicken and a soda before I catch another bus, this one destined for El Salvador.

CHAPTER 10
The Angel

The bus crosses an old metal bridge, and it sings as the tires roll across its grooved frame. Below us a sickly, rock-filled trickle meanders toward the sea. A faded sheet-metal sign that can barely be read says '*Bienvenidos a El Salvador.*' The usual chaotic border carnival greets us as we arrive.

Upon entering El Salvador, the rugged mountain landscape of Honduras settles down to a simmer, and rows of muscular, thick-limbed trees appear at the side of the road, providing intermittent shade from the ever-present sun. This country is much more densely populated than Honduras; there is seldom a moment when at least a few houses or businesses aren't in sight. For a time I survey the modest vista, then the glades and orchards of trees on the left side of the bus suddenly break and the country opens up to reveal a gigantic volcano floating above the horizon. It looks exactly like the volcanoes of my childhood dinosaur books, a perfectly symmetric, mist-shrouded gray cone, complete with a steaming cauldron, towering over a vernal prehistoric world.

The vaporous volcanic visions lull me into a daydream. I recall that young child who wanted more than anything to search for dinosaurs. How did that path lead me into a life of running virus scans, troubleshooting system problems, replacing crashed hard drives and installing software? Where is my career going now? I consider the myriad of famous men who accomplished great things at ages younger than mine, many of whom died long before even reaching my age: Mozart, Keats, John Lennon, Jack Kerouac... I wonder if they are satisfied, watching from somewhere, as their earthly successes are commemorated. What will I be thinking of if I am ever in such a position? Will I be satisfied with my achievements? Have I maximized my potential, whatever that is? Have I even discovered my potential? I wonder. When I do hit my golden years and can finally retire, will I sit and reminisce in quiet confidence, smiling contentedly as I review the portfolio of achievements of a successful lifetime? Or will I simply let go a heaving sigh in exhausted frustration as if to say, 'Thank God that's over!'?

I disembark from the bus at the station in San Salvador to look for a suitable hotel, and immediately I notice that this does not look like a friendly place. With the exception of Panama City, I find the capital cities are the least interesting places in the Central American countries. San Salvador is the ugliest conurbation I've ever seen. It looks like someone took a gigantic electric mixer to the city. While walking along the street in front of the bus station, although granted not in the most desirable of neighborhoods, I come across several spent bullet cartridges among the crushed soft drink cans, scattered plastic bags and a broken windshield wiper. This is probably not the ideal spot for a relaxing vacation, I think. This is probably not a place I should be at all.

A middle-aged woman with dark, ragged hair and a faded red T-shirt approaches me and asks me in Spanish if I am lost. I may not be the brightest of world travelers, but I am smart enough not to tell a stranger in a rough part of town that I'm lost. She tries a different tack.

"Are you looking for a bus? I think you are perhaps at the wrong station."

"The wrong station?" I ask, trying not to reveal my concern.

"Yes, the wrong bus station. This is San Carlos station. This place is not safe for *norteamericanos*. I think maybe you want San Benito station in another part of the city. You have to take a bus from here. Come, I will show you."

She seems honest, so I don't resist. In truth, I am more than a bit uncomfortable with my present surroundings, and if she can help me get somewhere a little more up-market, I would certainly be grateful. She directs me to a chicken bus and indicates to me that I should get on.

"*Trés paradas*," she says, holding up three fingers. Three stops. She even pays my fare. Though the fare is not much, it must be a considerable sum of money for her.

I protest, but the bus is already pulling away. She smiles at me, and all I can do is smile back, wave, and yell, "*Gracias*," as many times as I can before I'm out of earshot.

I am reminded of something Blue said to me in one of our conversations. "The most important lesson of world travel is this: Anywhere, anyplace, people are much more likely to go far, far out of their way to help you, than to harm you." From my paltry experience, I have to agree.

One night in San Salvador seems to be sufficient for my purposes, and I'm eager to find another place with a bit more natural beauty. Luckily, my American dollars are once again legal tender. After purchasing a few desperately-needed T-shirts, socks, underwear and trousers along with a very cheap plastic travel bag, I decide to head south to the Pacific Coast. I board a chicken bus bound for the region of La Libertad. The desk clerk at my hotel recommends it, and says it is popular with foreigners. It seems to be relatively easy to reach, and it is familiar to the surfer crowd.

In spite of the change in scenery, I still can't stop thinking about being caught by the police. I have made a lot of mistakes along the way and in doing so, I have turned a relatively small problem into a large one. I mentally list the missteps that have exacerbated my situation. I departed my hotel without checking out, I left my baggage there, and I crossed two international borders in my hurry to escape. What was I thinking? On top of this, I'm still annoyed at Blue for his actions during my visit. How could he violate my trust like that? I'm just trying to enjoy a simple trip, and I keep screwing it up. I turn my face toward the window and try to forget my anxiety.

It is easy to find distraction on the Central American roads. Incongruousness is the norm; irony is routine. Reality is a variety show. I spy a man dressed in a powder-blue tracksuit with white racing stripes, furiously pedaling a bicycle through the traffic while taking deep drags on a cigarette. A chicken bus that was obviously once a US school bus but now is a bursting cornucopia of color pauses for the briefest of moments in heavy traffic, and a man climbs straight up a ladder on the back of the bus in one fluid motion, balancing a huge open basket of fruit in his arm and barely making it to the roof as the bus resumes its bumping journey. A few miles further along, on the side of the road, dozens of black-faced vultures pick at the carcass of an unfortunate horse, while barely a hundred yards away, a newborn foal struggles up on shaky legs. The miracle of life goes on!

We continue on our way, passing more tire shops. I am amazed at the number of them I have seen on this trip. Who can possibly be buying all the tires? Are the roads really that bad that a plethora of tire shops only miles apart can thrive here?

Finally, we reach La Libertad. La Libertad seems to be where everyone in El Salvador goes to take a break from the frantic city, and goodness knows I need a break. I've had enough trouble in the last several days to last me for the rest of my life. I'll try to lie low here for a couple of days, at least, until I'm feeling better.

After climbing off the bus in La Libertad, I stand along the roadside scrutinizing taxi drivers, trying to find one who looks honest, experienced, and preferably, elderly. I wave one down who seems to fit that general description, get in the taxi, and hope the driver is knowledgeable about the area. I am once again in the unfortunate position of not having any idea of where to go, so I ask the driver for a recommendation. I am looking for a low-priced but clean and safe hotel on the beach somewhere, I tell him in Spanish, the more secluded, the better. He considers this for a moment, his cracked, dirty fingertips tapping out a nervous rhythm on the well-worn steering wheel, then his eyes light up and he pulls out into the busy road.

I wouldn't necessarily call La Libertad beautiful, but it does have a certain laid-back appeal. I can definitely envision spending a few days here, reading in a breeze-cooled hammock, strolling its peaceful beaches, dining on local seafood, lingering over a few drinks at a cabana bar… this may be just the stress relief I need. The rumble of the ocean and the distant screeching of seagulls bring me a sense of serene relaxation in a way that I have always found magical. Perhaps it's a throwback to ancient times when the sea represented such a bounty of food that it calms us just to know that it is nearby. It's so much easier to sleep with the gentle roar of the surf in my ears. I am reminded of my time by the sea in Manuel Antonio Park in Costa Rica, before this whole mess started, back when all I had to worry about was my life falling apart.

I rent a bungalow for myself overlooking the sea, and there is a steep grassy path cutting down the hillside to the beach. I am somewhat surprised at the grayish color of the sand, which is probably due to the presence of volcanic dust, I surmise. The dark color allows it to pick up heat in the daytime more readily than white sand does, and it is difficult to walk on when the sun is out. I have either to run to the wet sand, which is cooler than the dry sand, or to dig my feet deep into the dry sand, beyond the range of the heat. Up ahead, the ocean is a bright cerulean blue that beckons me for a swim.

That night I stroll the dark beach with only the light of the full moon and its glistening reflection on the waves guiding the placement of my bare feet. I walk some distance, until my peripheral vision detects movement on the wet sand and it startles me. Suddenly, I notice that I am surrounded by small, black creatures squirming on the sand. They are oblong and about five inches long, with the sheen of wet leather, and they are crawling toward the water from all directions. I bend down and realize that they are baby sea turtles, newly hatched, clumsily hurtling themselves into the waves with tiny legs that look like miniature paddles. There must be a hundred of them. They are making the first and most important journey of their lives, from the grassy mound where their nest must be hidden, to the ocean, where they will live the rest of their days. Of the hundred or so in front of me, I wonder how many will survive into adulthood.

Perhaps five, maybe six. The rest will provide sustenance for all kinds of sea creatures. As I watch, I realize that the turtles and I are in a similar situation, hell-bent on finding our purpose in life and doing our best to tackle the obstacles that separate us from our goals and dreams.

The waves crash down mercilessly on the tiny turtles, which struggle against the seemingly overwhelming power of the sea with desperate determination. Whenever one is washed back ashore, it turns and tries again, never giving up until its minute black body becomes one with the immense blackness of the ocean. The turtles paddle swiftly, ceaselessly, into their unseeable, unknowable futures. Soon, all but one of the turtles disappear out to sea. I turn to walk away, but from the corner of my eye I can see the one lone turtle continually being pushed back to shore by the unyielding waves. He is getting tired, this turtle, and I know that he must make it out to sea tonight, or he will die on the beach, rejected by life before even living. I turn around and pick up the little turtle. Its tiny legs struggle wildly as I lift it from the sand and place it into the foamy sea, into its uncertain new life. The turtle disappears without a look back.

. . . .

The best thing for me to do at this point is just to relax and take it easy, I decide the next day. I take a morning jog along the beach before the heat kicks in, and then have a late breakfast at the hotel. Having no plans for the day, I spend most of it walking and lying in a hammock by the beach.

I spend an hour watching leafcutter ants. They have discovered a discarded blue plastic shopping bag caught in the brush and have somehow mistaken it for a giant leaf. With surgical precision, their scissor-like jaws slice the bag into quarter-inch squares, and they carry it piece by piece to their nest. A winding double line of ants, one lane moving in each direction, stretches the length of the fifteen-foot circuit. Their swollen heads and enormous mandibles look very menacing, and I imagine that the bite from just one of them would be tremendously painful. But they have no interest in me. Wrapped up in their work, they do not seem to notice my presence, and not one of them seems to realize the futility of their task. The bits of plastic bag will give them no benefit whatsoever, and will take up valuable time, energy and nest space. I can't help but wonder: How much of what I have spent my own time on has been just as useless?

The wind picks up and clouds roll in from the sea. I feel the air take on a sudden chill as palm leaves begin to rustle and hiss. The sea turns angry and its color transforms from deep sapphire to smoky jade. The surf tumbles and crashes, purging itself of the detritus of man and marine life: shells of a thousand shapes and colors, torn bits of fishnets, bleached chunks of rigid coral, palm fronds, assorted plastic bags and paper labels, pieces of weather-beaten wood. The surfers love this change of weather and are in their glory, although many have donned wetsuits due to the drop in temperature. Eventually the wind grows too strong even for them, and the sky dims as the sun succumbs to the brewing storm and slips behind the sodden gray clouds.

I love to watch storms over the sea. It's a display of the awesome power of nature. It was like this before we arrived on this planet, and I imagine it will be the same after we're long gone. A flash of lightning brings depth to the swirling charcoal clouds, and gradually the light sprinkle gives way to a downpour. I head for my cottage to watch through the window.

I dreamed I was walking through a gigantic woods. The woods were wild and rugged, and they unfolded in every direction. Much of the path I wandered was shrouded by heavy mist, so I could not see beyond a dozen yards. I did not carve my trail- it had been here long before I arrived. Though in many places I found it to be the only route, in other places I longed to venture beyond its edges. But I could not, for one reason or another- the terrain was too steep, the vegetation too thick, or my knife blade too dull. I dreamed of verdant, fertile valleys, cascading waterfalls, wondrous meadows turned golden in the sunlight, fields of tall grasses rippling with the breeze. I saw such beauty it nearly brought me to my knees. But I also passed vast stretches of bleak, barren wasteland. I passed dry, dust-choked rivers, empty forests of ashes and burnt stumps, lonely, desolate places that brought me to such despair that I had to force myself to go on. I dreamed of danger, of fearsome creatures lurking in the forest, not far away. Sometimes these creatures came within frightening proximity; sometimes I had to fight for my very life. Some of those times I didn't fare very well, and I had to continue with unhealed wounds and treat them myself as best I could. I dreamed of a fascinating world filled with infinite possibilities: I dreamed of life!

Morning comes and the sky has lost its fury; it is at peace with itself and the sea once again. I stroll along the beaten coast, savoring the fresh, cool air and surveying the debris that the sea has ejected. Something small and black catches my eye in a pile of shells up ahead. My feet splash droplets of water around my legs as I pad through the shallow surf toward it. When I realize what it is, it catches me by surprise. It is a dead baby turtle, washed up by the storm. I feel warm saltwater trickling down my face- but how can this be? The seawater hasn't splashed higher than my knees. Within seconds, I find myself seated at the water's edge, sobbing— loud, real sobs, for the first time in maybe twenty years.

. . . .

Over the next few days, I meet several other people staying at the beachside bungalows. There is the Sepulveda family I meet at breakfast, with whom I exchange greetings of *"Hola"* when we pass. They often invite me to dine with them, but they have young children and I would feel like a fifth wheel if I were to join them. There is the young couple from San Salvador, a couple of 'surfer dudes' from the USA, and a Guatemalan businessman, Ricardo Gomez. Ricardo is traveling by himself too, and speaks fluent English. I see him sitting a few tables away at lunchtime and wave. We exchange greetings and he invites me to join him for a 'bachelors' lunch.'

"So what brings you to El Salvador?" I ask.

"This!" he says, spreading his arms and looking out over the ocean.

"It is nice, isn't it?" I agree.

"That's why I'm going to buy some property here. So many people want to come to La Libertad. I want to build a summer house here, while the prices are still cheap. My wife and I looked at places in Miami, but they were too expensive and it's too far. Here in La Libertad, we are just six hours away from Guatemala City, any time we decide to come!"

"Wow, I'd love to have a summer house here."

"Are you here on vacation?" he asks.

"Well, sort of. More like an exploration. I'm doing a bus trip across Central America. I started in Panama about three weeks ago, came through Costa Rica, Nicaragua and Honduras, and now I'm here. I fly home from Guatemala next week. I can't believe it's going by so quickly."

"That's a very long trip!" says Ricardo. "Which country have you liked best so far?"

I have to think for a bit. "Hmm… that's a tough question. They've all been nice. I met some great people in Panama, saw a lot of wildlife in Costa Rica, really enjoyed the colonial architecture in Nicaragua, stayed with some friends in Honduras, and I really like La Libertad so far. I originally planned to stay in San Salvador, but it didn't appeal to me nearly as much as this."

"That's understandable. La Libertad is the place to be. That's quite a trip for a *gringo*. Most of the Yankees we get here are either young backpackers staying along the beach, or businesspeople. A few tourists come down this way, but most don't leave the resort a few kilometers down the coast. I guess they're afraid we're all *bandidos!*" he says with a chuckle.

"I hear you!" I say, "I don't really understand it either. Obviously, I don't agree with them. Although there are some rough places around here, no doubt."

"Well, we have bad neighborhoods, just like you have bad neighborhoods. Ours are just a little bigger and a little badder than yours. As long as you pay attention and don't do anything stupid, you should be all right."

"So far it's been no problem."

"I imagine you must find the weather much better here than back in America?"

I nod. "It's very pleasant here by the coast, with the sea breeze to moderate the heat. At this time of year, it's beginning to get cold back home, and the leaves will be starting to fall."

"Yes, I think it's nearly time for your Halloween holiday."

"That's right, on the last day of October."

"So you will be back in time to hand out chocolates to the little ones?"

"Oh, yeah. I seem to catch that delightful moment every year. You're familiar with it, obviously?"

"I lived in Houston for seven years," he says. "I made the mistake of living in a large community of townhouses. People used to drive into our neighborhood with vanloads of kids on Halloween. It was the perfect place for them – safe, no busy roads, and the houses were very close together."

"I planned it out pretty well as far as Halloween is concerned," I tell him. "In my area, the houses are spread pretty far apart, so the kids have to earn their treats. But we still go through several bags of candy a year."

"There is one thing about Halloween that I have never been able to figure out— perhaps you can help."

"Sure… what's that?"

"Where does all the missing candy go?"

"What do you mean, the missing candy?"

"I'll try to explain. Let's say you spend ten years in your child-hood going out trick-or-treating, and each year you bring home a bag of candy— is that reasonable?"

"That sounds about right," I say.

"Then, as an adult, you hand out the candy— let's say each year you hand out about one big bag of candy over forty years of your adult life. So in your lifetime, you bring home ten bags of candy, twenty if you count your wife, but you hand out forty. What happens to the other twenty bags? If each house has a lifetime net loss of twenty bags of candy, where does all that candy go?"

I think for a minute. "That, my friend, is a question for the ages. In all my life, I have never thought about that. You have a very analytical mind."

"It comes from being a businessman," he laughs.

The waiter comes to take our order. He's grinning and has obviously overheard the last part of our conversation.

"You're American, *señor*? My brother lives in Cleveland."

"Cleveland… well that's a bit of a ways from where I live." I tell him.

"I want to move there too; I'm just waiting for my brother to find me a job."

"And why are you so interested to go to America?" I ask, feeling a hint of pride.

"It's a great country. I want to have a big house, and a car, and work in a big city, like Cleveland or New York."

"Well, it *is* a great country; that's for sure, and it's my home, but we have got our problems. You might find this difficult to believe, but not everyone in America lives like that, you know. Some people have to really struggle to get by."

"But I will work hard. I am a good mechanic. I know how to fix all kinds of cars. Here in La Libertad there's not enough cars to fix. I have to be a waiter also. But it helps me learn English for when I go to live in America. Here you can work your whole life and have nothing. You can be the smartest person in school and there is no work. Only the same thing day after day to survive." Something about the waiter's comment catches my attention. 'The same thing day after day'... where have I heard that before? Hadn't I been thinking the same thing myself before I came here—in essence making the exact reverse of the trip this waiter is dreaming of? Is this perhaps just the way the human mind is programmed to think, regardless of one's circumstances?

Ricardo and I order a plate of fish tacos, and they are served with wedges of sweet lime. A couple of freshly-mixed margaritas provide a tasty accompaniment. The weather is perfect for a laid-back lunch and some nice conversation.

Ricardo's analytical mind apparently benefits him with his work. He is attired in a kind of tropical version of business casual: pressed khaki trousers, a short-sleeved mango dress shirt, brown loafers and a matching leather belt. Aside from the mango short sleeves, it reminds me of how I would dress for work. He does have one thing I don't have, however— an air of quiet confidence and sophistication that one can only achieve by building a successful business from the ground up.

Ricardo picks up a taco and takes a bite. Then he throws the ball into my court. "So what about the American politics, then? Do you like the President?"

"Well," I reply, "That's a pretty big question. It's actually embarrassing to me that people here seem to know more about American politics than I do. Everyone knows who our president is. But I'll bet there are very few Americans who can even name the Prime Minister of Canada or the President of Mexico, our two neighbor countries, let alone any other world leaders."

"But," Says Ricardo, "You have a big country. Maybe it's enough that people know your government."

"Maybe. If they do," I say, shrugging my shoulders. "That might be giving them too much credit," I grin.

"So let me guess… you would be a Republican."

"No, but you're close!" I reply. "See if you can guess."

"Well, OK, then Democrat? How's my guess?"

"Ha!" I say. "Falling into the old trap. Nope, still wrong. I'm an Independent."

"Ah… in the middle of the road. A good place to get run over!"

"No… wrong again. Three strikes, you're out! No, that's one of the fallacies about Independents that people in the two big parties think. Being Independent doesn't have anything to do with being undecided or middle-of-the-road. I'm actually very committed to my opinions on the issues. It just means that I don't follow party lines. Just because I have a certain opinion on abortion, for example, doesn't mean you can predict my opinion on gun control, or capital punishment, or fiscal policy. In my opinion, there's no sensible connection between these issues. Each issue should be examined separately and logically before you decide your position on it. Being an Independent involves much more commitment and intelligence than just following the party line like a sheep."

"A sheep! Is that what you think of all of your countrymen?" Ricardo says with a laugh.

"Well, no, not really. Sometimes. It's something I'm trying to avoid, myself. I want to think a little deeper about things than everybody else. I want my own opinions to matter. I like to question everything. I think you'll find that a lot of people just accept what others tell them without question, for the most part. Not me. At least I try not to."

"So it's not a way of being neutral, then?"

"No, definitely not, not neutral or undecided, noncommittal, wishy-washy or anything like that. I explain it like this: Most people seem to think of political philosophy as one-dimensional— as if a person can only be left or right on the axis. They talk about left-wing, right-wing, and center. I'm an Independent. I'm not on that axis at all. I'm floating above it, on a separate Y-axis, looking down and choosing my positions. I have some very firm political viewpoints, probably even stronger than those of people who follow the party lines, because I thought through the issues myself and came to sensible conclusions based on logic, without fear of being branded a member of the 'wrong' party. I just don't see any linkage between widely different issues like health care and farm subsidies and immigration policy. In fact, you could argue that the party lines are mismatched and would make more sense if they were rearranged. For example, a position like pro-life should go with gun control and against tobacco subsidies. I would think, anyway."

"So what do Independents believe in, then?"

"Whatever we want to! That's just it. Independents aren't a political party. It doesn't even mean that I'll vote for or even agree with any Independent that's running for an office, just because he's an Independent. We all think differently. I might not agree with any of them."

"Complicated politics, and you're a complicated person. I like that." says Ricardo. "Here, they're all bad. We just hope for the one that's less bad than the others."

"Well, that we have in common, I'm afraid! It seems that more and more often I'm trying to choose the least distasteful person to vote for. I guess everywhere in the world it's the same."

The clouds have opened up and the sun is beating down. The fish tacos seem to leap off the plate and the margaritas take the edge off the heat.

"It sure is a hot day," I say as I take a sip."

"It's a normal day," says Ricardo. "You haven't seen a hot day yet."

"Oh, I've seen a few. Down in Panama and Nicaragua I saw some hot ones. Thank God for showers!"

"The world is getting warmer, they say. Or is that politics again? At least in your country, right?" says Ricardo with a mischievous grin.

"See, now there's the perfect example," I say. "I really wonder about our country sometimes. Global warming isn't about politics; it's science. It's something that should be determined by scientists: either the world is getting warmer, or it isn't. If it is, then mankind's actions are either contributing to it, or they aren't. I can't imagine any-one not agreeing that both of those points are scientific matters, and should be determined based on the analysis of valid scientific data, not based on people's opinions… but you have so many politicians arguing with scientists, as if the scientists had some kind of political agenda or score to settle. To be honest, I really can't understand why there is such a great disparity between the beliefs of Republicans and Democrats on this issue. Does it mean that one political party is bet-ter at scientific analysis than the other? How could that be? No, what it does mean is this: the majority of people in both political parties go about making decisions in an uninformed way. I'm not saying that the people are necessarily uninformed. I mean that they make decisions that way. This is not how our country should be run, by people making uninformed decisions and taking up certain points of view because of some political group they've boxed themselves into. As an Independent, I like to think of myself as above all the crazy politics, at least as much as possible, making decisions based on facts and data, rather than on feelings or political affiliations."

Another round of fish tacos arrives along with more icy margaritas. The roar of the ocean in the background fills a break in the conversation. A very welcome breeze swishes through the dry palms overhead.

I pick up my margarita. "One more of these and they'll have to carry me out," I say.

"Don't worry. It won't be the first time I've had to do that," he smiles. "Once I buy my property here, I will have to do it about once per week! What about you—do you invest in property at all?" asks Ricardo.

"No, to me it's always seemed a bit out of my league. I'm more of a stock market guy."

"Oh, and let me guess – you have a system," he smiles.

"I do! Did I tell you this before?" I return the smile.

"No, but I'm sure you will now."

"I don't mind telling," I say. "It's worked for me. It takes a little bit of effort though. First, I have subscriptions to several of the major financial magazines, and I read these thoroughly every month to be sure that I'm well informed of what's happening in the market. Second, for any particular stocks that I'm thinking of trading, or any investment sectors I'm interested in, I research these in detail on the Internet, through talking to people knowledgeable in that sector, and any other way I can find. Then, when I'm ready to make an investment move, I put all of this information together and do exactly the *opposite* of what I think I should do. You might find it surprising, but I've had about a sixty-percent success rate with this method! I don't want to think too much about what that might mean about my financial skills, so I just try to take comfort in the fact that, so far, it seems to be working."

Ricardo has a good laugh. "That's the only system I've ever heard that makes sense!"

"It was a lesson hard learned," I tell him. "The US economy is like the New Jersey rain— there's always either a drought or a flood. There can never just be a nice, steady sprinkle." He laughs again, perhaps just to be polite.

"So what business are you in?" I ask him.

"Every business!" he says, still smiling. "The Central American countries are very small, as you have seen. If you restrict yourself to one type of product or service, your business will be very limited. My company imports many kinds of products from the USA, Europe, China… all over the world, and I sell them in Guatemala. I handle medical products, equipment, cleaning supplies… mostly things that are used by hospitals. But my family also owns some commercial properties."

"Well, you're obviously a good person to know in Guatemala. Isn't it hard to start a business there?"

"It's not so hard. Like you, I have a system. My system is easy— just work hard eighteen hours a day for fifteen or twenty years and you will have a healthy business. My system works anywhere!"

"I'm sure you're right about that. You've obviously worked hard and achieved a lot. It must be difficult to be a wealthy person here with so much poverty around you," I add, "Do you find yourself giving a lot to charities to help the poor?"

Ricardo turns the question around very quickly. "Yes, of course I give some; what about you?"

"Well of course I give to some charities, like my church, for example, and some other local organizations. But living right here in Central America, you see the poverty all the time. Are the affluent people here doing enough to improve the living conditions of the less fortunate citizens?"

"First of all, I am not rich," he asserts. "I probably make less money than you do. I can live a decent life because the cost of living is lower here than it is in your country. But let me ask you something— why do you think I should give more than you?"

"I didn't mean that you should give more. I was just thinking that I donate to charities in the US, and wondered if you do the same in Guatemala."

"At my company we have a program to help the local community in lots of ways. We also provide our staff with free breakfast and lunch. Otherwise, some of them might not eat anything. But something you said made me wonder. You basically said you give to your church and some other charities, but you don't even seem sure where the money is going. I am thinking that you're donating more for yourself than for others. Are you sure that the main reason you're giving to charity is to help other people, or could it be mainly to soften your feelings of guilt for having so much?"

"Well, I like the idea of helping others. I think we all need to do this."

"And what people have you helped?" he asks.

"A lot of the people in my neighborhood come by to collect donations for causes like cancer, sick children, and things like that."

"And do you donate because you want to fight these diseases, or because you want to help your neighbors?"

I consider the question. "A bit of both, really."

"Do any of the people collect to help the poor people of Guatemala, or El Salvador?"

"No, those aren't the usual type of things people collect for."

"But you are very concerned that I should be helping them. Do you think I should give more to these people just because I see them every day, or because geographically I live within the same political boundaries that they do? The way I see it, they are just as much your responsibility as mine. Just because you live far away and you do not see these people day after day in your life does not mean that I am more responsible for them than you are. We all share the world. It seems ridiculous to donate to your rich churches and rich organizations just because they are located within your country's borders, and ignore all the poverty down here because it is on the other side of some imaginary line."

I imagine how Ricardo must view me, as a sort of naïve, misguided Robin Hood, a rich man giving to the slightly-less-rich. I hadn't wanted to provoke any sort of moralistic confrontation with him; I'm just trying to have a friendly conversation over lunch. He is right, though; there is a world outside my immediate neighborhood, a world in which feeding one's family and keeping them healthy are an ongoing challenge, and the idea of lifting them out of their daily misery is an impossible dream. Even though I realize this cognitively, there are still so many ways that I am insensitive to it. My small donations to my church and to local fund drives are not going to do much to alleviate world poverty. This trip has opened my eyes a bit more. Blue definitely had it right. If you travel enough, you will realize that you are rich.

I make the decision to donate more in the future to charities that directly assist families in dire circumstances around the world to get on their feet- I will need to identify some established organizations that offer micro-loans that enable people to start small buying-and-reselling businesses, groups that donate animals and livestock to families and communities that can raise and tend them in order to reap ongoing benefits such as milk and eggs, and other aid groups with the plant-a-seed philosophy. It sure beats hearing my kids cry from receiving too many Christmas gifts. I mention this idea to Ricardo and he agrees.

"This is the type of assistance that works," he says, "Making a small investment that, with the commitment of the people that receive it, can grow into something that can sustain them."

"I think you're right," I tell him, "That in the US we focus too much on internal issues and don't view ourselves as citizens of the wider world. Our country is so big, we tend to lose sight of the fact that there is so much more world out here."

As our conversation evolves, I explain to Ricardo my thoughts on the strange phenomenon of celebrities crusading for charities. "These are people who have had an extraordinary amount of good fortune shine into their lives, and they want to give a little of it back. The trouble is, they want to give it back with my money! I can't imagine anything more ridiculous than a multi-, multi-millionaire getting up in front of a crowd of us working folk, asking us to crack our wallets and donate to a charity. If they really feel that strongly about helping a charity, if they really are serious, why don't they give away more of their millions? Why do they feel that they're entitled to live their lives in the five-star luxury that the rest of us support through movie tickets, DVDs, concert and sports tickets or whatever, and then ask us to give more of our hard-earned cash to their charities, so they can feel better and less guilty? My response to them would be: before you ask *me* to give, first *you* give away enough money so that your net worth becomes equal to mine. Then, also promise to donate any income that you earn from now on that is in excess of mine, and once we are on equal footing after that, then I will match your additional contributions dollar-for-dollar. Then we'll see how committed they are to those charities. I imagine I'll wait a long time for such an event."

The fish tacos are reduced to a pile of crumbs, and I am tempted to order another round of margaritas. But it is time to take the next step in my onward trek. I have to get back to San Salvador tonight so I can catch the morning bus to Guatemala City.

I ask Ricardo whether he'll be back in Guatemala City in the next couple of days, when I plan to be there. Unfortunately, he has to leave for San Salvador tomorrow to sort out some legal issues related to his business, and won't return to Guatemala City until the following week.

"Guatemala is a great country," he assures me, "Be sure to visit Lago de Atitlán and the pyramids and ruins of the Maya at Tikal if you get the chance. And of course, La Antigua Guatemala, the old colonial capital. Your hotel will be able to set up a tour for you." Ricardo seems to be under the impression that I will be staying in a posh hotel rather than the concrete-block *pensiones* I have been frequenting in the cities, but I assure him I'll do my best to see as much of the country as possible during my short visit.

I check out of my bungalow, and as I'm heading to the street to jump into my taxi, I see two police cars pull up in front of me. The sun is blazing before my eyes, and, instinctively, I tip my head down so the visor of my baseball cap blocks its rays. Fortunately, it also shields my face from the policemen, who walk slowly but purposefully toward to hotel entrance. Are they looking for me? Or is it just a coincidence that two squad cars are here at some isolated beach hotel with only ten cabins and maybe fifteen guests, on a quiet morning? Maybe they are local police, I reason, or maybe they know someone who works here, or perhaps they have come to enjoy an early lunch at the beachside restaurant, but none of these explanations brings me any comfort. No, most likely they have come to look for me. It's time to leave the country again, right on schedule. I hand my taxi driver fifty dollars and tell him to take me all the way to San Salvador.

This time, I know enough to depart from the San Benito station, so I ask the driver to drop me off at a hotel in that district. Even this area looks a little rough, so I restrict my wanderings to the main roads and make sure I'm back in the hotel before dark.

In the morning, I hop aboard the first bus to Guatemala City. As I take my seat, a quick glance reveals that the girl sitting across the aisle and behind me one row is stunningly attractive. I make a mental note to take a better look when the opportunity arises.

The bus pulls out from the station into the traffic-congested street. One of the usual horribly violent American films comes on the video screen, conveniently subtitled in Spanish. Ignoring the video, I watch the continuing drama of El Salvador life unfolding just outside my window. A squat man wearing a straw cowboy hat hurries past the bus carrying a squealing baby pig over his shoulder, no doubt en route to meet its maker. Further along, a crippled beggar in filthy clothing scores a gratis soft drink from a kind-hearted young vendor. Crumbling, tile-roofed cottages and broad-branched trees punctuate the sun-dappled landscape. Everyday life proceeds with its beautiful chaos.

I decide that the time is right to have another peek at the girl behind me, who by now has moved a few rows back to have a nap. I pretend that I have to use the rudimentary lavatory facility at the back of the bus, and make my way along the aisle, lightly gripping alternate seat backs on the way in case the bus takes a wicked bump, a fairly routine occurrence.

The objective of my slightly obsessive stalk is stretched out across two seats, sleeping quietly, and this affords me the opportunity to have a somewhat longer gaze than decorum would have allowed, had she been awake. Even so, I am taken aback. My mouth drops open. The significance of the moment slowly dawns on me. She is absolutely, flawlessly beautiful. Within five seconds I realize that she is, in fact, the most beautiful woman that I have ever seen… a perfect ten out of ten, as Blue would say. Of course I have heard about 'tens' before, the same as I have heard about yetis and the Loch Ness Monster. But I have never actually seen one before, and I certainly never expected to now. Yet here she is, reclined on the seat before me, an angel in repose, her flaxen hair draped behind her, her skin exquisitely toned, the color of milky tea. She is radiant as the sun— her glowing face a beaming star, a shining, golden circle of heavenly light from which I perceive great life-giving warmth. I am overcome with emotion. I can only stagger back to my seat, whispering "Holy shit!" in amazement a dozen times to myself.

I've got to remember the details of this moment. I try to etch the image of her beauty indelibly on my mind, so I can accurately relate it to my friends when I return, and so I can conjure her in my memory through the years of my life. My description of her falters and sputters as I try to find words to describe her. Perfect face, great hair- what does it mean? It is like describing the perfect summer day- details about the temperature and wind velocity are useless, as are any facts at all; it is the idea that the day creates that is the beauty.

Once I collect myself, I decide to move to a new seat a few rows behind the Angel, so I can at least admire her from a distance. I consider whether I should make some excuse to speak to her at some point, and if so, what to say. I worry about my new fixation and wonder whether I am being rational, or whether my mind is exaggerating her attractiveness after traveling alone for so long. Is this normal? Have I finally gone over the edge? I force myself to try to focus on the breathtaking scenery on display outside my window, but my eyes magnetically turn to her.

As we approach the Guatemalan border, the bus conductor advises everyone to keep their passports handy. I strain to see the Angel's nationality. My heart skips a beat when she pulls out an American passport- at last, a talking point for me!

By this point I have become a shameless stalker. I listen to her speaking fluent Spanish with her female companion, who holds an El Salvador passport. Even her voice is magnificent.

All of the bus passengers line up at the Guatemalan immigration post. As usual, moneychangers and hawkers of all sorts frantically surround us as we disembark. I ignore them and nudge my way through the crowd. Somehow I lose track of the Angel in the commotion. I wait in a queue with about ten other people and receive my entry stamp. Then, in what constitutes a serious deviation from the norm for me, rather than stand outside and absorb the pleasantly chaotic ambience as usual, I double-time it back to the heavenly body of the Angel.

Back on the bus, the Angel is awake and, at least for now, not conversing with her friend. I can't miss this opportunity. "Where are you from?" I blurt out almost too soon, knowing she will realize that I am an American and feel that instantaneous bond that all Americans feel when traveling outside the country.

Girls have always been a bit of a mystery to me. I remember one day in elementary school, I pulled my teacher aside after class (well, I guess it was more a matter of standing annoyingly in her personal space than 'pulling her aside') and asked her something that I had been wondering for some time: what is a *period*? The teacher immediately got a bit flushed and started to stammer a bit, which I had never heard her do before, but I stood before her as a truly perplexed child, and, obviously feeling the call of her profession, she swallowed heavily and answered as best she could. It ended up being a rather lengthy and delicate interpretation that ensued, brushing over tender topics like female anatomy, hygiene and pregnancy, and in the end she advised me to continue the conversation with my parents when I got home, in order to get a more clear idea. The whole incident confused me to no end, as I just could not fathom what all of that had to do with the little dot at the end of a sentence. But anyway, back to girls…

When I was young and single, my attempts to get a date were comparable to those of a young child learning how to fish. Though he may have learned from those with more experience exactly how to bait his hook, all the specifics about where to cast his line into the water, how to reel in a fish and so on, he is still so surprised when he actually gets a fish on the line that he doesn't know what to do, and ends up dropping his fishing rod into the water. In the unfortunately rather rare circumstance that a girl actually responded positively to my affections, I would be overcome with shock to the point that I would freeze and remain motionless, waiting for a cue from somebody offstage to tell me what to do next. Now here I am with twenty years of marriage under my belt, and I find that relatively little has changed. It's amazing that a pretty face can still leave me stuttering. If I am still awkward around girls at this age, it seems that there is little hope for me. But the girl on the bus doesn't seem to notice.

"Oh… Hi," she says, "I'm from North Carolina."

"I'm from New Jersey. I noticed your passport when we stopped at the border. I didn't realize you were American." Shit, I think. Now she knows I have been looking at her. I quickly add, "You speak Spanish so well."

"Thanks," she says with a glancing, almost shy, smile, "I'm really not that fluent yet, but I'm trying. It's taken a long time to get this far."

"What brings you down here?" I ask.

"I'm in the Peace Corps. I've been living in El Salvador for about eighteen months."

"Wow, eighteen months. No wonder you're so good at Spanish. So, what's it like to live here for that long? Do you like it?"

"I love it," she says, and her radiant eyes confirm her accolade. "This is my new home. I've been living with a Salvadoran family… that's the mother over there," she says, indicating her traveling companion. "She has a husband and two young kids. I feel like part of the family now. I can't imagine how I could ever leave."

"Will you have to leave soon?"

"I have about half a year left. But I'm looking at some other options. I really want to stay here." Her smile is breathtaking. Does she know it? I am on the verge of being irretrievably enchanted. I try to continue the conversation nonchalantly, as if I speak at length to women this alluring every day. Desperately struggling to appear at ease, I rapidly scan the crevices of my brain for interesting conversational material. "What are your living accommodations like?" is the best I can come up with.

"Well, I have my own small room in the house. It's not a room like we would have in the States; it's more like a sort of separate area. The whole house isn't much larger than, say, an American living room. But it has, not really a kitchen, but a food-preparation area, and there's a table and chairs, and places to keep all the clothes and food and other stuff. It's all you need, really. In the States we have too much stuff."

Hey! She sounds like me now! "I think you're right about that," I say. "So many people in other parts of the world make do with so much less. We've really got too much. And it's not like we're any happier for it. In a lot of ways, I think people are happier here, even though they don't have nearly as much."

"In a way, they have more. They have family closeness to a degree that we'll never have in the States."

"That's an important thing. But, what about health and safety? Have you had any problems here? I mean, those are the things I would worry about living in a village in El Salvador."

"There are some health issues. I've had a few parasites since I've been living here," she confides. "But I just go to the doctor in another town and I can get the medicine to treat them."

"You mean like tapeworms and roundworms and that sort of thing? Geez, I wouldn't want to have to deal with that. I don't think I could handle knowing that something like that was living inside of me. I had a hard enough time with a botfly larva, and I sure wouldn't look forward to repeating that!"

"Oh, you did? Well, it's just nature. People have been living with those things all through history, except for maybe the past fifty to a hundred years. And that's just in the developed countries. And even *there* people get them sometimes. It's not a big deal. I know the signs to look for, and if I think I've picked up something, I go to the doctor and get it treated. It's really easy."

"And what about the local people?" I ask. "Do they all get treated as well?"

She glances downward. "No, they usually don't."

"They don't care?"

"It doesn't really bother them. They don't think about it the same way as we do. And a lot of times, they don't have the money." She looks up and gently shakes her hair out of her eyes. It almost makes me shudder. This is the sexiest conversation about parasites I've ever had. "Like I say, they've been living with it forever."

"What about crime? Is it really as dangerous here as people say?"

"I hear a lot of things about crime, but in all the time I've been living here, I haven't had any problems. There are some things you just don't do, like walking in certain places after dark, for example. There are some places that are known for crime problems and I try to stay away from there as much as possible. But, like I said, I've never had a problem. In fact in my time here, I've met some of the nicest, most caring and giving people I've met anywhere."

"I haven't had any problems with crime either." To myself I add, 'except, of course, the minor one about me being an accused sex predator, hopscotching international borders to stay ahead of the police.' "But the perception back home of this place is terrible."

"Yes, I know. People tend to fear what they don't know about, and not many people seem to know about Central America, unless they're from here."

"So, did you major in this sort of thing in college? How did you end up doing this?" I ask.

"I double-majored in social work and biology," she explains. "This seemed like a great way to use both. In fact, I'm not sure what I want to do after this. Like I said, I can't imagine going back to the States now, and leaving my Salvadoran family behind. I just love my little 'sister' and 'brother'. I don't want to think about them growing up without me."

"What sort of other options are you looking at for after the Peace Corps?" I ask.

"Well, there are some other service organizations and charity groups that have operations in El Salvador. I'm talking to some people now, through e-mail."

"You have e-mail?"

"I have an e-mail address, but I don't get a chance to check it very often. There aren't any computers in my village, so I have to get to a bigger town and find an Internet café. Then I can check my e-mail, check in with my parents back in the States, and look for some kind of new assignment down here."

"Would you mind if I e-mailed you?"

"Sure, I'd really like that. I like to hear what's happening in the outside world. I can only check it every couple of weeks, but it would be nice to keep in touch with you."

She writes her name and e-mail address on a scrap of paper and hands it to me. I can't believe my luck! Not only is she a 'ten', but she's got the personality to match. She is a beautiful, beautiful person, inside and out. She is a shining beacon of youth, optimism and beauty, bubbling with enthusiasm for life. I vaguely remember that feeling from maybe a quarter-century ago. And now I've got her e-mail address! Maybe she is The One, the true and perfect soul mate for me, and I'm finally, *finally* meeting her after all these years. She is half my age. Will it matter? Will I be looking forward to retirement when she decides it is time to have a family of her own? Will I be settling into a rocking chair when the yearning hits her to travel the world? Would it be fair to her?

Hey! What am I doing? I'm a middle-aged, married family man, chasing after a girl in her mid-twenties. This doesn't make any sense. I expect I am following a natural pattern of behavior that is deeply etched in my psyche. Almost automatic, reflexive, a relic from an earlier mindset. But there is no reason, no purpose to it. I love my wife and am a devoted husband and father. There is nowhere for this to go, nor do I want there to be. But I cannot deny the attraction- it is beyond my control or my ability to reason away with logic. The feelings of emptiness and helplessness are deeply frustrating. Why should such feelings exist after so many years of marriage? There is nothing positive that can come of it. I wish I could turn the feelings off, but I know there is no way. I realize it is just one more weight to deal with as I move through life. I will try to take the energy and focus it on more constructive pursuits.

Not only that, but I am missing Guatemala!

CHAPTER 11

Reflections of Blue

Guatemala brings with it a return to the rugged hills and dilapidated rurality of Honduras. The people are different, however. In this country, the Mayan heritage is much more evident. I observe substantially more people of native blood and customs than the Spanish or mestizo heritage that seems to predominate in the other countries. Here in the countryside, the clothing, too, carries with it a style that is more redolent of Amerindian culture. Earthy tones of ochre, cornsilk and crimson adorn the shoulders and backs of the local women in bold, thick stripes. But to me the most notable features are the outlandishly out-of-place straw fedoras on many of their braided heads.

Beams of sunlight break through a cloud to direct an ethereal light on an emerald mountainside, giving it an almost divine glow. The bus rounds several hairpin turns along the edge of the mountains, and from my seat high above the road I can see far down into the fecund valleys, spilling over with lush vegetation and speckled with compact, whitewashed farmhouses, their red tile roofs contrasting sharply with the luminescent green of the vales.

As the bus enters Guatemala City, I am struck by the graffiti I see on the walls. It seems that everywhere in the world, people are overcome with the desire to paint on walls. I wonder why I have never felt such a desire. Am I missing something? Yet everywhere, in every part of the world, it looks exactly the same, as if the same handful of quasi-artistic miscreants has scoured the earth, covering every available space with the same inflated, bubbly letters and indecipherable scribblings. Perhaps it is a craft passed from father to son down the generations, or perhaps it has evolved identical characteristics in different countries by separate routes through some sort of bizarre evolutionary pressure, in the same way that birds, bats and insects all developed wings. I shrug my shoulders, realizing once again that there are some things in life that I simply will never know.

I recall my discovery that in Central America, the capital cities are not the best places to be. As I stroll the streets of Guatemala City, I stumble across a travel agency, offering shuttle service to other cities, Lake Atitlán and la Antigua. I remember Ricardo mentioning these last two places. It seems that Lake Atitlán is some distance away, but la Antigua is quite close. My time is short; I don't want to wait for a shuttle. I decide to take a taxi from the hotel across the street.

A half-hour taxi ride later, I arrive in Antigua, a lovely place that enchants me immediately. The capital of Guatemala in earlier days, the city brims with activity and color. Immaculate colonial-style homes of multicolored stucco, complete with wrought-iron balconies and rooftop gardens line the roadsides. I notice a sprinkling of swanky but unpretentious restaurants and trendy bars, much more enticing than those I've seen in Guatemala City. Great stately palms and fluorescent purple jacaranda trees frame glorious golden churches and the ruins of centuries-old Spanish estates. But usurping the grandeur of all this is the imposing presence of Volcán de Agua, a gigantic green monolith that dominates the horizon.

Agua (water) was the source of a devastating mudslide that destroyed the previous capital, several miles from here, in 1541, and seems to threaten Antigua to this day. Further afield, but even slightly more menacing is its brother, Volcán de Fuego (fire), a continuously active volcano that steadily spews thick gray smoke and occasionally lets out a thunderous groan. As if the presence of these two volcanoes were not enough, the dilapidated state of the ruins is a constant reminder that this is earthquake country. Still, the people seem to pay little mind to all of this, and life goes on in its day-to-day splendor.

The city (really not much more than a town) is dazzlingly beautiful. I can't get enough of it. I walk quickly up and down its lively streets, almost afraid that I will miss something, anything, in this open-air museum. I find a very pleasant hotel not too far from the center of town, then enjoy spicy fried chicken for lunch at a nearby restaurant. As I continue my walk, I notice the abundance of Spanish language schools and make a mental note to check in with one later, to see how much they charge. Finally I head to the central park for a rest.

I'm sitting on a bench in the shade in the leafy town square, watching the locals and the gringos. The Americans seem so much louder, always calling to each other, taking too many pictures of the same things, and walking around in either brightly colored sneakers or flip-flops. I wonder to myself whether there is any place in the world where you will not see them. I am just about to get up and continue my walk, when I feel a hand on my shoulder. My heart jumps! The police? I slowly turn my head. It's a large and strong, yet aged hand, speckled with dark sunspots, with thick blue veins weaving under the leathery skin. I turn around and squint up at the contrite face of Blue Sunshine.

I breathe a sigh of relief, although he probably takes it as one of disappointment.

"I don't suppose you're too pleased to see the likes of me," he says. "Can I buy you a beer?"

I glance around the square as if to see whether there are any better options. "Sure," I say after a brief hesitation, and he leads the way to a quiet restaurant with a bar, on one of the side streets. We grab a table for two near the center of the room and sit down across from each other, me facing a wall-size reproduction of Frida Kahlo's self-portrait *The Broken Column*.

"So what are you doing here?" I ask, "This is a long way from your neck of the woods."

"Well, you can imagine I was feeling pretty bad about what happened last week, so I figured I'd find you and apologize."

"I appreciate that, but how did you find me? I didn't exactly leave a trail of crumbs."

"No, but you did tell me you were headed to Guatemala. And every American who comes to Guatemala goes to Antigua. And then it was just a matter of time before you'd end up in the town square."

A chill goes up my spine as if it were Frida's metallic pillar. Am I that easy to find? I think I'm going to have to move on quickly. But first I'll see what Blue has to say.

"I trusted you, Blue. You violated that trust."

"Yes, I sure did mess things up. I thought you were ready. You seem so much like me when I was younger. I was ready then. I just assumed you would be too."

"You didn't even *ask* if I was ready. You just assumed it. And I *wasn't*, by the way."

"I know that now. I should have then. I'm sorry, Doug. Please forgive me."

I stifle a sigh. "It's all right, Blue. I guess it wasn't so bad of an experience. I just was not ready for it, and really... to do that to someone without them knowing..."

"No harm was meant, son. It was a mistake."

"All right, let's forget it then. How is Luz?"

The waiter interrupts us with two menus. Blue orders two of the local beers and some tortillas to snack on. As soon as I shift the colorful fabric that keeps the tortillas warm in their basket, their heavenly, steamy aroma hits me. I have begun to love the smell of fresh corn tortillas, especially those made by hand like these. But I have also become discerning about them. Their shelf life is exceedingly short; if they aren't still warm from the grill, it has expired, and no manner of re-heating can resuscitate them.

"Luz is well. She sends her regards. So how has the trip been going?" he asks.

"Mostly good." I reply.

"That's good. You enjoyed El Salvador? Hope you spent some time along the coast."

"Yes, I did. La Libertad. Very nice. I met a great guy there. Business owner. Fascinating."

"Good, good. I knew you would love it in this part of the world. You OK with your… your issue? The one you were talking about when you came to my place?"

"Yeah… for the time being."

My thoughts turn to something that I've been thinking about since that night. "Blue, let me ask you something. Those mushrooms… Do they… do you think weird thoughts when you eat them?"

He chuckles. "Sure do. Just like you probably did. Existence, meaning, philosophy… you know."

"But how… how can a mushroom…do that?"

"Well, in all the years I've known about them, that's one thing I've never been able to work out. Don't suppose it really matters *how* it works, just that it does."

"And they make you think the same kind of thoughts as I did? Do they… put the thoughts there?"

"Remember what I called them? Entheogens. God generators. Something they've been considered for generations immemorial, long before modern politicians started grouping them with amphetamines and narcotics."

"Yes, I remember your theory."

"All kinds of what they refer to as 'drugs,'" he continues, making finger quotations as he says the word, "Are woven throughout the fabric of American culture. They're everywhere, and they always have been. We all know that they have been a fixture in Hollywood and the entertainment industry for decades, and that does not seem to be changing. It's just considered normal. We all also know the slang that revolves around marijuana and cocaine, whether we want to or not, just from watching movies, where they are almost universally treated as harmless, everyday household products. You might accuse the motion picture industry of dulling our senses to them, but I really feel that this is a case of art imitating life rather than the other way around. It really makes the so-called 'War on Drugs' look silly. That is, if you don't think too hard about the fact that so many people are losing their lives due to the distribution system being de facto handed over to organized crime."

Blue looks down for a moment and notices that both of our glasses are empty. He signals for two more beers. The waiter brings them over and also brings a fresh basket of tortillas, much to my delight. I can tell that Blue is on one of his rolls and I am unlikely to get a word in for a while, so I sit back in my chair and listen.

"It's crazy," he continues. "In the US, for example, I can own a gun. I'm not saying that's right or wrong… I'm just stating that fact. I certainly don't mean to open up a discussion about gun rights. That's a whole other kettle of fish. But right or wrong, I can own a gun. I can hold one in my hand, no problem. But if I have in my pocket a piece of a certain plant or mushroom that grows of its own accord on the earth, with my sole purpose being to ingest it and enjoy an experience in my own mind, by law I can be thrown in jail for maybe ten years. It doesn't make sense."

"Not to you, but that's the way it is. You're lucky, Blue, real lucky that you haven't been caught. I think you're playing with fire."

"That's my choice. For me, it's helped me. I enjoy it."

"But what is it, that it does?"

"Why don't you tell me what it did to you?"

"To me? Well, I started having all these crazy thoughts, that's all. Thoughts like I've never had before. About my brain and my mind and my self. Weird things." As I speak, Frida's hirsute eyebrows seem to scrutinize me.

"Were they really crazy?" asks Blue, "Or were they just new to you? And deeper than what you're accustomed to?"

"Well, I don't know. I guess you could say that."

"Contemplating your own existence and the nature of the universe doesn't make you crazy, son. Philosophers have been doing it for centuries. It's what religion is all about."

"OK, but there were no answers, only questions. So what does that do for me?"

"Asking questions is the first step toward understanding. If you don't have the interest to ask, you can't have the intelligence to know."

"All right," I admit. "The questions were interesting. They just weren't practical or relevant. Why does someone like me need to understand the universe?"

"I wouldn't worry about that. We'll never understand the universe. I mean *people* never will."

"You don't think so?" I ask. "Look at how far people have come in the last two hundred years, in our understanding of astronomy and space, medicine, microbiology..."

"Long way to go..."

"...And a long time to do it, hopefully. People might be around for millions of years. Billions. Trillions!"

"When it comes to the universe, we're like ants trying to figure out how a car works. No, worse than that. We're like ants trying to figure out the universe. Because there's really no difference between our minds and ants' minds when it comes to figuring out the complexities of the universe. Every time we make a new discovery, it raises ten thousand more questions. The deeper we look into space, the more things we see that we don't understand. The ancient folks thought they had it sussed when the gods ruled the skies and the earth was the center of the universe. Now we know so much more… but also we realize that we're further back on the learning curve than we ever thought! The ancients didn't know about galaxies and quasars and black holes…"

"It's incredible. The vastness and complexity of space. God must be having a laugh each time we think we're getting closer to understanding it."

"And yet," says Blue, "We can't even understand ourselves. The universe that exists in our own mind. The universes— plural— that make up each person's mind. Completely separate and utterly unbridgeable."

"Not unbridgeable," I say. "We have conversation. That bridges it."

"Yes," Blue agrees, much to my surprise. "Thankfully we have developed language, to transfer thoughts from one person to another. In fact, I should say, it's a good thing we developed language, so we can think."

"You don't have to have a language to think," I say, immediately regretting it, as I can see in his eyes that he was waiting for that response. I grab a tortilla to chew on.

"I believe you do," he says. "When you think, don't you think in language?" Before I can answer, he continues. "Here's a question for you— do you think it's possible to think of anything that can't be described in words?"

"Yes," I joke, "I'm thinking it now!" He patronizes me with a smile. "To think about something that can't be described in words…

I guess so; isn't that what visionaries do? People who invent new things that haven't been thought of before?"

"But those things can be described in words. Before they're built or developed, that is. I would say that it's impossible to think of something that cannot be described in words."

"But how can that be?" I ask. "What about someone whose language skills are not good? What about a child just learning to talk? What about humans before language was developed?"

"I believe that language and thought developed concurrently," he says. "Before a child can speak, they are only aware of needs. They can perceive things they can't speak about, and recollect them, of course. But to think of something entirely new, that doesn't exist, would require words. Think about the conditional tense, what 'could' be or what 'would' happen if… Or the composed past, the complexities and nuances in meaning. Were such things thought of before words could express them, or did the ability to think contrary-to-fact tenses and such develop as the language did?"

"I don't know," I say, flabbergasted, "This is all making my head hurt. Do you sit around and think about these crazy things all day?"

"I'm a philosopher," he replies, "So in a way, I do. You don't just want to glide through life without considering what it's all about, do you? You know the old saying; the unexamined life is not worth living."

"I think that's for the non-examiner to decide. My life is just fine the way it is."

"It's good to hear you say that. I think we may be getting somewhere with you."

Blue takes a sip of his beer, straightens up and bends over the table a bit to ask me a question. "So what were these 'crazy' thoughts that the mushrooms put into your mind, if I may ask?"

"Oh, it was just silly stuff. Things that seemed to make sense at the time, but that I later realized was pure crap." I hesitate. Should I tell him? Well, why not? He probably already knows. "All right, if you really want to know… I thought I might have multiple personalities within my mind, for example. Crazy things."

"And you don't?"

"Well, of course not. Do you?"

"It depends on the definition of 'personality.' That's a manmade term, of course. So if you define it as the sum total, or externally visible characteristics of a person, their particular set of qualities, or whatever, of course there is only one, by definition. But there's nothing to say that that set of qualities doesn't come from different sources within the person."

"Oh, come on, Blue. If you think this fungus that grows in the dirt can impart new wisdom to you, that's one thing. But to support such a ridiculous idea just because…"

"I didn't say I support it. I didn't say I didn't. I didn't even say that thought came from the mushroom. Maybe it came from you, where all your other thoughts come from. Perhaps you were just uninhibited in your thinking at the time, and the mushrooms facilitated that. Maybe the idea is wrong; maybe it's not. But you did consider it, and there's nothing wrong with that."

"There's nothing right with it, either. How could that possibly help me?"

"Look, we may be social creatures, but let me tell you, in our minds we are utterly, utterly alone. There's no way to cross that boundary into another person's thoughts. When I was with Caroline, I remember lying there next to her so many nights, thinking we were as close as two people could be. And yet, I had no idea what was going on in her head— none! How can that be, I would think. It's as difficult to get inside another person's head as it is to visit another universe! It's true— no matter how much you want to and no matter how much the other person wants to let you, you can never really know them. They will always remain an unfathomable mystery. But then I realized that even my own mind is a mystery to me."

"Blue! Certainly you must know your own mind pretty well after living with it so long! You *are* your mind. How can you not know it?"

"Well, sure, I know the basics… I know what I like and what I don't like, for example. But if I look deeper, I'm not sure why I like some of the things I like, or why I don't like some of the other things. Where does it come from?"

"Good or bad experiences with them in the past, probably," I postulate.

"It's easy to dismiss it that way, but that's not always the case. Let me give you an example. So… I like books. When I see a bookstore, it draws me in and I can spend hours inside, just perusing the pages."

"Well, obviously, you like to read. You're an intelligent guy, and you probably got at least some of your information from reading."

"But here's the thing. I like to read, yes. But I like books for some other reason that has nothing to do with reading. I like the look of books, the feel of a book in my hands. I go into bookstores just for this feeling. How do you explain that?"

"Hmmm… well, if I were your analyst, I'd certainly lock you up and throw away the key for that!"

"Funny. Well, maybe that's a bad example. But I'm sure you've reacted in different ways and thought in certain manners, and wondered afterward, why did I do that? Why do I react in that way? Even with a whole lifetime to work on it, I don't think a person can even begin to really understand himself. Why he's obsessed with achieving certain goals, why some things are important to him and others aren't. Or why a certain woman appeals to me, and another doesn't. I simply don't know, so how can I possibly explain it?"

It suddenly strikes me that my fear of the seeing the sun is one such thing that I don't understand about myself. I mean sure, you don't want to stare right at it, but my aversion to even looking at sunrises and sunsets is a little over the top. I know it cognitively, yet still I enable this phobia. Maybe… maybe it's a fear of life itself! God! Maybe Blue is right again, as usual. I can't explain it because, as he says, I don't understand it myself.

Two more cold beers appear on the table, condensation dripping down the bottles onto their white cardboard coasters. A few more patrons have entered the restaurant and are chatting amongst themselves, mostly in American-accented English, and the waiter rushes around to serve them. Frida continues her melancholy vigil.

"What you experienced on the mushrooms is the beginning of what they call 'ego death,'" explains Blue.

"Whoa. That sounds pretty serious." I feign a concerned expression.

"It's just a term. It's tricky to explain, but basically it means that you reached a point at which you questioned your sense of self, and your separation from the rest of the world, particularly other people. You considered that you might have multiple personalities. That's actually not so odd. But maybe the opposite is true: Maybe *you* exist in several different people."

"Uhh… I'm pretty sure I don't."

"Let me ask you this: In the past, when one of your daughters was hurt, did it hurt you too? Have you ever wished you could take on their physical pain, so they could be free of it? Or to go even further, did it ever feel like it hurt you more to see them in pain than it would have hurt to bear the pain yourself?"

"Sure, but that's called love. It has nothing to do with a personality disorder!"

"I'm not talking about a disorder. I'm talking about pain that you feel from someone else being hurt. To me, that indicates so kind of overlap in self. Someone I love gets a broken arm, and I hurt from it! We're connected!"

"You sure do have a unique way of looking at things, Blue."

"It comes from doing a lot of thinking. A fisherman has to think about something other than worms and water!"

"Maybe… it comes from doing a lot of *drinking*! Put that in your pipe and smoke it!"

We both laugh.

I take a break to use the restroom. When I return, Blue seems to be pondering the dregs of his beer. He looks up at me. "If I can share with you a bit of wisdom that entered my mind while I was digesting a certain fungus…"

"Of course! Your normal thoughts are pretty wild," I say. "Your thoughts on mushrooms must be deeper than the ocean!"

"I'd hold off on that judgment for a few minutes," he says. "This idea is quite simple. Just listen to me. People's minds are like... onions."

I momentarily consider how if anyone but Blue had just said that, my eyes would widen. They don't. "They make your breath smell bad?" I counter. "Sorry, I know you're on a roll."

"They grow in layers," he explains. "When a child is growing and just developing, his mind is simple. It has only a few layers, mostly based on taking care of bodily needs and tangible desires, things that provide momentary satisfaction. Their thought patterns are simple; other people can understand most of them, and even predict their reactions. Friendships that form at this age can be fleeting. Ten years down the road, two people that were playmates as infants may have little in common. Although those first few layers may have been similar enough at the time, those early layers are now buried underneath subsequent ones that may be very different. On the other hand, those who are able to maintain friendships through into the teen years and beyond, tend to develop their onion layers in tandem and become very close. They are able to see deep into each other's souls because they share the same makeup. Their personalities, or selves, developed concurrently, and together. I think there's some carryover of 'self' between them. They may remain lifelong friends. Do you see what I mean?"

"I think I'm following you," I say.

"As a child grows older, the thought patterns become more complex. By the time a person is in his or her twenties, their thoughts are quite intricate. There are enough layers in the onion that significant parts of the psyche are not shared, and are in fact unshareable, with their partner or spouse. Still, when two people are so young, there are plenty more layers to be added, and as a couple goes through life together, they then add similar layers as they share life experiences. Now take for example two people in their fifties. They meet; they like each other, but even if neither one has ever been married before, it is much more difficult for them to get to know each other than it is for the twenty-year-olds. Their living patterns are established, and there is a vast ocean of layers in each of their minds."

"All this talk about onions is making me hungry," I reply. "The tortillas are great, but they just don't fill the spot alone."

"Let's get some dinner," says Blue. "I know a place near here that serves some great steaks."

"Really? I didn't think you spent any time here in Guatemala."

"Remember what I said? Every American comes to Antigua."

We walk through the cobbled streets, past Mayan women selling trinkets to the tourists, past artists' shops with rows of oil paintings on display, secluded bars, convenience stores, old colonial buildings with chipped but colorful stucco, masses of people swirling through the narrow lanes searching for the shade, and others seated on the curb resting, selling things, or just watching life go by. Soon we reach a classy restaurant with white linen tablecloths, crystal wineglasses and jacketed waiters.

"Is this still Guatemala?" I am incredulous.

"Not very representative, I'm afraid. But this restaurant always reminds me of the place in St. Louis where I first saw Caroline."

"Maybe you're subconsciously looking for her again?"

"You never know. But I've grown lots of onion layers since then!"

The maitre d' shows us to a table for two by the window.

"I'm tired of beer. Do you like wine?" asks Blue to my surprise.

"Sure. A good red would be great."

He orders a Malbec from Argentina. "Great wine the Argentineans make," he says. "I think it's underappreciated." We order a couple of steaks, although *tres cuartos*, or three-quarters done, is the rarest that Blue recommends. The wine is perfect, and the steak is exactly what I have been craving for the last few hours. Although it is small, I feel I couldn't have eaten anything larger after munching on tortillas for the previous two hours.

"Feeling all right?" asks Blue.

"Right now, I feel like I've died and gone to heaven!"

"And that's a good thing, I suppose? He asks with a wink.

"Well, the heaven part, yes; the dying part I'm not so sure about."

"And what do you envision as heaven? A palace in the sky covered with jewels?"

"Not so much," I reply as he chuckles. "Jewels I don't really care about. I do think it's a place, or maybe a state of mind, that you achieve when you're satisfied that you've done good for the world, or good for other people, during your lifetime."

"And what part of you has this state of mind, considering that your brain or body won't be traveling to heaven with you?"

'Wait a minute.' I think to myself, 'Here is where the mushrooms help! I think I can handle this question.' I explain to Blue how my spirit couldn't possibly be connected to the atoms that my body and brain are constructed of, which are known to be lifeless.

"That sounds like a reasonable point. You have to wonder what would be left of a person if he truly left his body," says Blue. "Without any concern about meeting your body's needs, eating, drinking, interacting with people, pursuing your interests, thinking about the future, or anything we spend our time doing, what could you possibly even think about? At the very least, it would be horrifically boring. Can we even imagine that it's possible for us to be entirely separated from our bodies? Even so, many people imagine that somehow we would still have the sensory abilities to see, hear, feel and the like. Things that are absolutely dependent on having the sensory organs of the body. There are many living people who do not have all of these sensory abilities. People with eyes who are blind, people with ears who are deaf. How can we imagine that a soul without any body at all can have these senses? On earth, sensory deprivation can be catastrophic for a person. Imagine what it would be like to be trapped in a body that cannot see, hear or feel, and has no need to eat or experience anything, and yet be conscious. It would be a nightmare!"

"Maybe the senses are recreated in a spiritual manner after we die," I hypothesize.

"In that case, would they be limited like the human senses? Would such spiritual hearing include ultrasonic and subsonic sounds? Would spiritual vision only be able to see light in wavelengths of what we know as the visible range, or could we then see infrared and ultraviolet light? And if so, why not X-rays, gamma rays and radio waves? If the limitations of a physical eye aren't there, why would the range of vision be limited? In fact, if we could see without eyes, there would be no need even to be present to see something. And what about touch? If touch were not dependent on skin or nerves, could we then touch something without being near it? And could we remember things stored in our brain cells, after those cells are gone? I'm not saying that your theory isn't possible; I'm just saying, it's much more complex than what you might initially think."

"That just brings us back to the point that there's so much we will never know," I say.

"No we won't. But it is interesting to think about!"

The wine starts to go to my head after the beer of the afternoon. I think about all the things I've learned about myself on this trip, not just from Blue, although he has been a big part of it, but from all of the people I've met and the experiences I've had. In some ways I feel as if I've woken up after a long sleep. The depression I came here with has ebbed and flowed since my arrival, but I've had time to consider that too. My cheeks reddened with drink and my body slightly slumped in my seat, I look across at Blue, who seems to mirror my position. Perhaps he really is an older version of me. I'm emboldened by my realizations and vow to make a long-needed change.

"Blue, remember how I was feeling when we first met on the bus? I think I know now what the depression was all about. I haven't been myself. I mean I haven't been my *real* self. I've been afraid all of these years. The old me would have been afraid to take this trip, and I've had nothing but… *almost* nothing but… good experiences. I'm not afraid anymore. And the reason I haven't been my real self is that I was so afraid of disappointing others. I was being what they wanted me to be, instead of who I am. I'm a different person now. I can think for myself! I am an independent mind! I refuse to be a sheep anymore!"

"You don't think for yourself, Doug; the system does it for you. That's just the way it is."

"The *system*! That sounds like a conspiracy theory or something," I counter. "I'm not paranoid. I don't have to follow any system!"

"OK, not the system. The culture. Society. That's where our opinions come from. Don't even kid yourself that they come from inside of you. We're a society that has been conditioned to think as a group. You're a sheep. I'm a sheep. We're all sheep. Don't fight it— embrace it."

"No! I *will* be my own person. Distinct and with my own opinions and thoughts."

"Constrained by the limitations of language, and within the socially accepted limits of our time. Or you will suffer greatly! Remember what I said about slavery? How it used to be acceptable and now it's not? What about your religion? What about arbitrary laws against consuming plants— that you agree with! You are a product of your time and culture and your opinions were created, not by you, but by this… *system*! I'm sorry Doug, but you are *not* yourself. You are but one of all of us."

. . . .

The sun is setting in Antigua, early as in all of Central America. With the sunset comes a welcome coolness to the air, but with it the unwelcome thought of Blue's departure, and my own return to Guatemala City in the morning. Every moment I stay in this tropical gringo paradise is another opportunity for the police to find me.

"Blue, thank you for everything. It really has been my great pleasure to talk with you— and eat and drink, and fish with you. I'll never forget the things we talked about. I don't imagine I'll have any conversations like that for a while!"

"I think you will. But you'll have to do most of the talking! Doug, it's been a real pleasure to have your company. Thank you for sharing your time with me."

"You take care, my friend. I'll be back again, I promise."

"Come down anytime. Bring the family next time. I'd like to meet them."

"I will. And next time you're in the States…"

"Don't know if there will be a next time, but we'll see. Good luck, and watch out for botflies! Stay well."

We shake hands and I watch him walk off toward the cheap hostel where he is spending the night. He has a lot of wine to sleep off before his bus leaves tomorrow morning. Me, I'll take the shuttle into the city early tomorrow. As the last rays of the Antigua sunset silhouette the volcanoes, so the last traces of Blue Sunshine disappear from my sight.

CHAPTER 12

Starlight

It is late in the afternoon in Guatemala City when I decide to adopt Scroungy. Actually, it is Scroungy who decides to adopt me, for some reason that I can't fathom. Scroungy has to have been one of the world's most unfortunate dogs up until this point. Skinny and bedraggled, he has obviously been living on the streets for most, if not all, of his young life. Most of the hair on his face is missing, as is the fur from several large patches on his body. His wrinkled, black, bare skin looks like worn leather, and it makes a strange contrast to what remains of his scraggly brown fur. When he is lying down, he looks like an ancient, discarded mink stole that has been through the washer and the garbage disposer, and then somehow has come to life. He seems not to realize the desperation of his circumstances, however, as he ambles forth with a bumbling, almost idiotic happiness that makes me question my own negativity almost immediately. I first notice him walking alongside me, but on the opposite side of the road. Stray dogs learn early, I reckon, to stay out of the path of vehicles here, as maniacal, distracted driving seems commonplace, and speeding vehicles are not very forgiving of naïve dogs learning the ropes of street living. I am amused by the way he seems to be keeping pace with me, and every so often he seems to glance over at me. Is the sun making me feverish, or is that dog smiling at me? I reach the main square, the traffic turns away, and Scroungy trots up to greet me as if he has known me all his life. How is it that dogs recognize dog-lovers when they see them?

Scroungy's unbridled enthusiasm in greeting me, along with his ridiculous optimism, makes me smile right away. We have instantly bonded. I am afraid to touch him due to the almost certain presence of fleas or mites, but it becomes clear that Scroungy and I are now a team. Even if I were to bolt down the street to try to lose him, I am convinced that he would follow me, and anyway, I don't want to bolt; I could use some company, and an optimistic counterpart to my occasional negative mindset couldn't do any harm.

Not surprisingly, it appears that Scroungy has not had a good meal for some time. I continue along the street, dog at my side, looking for a shop that might sell dog food. I spy an open-air stand along the roadside, but they've got no dog food, and flea shampoo is out of the question. However, they do have cans of Vienna sausages, and these Scroungy devours with great abandon. I realize that from this point onward, I have a new friend for life. There are worse things that could happen.

One great advantage to staying in a cheap hotel that I never considered before is that for the price of just a few extra quetzals handed to the desk clerk, I can bring my dog upstairs with me into the room. I'm sure Scroungy is infinitely grateful for this, as am I, since I really don't want to leave him outside anymore. He has a contagious cheerfulness about him that is almost unreal. I fashion a souvenir ceramic pitcher into a makeshift water bowl for him, in case he gets thirsty during the night. The sudden thought strikes me that I'm not even sure whether he's housebroken or not, indeed, whether he has ever even set foot inside of any building before. But there is little risk with the bare linoleum floor of the hotel. I put down a dry towel for him to sleep on, and we both drift off into the night.

I am in my early thirties. My body is still strong, and there's not a trace of gray in my hair. A brisk but fresh spring wind swirls through the leaves outside; it feels good to be alive. Two-year-old Estelle toddles across the floor toward me, beaming with the utter joy that only the very young can know. I reach down and place my hands gently under her arms. The ruffles of her frilly cotton dress rustle and fold between my fingers. She is so light it feels like I could lift her up to the sky. I bring her up above my head and she squeals with delight. Slowly I lower her to my chest. She smells like baby oil and sour milk. "Do you have a big hug for Daddy?" I ask, and she throws her arms around my neck and clasps me as tightly as her soft little arms can manage. Now this is the kind of moment that should last forever. But of course it doesn't; the honking of a car horn awakens me and twelve years of life evaporate, and I am in Guatemala City with graying hair and a troubled mind.

It is one of the great mysteries of my life. What happened with Estelle? When did we start to drift apart and why? What, if anything, could I have done differently to prevent it? In some ways, I am reminded of Blue's story of Caroline, how one day he realized that the Caroline he knew and loved just wasn't there anymore, and I desperately hope that this hasn't happened with Estelle. I miss her so much. I miss her when we're in the same house. I've missed her for years. I wonder if somewhere deep inside of the silent, self-imposed adolescent isolation, the old Estelle is tucked away like a seed, waiting for the warm sunshine of early adulthood to awaken it, and

I dream that if it is, it will then burst into magnificent floral bloom, bringing with it all the beautiful colors of her glorious youth, tempered with the delicate blossom of new womanhood.

I'm sitting on the edge of a creaky cot in a dumpy hotel in Guatemala City, with a mangy mutt sprawled across the floor next to me, and thinking about home. Well, not so much about home, but about my family who lives there. It's been some time since I've received a lukewarm, vaguely encouraging nudge from Dawn, or some unsolicited fashion advice from Celeste. I might have to telephone home to get my fix.

Not surprisingly, my hotel room has no telephone. I walk down the austere concrete staircase, Scroungy's unclipped toenails clicking at my side, to what passes for a front desk. There is a phone there, and the clerk says it's no problem if I want to use it for five minutes, provided that I pay with my credit card.

Dawn answers the phone. The conversation begins awkwardly, with neither of us really sure what to say. Well, maybe it's only I who am not sure what to say, and my awkwardness is aggravated by a poor telephone connection.

"Hi, it's me."

"Hi, you," she says. "Finally, we hear from you. I thought you had found a new wife down there or something. How's the world traveler?"

"Good, pretty good."

"Is everything OK? We haven't heard anything from you in weeks, and now you're calling a couple of days before you're supposed to come home. You *are* coming home, aren't you?"

"Yes, yes… everything's fine," I stammer. "Don't worry. I just missed you all."

"Oh… well, we all miss you too. Where are you?"

"I'm in a little hotel in Guatemala City."

"Sounds terribly romantic. What's it like down there? How's the trip?"

"The trip is great. It's unbelievable." If only I could find the words to explain it to her.

"Well, you don't have to be quite so descriptive," she says sarcastically, and then after a brief pause, she asks more tenderly, "Did you find what you were looking for?"

"Yeah…" I reply slowly, perhaps realizing it myself for the first time, "Yeah, I kind of think I did."

"Well, are you happy? What's it like?"

"It's like… everything. It's a slice of life. I've seen so many beautiful things, I can't even describe them to you. It's just incredible. And yet, there's such poverty, such dirt, such deprivation. But it's been a fascinating, insightful journey."

"Doug, you sound like Dorothy after she just returned from Oz. But I haven't heard you this enthusiastic about anything in ages. What happened to you down there? Are you taking your medication?"

"No, I kind of stopped," I admit. "I don't think I need it anymore. I'm happy now. It's hard to explain. I'll tell you more when I get back. Oh, yeah, I got us a dog."

"A dog? What do you mean? We have a dog… did you forget?"

"Well, I sort of picked up this dog, Scroungy, along the way."

"Scroungy? What about Bonita?"

"I'm sure Bonita will love him. He's a great dog. We just sort of bonded. I don't even know how it happened. Now I just have to figure out how to get him home. He's not the handsomest dog, at least not at the moment. But we'll get that fixed up. He needs us!" It also might be nice to have a little more testosterone to dilute the estrogen sea, even if it's canine testosterone, I add to myself.

"Is that Dad?" I hear Celeste say in the background. She's obviously just come in on one of her quick passes through the house before going out again. "Daddy?"

"Hey, Celeste! How are you doing?" Dawn has handed her the phone.

"Hi, Dad; I'm just on my way to the movies with Katie. When are you coming home?" She sounds breathless from running around, as usual.

"Coming home soon, kiddo, just a couple more days."

"Awesome. Gotta run. Oh, wait, Dad?"

"Yeah?"

"I was wondering if you could maybe teach me Spanish…"

"Teach you Spanish? Sure, Celeste, no problem. When did you become interested in learning Spanish?"

"Just recently. I thought it would be cool to learn another language."

"Well, I'd be happy to teach you as much as I can. I'm no expert, you know…"

"But you know a lot more than me. That will be great. Carlos will be amazed."

"OK, who's Carlos?"

"This guy in school. His whole family speaks Spanish."

"And you haven't asked him to teach you?"

"I don't want him to think I'm stupid! There's Katie— Gotta run. Bye Dad! Love you!" then she turns and adds, "Oh, and Dad…?"

"Yes, Celeste?"

"Please take off those ridiculous sunglasses!"

"Bye Cellie! Love you too!" I yell, but I'm not sure she hears me, as the door has already slammed. She can't stand still for too long. She probably thinks she will get moldy. I say to Dawn, "Some things never change."

"At least she's happy. And that would give you a great opportunity to spend some time with her, if you could teach her Spanish."

"If she can sit still long enough. There's always got to be a boy involved in there somehow."

"Couldn't imagine it any other way. Better take what you can get, right? How's the Spanish working out for you, anyway?"

"I'm getting by. Haven't gotten myself in too much trouble yet," I lie, knowing full well that I have.

"Well, we're all looking forward to you coming home safe and sound to us again. You'll be surprised when you see me!"

I am never sure how to handle a comment like this, with its vaguely ominous overtones. "Any particular reason?" I ask.

"Well, right after you left I had some extra time on my hands, if you can believe that. When I was watching TV at night and you weren't here, I would think about how much you always complained about TV. And I realized that it wasn't any fun without you. I started thinking about myself just getting older in front of the tube, so one night I just turned it off, and I haven't turned it back on since!"

"That's great! Wow! So what have you been doing instead?"

"I've been working out!" she proclaims proudly, "Can you believe that?"

"Amazing! That's incredible, Dawn!" I tell her, and I really mean it.

"I really want to get in shape. For the future- for our future, together, Doug. I don't want to miss a moment with you. I want to keep myself healthy and fit so we can do all the things we want. Then maybe, the next time you have frequent-flyer miles, we can both go somewhere together."

"That's exactly what I want to do," I say. "Wow! Now I can't wait to come home!"

We chat a bit more, about the girls, about Central America, about the mundane things that come up during several weeks away from home— Did you pay the heating bill? Any news from the wider family? What are we going to do with two dogs? Soon, it's time to wind down the call, but before I go I ask, "Any sign of Estelle?"

"She's up in her room. I hear the music blasting. Let me go try to get her to say 'Hi.'" I hear Dawn tromp off toward the stairs. I sit and wait, wondering what I could say to my youngest daughter that would at least be of mild interest to her. Minutes later, she is on the phone.

"Hello?"

"Hi, Estelle; It's Dad. How are you?"

"Hi Dad, where are you?"

"I'm in Guatemala City. Remember when we were in Cancun? Well, it's…"

"I know where it is— it's between Belize, Honduras, El Salvador and Mexico."

"Hey! That's right, honey... how did you know that?"

"I've been trying to follow your trip on a map. It would have been easier if you could have called us before and told me where you were!"

"You've been following my route on a map?"

"Yeah. I know you started in Panama, so then you have to go up through Costa Rica and Nicaragua... Did you see the lakes in Nicaragua?"

"Yes, honey, I did! They're fantastic!"

"Did you know that Lake Nicaragua is one of the only lakes in the world to have sharks?"

"That's right, Estelle! That's right; it *does* have sharks! I didn't see any. But a good friend of mine told me there were sharks there." I am stunned and amazed. "I didn't know you were interested in this stuff!"

"I didn't either, but I missed you a lot, and one night I just decided to look at a map and see where you were. It looked like a pretty cool place. I was reading about it, and there's mountains, and volcanoes, and lots of animals..."

"There are, and I saw just about all of them. Even alligators- well *caimans*, they are here, actually. I went out in a canoe at night and looked for them by flashlight."

"Wow, Dad, did you really?" She sounds sincerely interested.

"I did! We saw one that must have been ten feet long-- nearly swamped the canoe!"

"That's awesome, Dad! When are you coming home?"

"Soon, Estelle... just a couple of days. I can't wait. I'll see you soon. Give Mom a kiss for me. Love you!"

"Love you, Dad."

I hang up the phone and just sit back for a moment in the chair. A minute later, remembering that I have borrowed the chair from the hotel desk clerk, I smile, offer the clerk his chair back, and Scroungy and I both race up the stairs.

Happiness grows in the cracks between work and the responsibilities of everyday life. Lying on my cot in Guatemala City, my new canine friend by my side, I consider the incredibly complex array of interconnecting pieces that make up my life, like an infinite, multi-dimensional jigsaw puzzle. I now understand Dawn's obscure reference to me as a prism. It isn't shattered after all. I can examine my life from a multitude of different directions and perceive it in a different color, a different wavelength, from each: from straight on, I am Doug Roth, the dedicated and highly competent, though frequently frustrated, IT Director. From above, I am Doug the faithful but regrettably high-maintenance husband. Move slightly to the side and I am Dad, the often exasperated but proud and devoted father of two wonderful daughters. From here, a hopeless dog lover, from there, a competent but somewhat clueless Central American explorer. But there are so many other things I am: a good friend, a weekend outdoorsman, a deep intellectual and over-evaluator of everyday issues, a former inquisitive child, a depressed adult, an aspiring independent thinker, and now even an international fugitive. The colors are endless; they flow through me and arc onward across the infinity of the universe like rays from a blazing supernova. Yet only I can see them all. But I am just one of a huge galaxy of stars; every person on earth creates his or her own unique celestial spectrum. It's wonderful to be part of it. And the greatest beauty occurs when my colors intertwine and blend with those of others: Dawn's, Celeste's, Estelle's… and Ted's and Rod's and Cal's, and Blue's, Luz's,

Maria's, Paco's, Ricardo's, the Angel's and everybody else's that I've known through the course of my life.

Like Blue's, my story is not yet over. I must face my future. I must look forward to the second half of life. I will try to savor every drop, and when it is gone, I will know that I have lived fully, to the best of my ability.

As my time in Central America is drawing to a close, I head to the market to buy souvenirs for Dawn and the girls. The market is full of brightly-colored serapes, handbags and wallets, necklaces of thick, shiny pebbles and polished silver, old coins, sweaters and the usual collections of key chains, T-shirts and souvenir kitsch.

I choose several woolen blankets to bring home as gifts. They are beautifully woven in Mayan patterns and it is obvious that they were made by hand. I ask how much they cost and the young girl behind the table quotes me the equivalent of twenty dollars each. It's amazing, I think; these blankets would surely go for over one hundred dollars each in the States. However, I remember reading somewhere that the shopkeeper's first offer generally leaves plenty of room for bargaining. I am not accustomed to bargaining for retail purchases in the States, but I know that it is a common procedure outside the country. I rouse my practiced negotiating skills, honed from my many years as a businessman, and do my best bargaining. In the end, I am able to get the offer lowered to about ten dollars each. I am impressed with my success, and I smile with smug pride. But as I reach for my wallet, I realize that the girl is not alone; under the table is an infant, by my estimate only a few months old, sleeping in a cardboard box. I pause for a moment and survey my surroundings. Dilapidated wooden buildings fester in the scorching afternoon sun. Scroungy is standing next to me in his furless, leathery glory, and about ten feet away, one of his many stray brethren is sprawled on the crumbling sidewalk beside me, greedily devouring the severed head of a rooster. Here in front of me is a young girl, probably in her early twenties, selling handmade blankets to tourists, while raising a newborn baby that she must bring with her to work and keep in a cardboard box. There is no maternity leave for this woman, no day care, no health care benefits, and probably no comfortable home to speak of. And here I am, a moderately successful American businessman with a 401(K), a health care plan, a comfortable home and a good family. Why am I doing this? Why am I bargaining with her? To save a few dollars? For me it is just a game. I can wear my smug smile because I beat her at the game; I am a skilled negotiator, a force to be reckoned with; I won't be ripped off by any third-world street vendor. But ten dollars is a trifle to me; it means absolutely nothing. I won't even notice it. For her it is not a game. It is her life. It is her baby's life. Every quetzal that she doesn't earn is less food for her family, less medical care, another thing for the family to live without. I am ashamed of myself. I am smart enough to negotiate, but not smart enough to understand. I hand her the equivalent of twenty-five dollars per blanket and she meekly tells me that she does not have the change for such a large amount of money. I motion to her to keep it and her eyes well with happy tears. She wraps up the blankets in brown paper and tapes the package shut. I smile at her as I walk away with the package and she smiles back, a grateful, teary smile. I turn away and vow always to accept the first reasonable price an honest Central American shopkeeper gives me.

I treat myself to a late lunch at a Mayan restaurant. The waiter brings me a wonderful drink made from pureed rice, milk and cinnamon. The main course is spicy chicken served in a piping-hot clay pot. The ubiquitous corn tortillas, rice and beans round out the meal.

My mind is temporarily at ease as I enjoy my lunch, then head back to my hotel for a rest.

My experience with the souvenir seller and my conversation with Ricardo reverberate through my memory. There are but days left of my trip. This trip has been all about me finding myself. Yet I can't argue that my circumstances in life have been remarkably fortunate. Have I done enough to help others? I have good intentions to rescue Scroungy and I've fed a few other stray dogs along the way. But what have I done for people? The one time I can recall was the relatively minor sum I gave to Maria, and that incident changed the course of my whole trip for the worse. But I do not regret my actions; it was another person's misunderstanding of my intentions, exacerbated by my misguided attempt to escape, that caused the problem. I really do want to help people, and by doing so, maybe I can help myself.

I have a reasonable amount of money left. I devise a plan to convert two hundred dollars into quetzals and give it away in small amounts to the less fortunate people that I see as I walk through the city. I must be discrete about this at all times; the last thing I need is a parade of people chasing after me for handouts of money. I develop some guidelines for my intended good deed: rather than hand money directly to people, I will instead leave money where poor people are likely to find it. If anyone should ask me for money, or for more money, I will ignore them; my charity will only go to those who do not ask for it. And of course, I cannot advise anyone of these rules, so they cannot skew my charity in their favor.

Armed with a nearly two-inch-thick wad of quetzals in small bills, I take a walk in the direction of the nearest shantytown I know, a place I have passed on my earlier wanderings. I have been advised to keep out of these areas, that they are unsafe, but then again, I have been told the same thing about the whole of Central America.

I recall the Angel saying that she had spent nearly two years working with the destitute and was treated with nothing but respect the entire time. Still, for my own safety, at least until I get a better feel of what I'm getting into, I stick close to the main roadway, along the edge of the shantytown. Scroungy trots next to me, his pink, extra-wide ribbon of a tongue flapping up and down with each step, his breathing a rhythmic huff, keeping time with our pace.

Plodding along the broken streets, it strikes me as surreal that so many people must exist in these types of circumstances in this modern world. Although I have by now seen quite a bit of poverty throughout the course of my trip, it is still a bit of a shock to walk here. I note with alarm that most of the structures that people use as living quarters are about the size of a small garden shed back home. They are haphazardly constructed out of scrap wood, worn and splintered from ages of weathering, discarded sheet metal signs, corrugated aluminum, torn pieces of plastic sheeting, broken pallets and anything else people might find. Usable nails being in short supply, some of the shacks are not held together by anything more than strategically placed rocks and broken cinder blocks, and those that weigh down the scraps used for roofs look like they couldn't possibly hold in a strong wind. Acrid smoke from scattered small fires burning scrap wood and bits of trash occasionally assaults my nostrils and momentarily interrupts the rhythm of my breathing. From what I can see inside, floors are dirt, packed hard from being trampled for years under legions of barefooted children. Everywhere the salty stink of urine is strong; flies and litter are ubiquitous. This, for much of the world, is home.

I weave down the dirt path that leads alongside the shantytown, parallel to the road. There is a dusty vacant lot, full of weeds, where a group of the neighborhood kids plays soccer. I have seen the kids here numerous times, and I note the piles of loose rocks that they have made to designate goalposts. I take a quick detour through the field and drop a dozen or so banknotes in various places, crumpling them first so the wind will be less likely to take them.

A little girl, maybe three years old, in a tattered mint dress, toddles in front of me and suddenly stops, just gazing up at me with dark almond eyes. "Hola," I say softly, and I reach out my hand with some money for her to take. She just looks at me. It seems to me that she has no idea what money is, and she probably is wondering why I'm trying to hand her a dirty piece of brown paper. She eyes me cautiously, then totters off.

I launch crumpled banknotes through open doors and shack entrances into their unlit interiors, onto dirt floors or tousled blankets, hoping their residents will find them and wonder where they came from. Then suddenly, out of the corner of my eye, I realize that I have been spotted.

"*Señor, señor, por favor, dinero! Por favor!*" pleads a distressed, tired-looking young mother, her baby on her back in a sling, and she follows me as I walk. Other people are looking. I remember the rules I set for myself and realize that if I pull out a stack of money now, I will be overwhelmed by a writhing mass of destitute humanity. It is a delicate situation. How can I give, yet how can I not give? My rational mind tells me that I will never be able to pull these people out of poverty. I will have to continue my task later, in another such neighborhood. It's not like there is any shortage of them. I turn around and walk silently and as quickly as I can, back toward the main part of town, by now with a train of about fifteen ragged followers. As I approach the more affluent central area of the city, my entourage peters out one or two at a time, and they slink back to the misery that is their everyday reality.

I think my experiences on this trip have helped me to formulate a new theory about life. I've made many mistakes along the course of my own life. The little ones are too numerous to count and probably aren't worth noting anyway, but the main one is this: I have been living my life according to other people's ideas of how I should live it, not my own. I am certainly not alone in this; in fact, I believe it is a widespread, almost universal, phenomenon. There are over six billion people in this world, with six billion different brains and probably an equal number of ideas of how to live, but are people living their lives in six billion different ways? I don't think so. Like Blue's theory about all the things that can be done in life boiling down into eight categories, I'll bet the number of lifestyles in existence can also be broadly categorized into relatively few ways to live. But Blue is also right that I can do little to change this. So what should I do? As a beginning, the second half of my life will be less about money and more about doing the things I really want: spending time with my family and friends, helping people and taking more trips like this.

Three Guatemalan policemen are standing on the street corner in front of my hotel. They look bored, alternately staring at the ground and chatting amongst themselves. As I approach, they look up. They stop talking. I feel a jolt of adrenaline stab through my body. Are they looking for me? I decide not to find out. Instinctively, I turn around and walk quickly in the direction I came from. Wrong move, I think. Any police officer with even the most cursory law-enforcement sense knows that's a suspicious act. Too late to correct it. They must be following me now. I don't look back as that would be even more suspicious. Is this all in my mind? No, I decide, they really were looking at me. I'm sure the Nicaraguan police have sent them my name and passport number. The officials at the border must have known about me when I entered Guatemala. They tipped off the police, who tracked me to my hotel. I had to show my passport to check in. I may as well have dropped white pebbles along my trail.

I break into a half-walk, half-run down the street. Scroungy has fallen into a half-trot next to me. I am trying hard not to be obvious, but I'm sure I am failing miserably. It's too late now. I'll never blend into the crowd like this. I swerve to avoid snagging my foot on a loose paving stone. I imagine I will feel a firm hand on my shoulder any moment now, but I keep moving. My nerves are shot; I am trembling.

Sweat trickles down my face and into my eyes, bringing sun block with it. My eyes start to burn and my vision becomes blurry. I can't see again, but I have to keep moving quickly. I bump into people several times. I don't know where I'm going. Now I try to look back to see whether I'm being followed, but my eyes won't clear. I blink hard several times, but it doesn't help. I can't see anything. There's a curb in front of me with a four-foot drop to the street. At the last moment, I see the curb just in time to jump over it rather than tripping over it. I land in the road on my feet.

And that's when I see the truck. It rounds a curve at breakneck speed. Where did *he* come from? I freeze for a split second like a deer in headlights. There's no time to scramble back up the four-foot retaining wall. Scroungy stands at the top of the wall bewildered, ears pointed skyward; he doesn't know what to do. The smell of gritty diesel exhaust floats in the oppressively humid air. The screeching of brakes pressed to the floor and the sound of rubber tires scraping across loose gravel fill my ears. Half a second until impact, and the driver sees me. His eyes are as wide as mine. Every muscle in my body goes rigid. My teeth clench like a vise. I avert my eyes from the truck, and then I see it- the gorgeous, pristine, streaming colors of the setting sun. A timeless, incandescent ball of magnificent fire in the sky. A star, red on the horizon, bathing me and all of this part of the world in blazing starlight. A magic moment of life, so close to the end. Is it possible to enjoy thoroughly and serenely the last half-second of one's life? It's as if a retaining wall in my mind has suddenly burst, and all of my emotions, unrestrained, come pouring through in a jumble. I realize that my experiences in Central America have been a microcosm of my life: I laughed so hard that my stomach hurt; I cried a few tears; I felt great love, frustration, despondency and fear. I stared in awe and wonder at the most amazing sights; I made friends; I shared my thoughts and dreams, and listened intently to those of others. I made my place in this world; I leave behind a healthy family that I nurtured from the beginning- my legacy. A bad way to die? It doesn't matter how you die; it matters how you live. Everyone dies alone. The fear is gone. Now that I know how my story will end, there is no need to worry about it anymore. The book of life is written, its last sentence in sight. Dying is no longer the preponderant thought in my mind. I have thought about death enough when it was not imminent. Now, when it is imminent, I am overwhelmed by an incredible sense of peace. I think about life. The final flickering of the bulb before it goes out is of no importance. Yes, we all die. But by far the more amazing thing is that we live, and *that* we must do to the fullest. Of this, I have no doubt: I *lived*!

ABOUT THE AUTHOR

D on Carswell grew up writing short stories and articles for his school newspaper and dreaming of traveling the world. Beginning with a backpacking trip through Europe at age seventeen, Don has traveled extensively through 89 countries and all 50 states. He has spent a great deal of time exploring Latin America, including a two-week solo bus journey across Central America that became the inspiration for *Look at the Sun*. Don shuns escorted tours and travels independently, giving him a unique street-level perspective of foreign cultures.

Don holds a BS in chemistry from Penn State University and an MBA from the University of Strathclyde in Glasgow, Scotland. While his career has focused on international sales, he is also a freelance journalist and travel writer, with his work frequently appearing in such publications as the *Sparta Independent*, the *New Jersey Herald* and *International Traveller*, an Australian magazine. *Look at the Sun* is his first novel. Don currently lives in Sussex County, NJ.